WASTRA

WASTRA

ROHAN KAILASAM

NU VOICE
PRESS

First published by NU VOICE PRESS 2023
An imprint of Hubhawks Pvt. Ltd
www.nuvoicepress.com

This is a work of fiction and all characters and incidents described in this book are the product of the author's imagination. Any resemblance to actual persons, living or dead, is entirely coincidental.

ISBN: 978-81-963184-0-6

Typeset by Saanvi Graphics, Noida
Printed at Thomson Press
Published by Nu Voice Press

AUTHOR'S NOTE

Dear Readers,

This book is a work of fiction that draws inspiration from the rich and complex history of Bombay's nefarious underworld. The story is based on true events, but the names of the characters and organizations have been changed to avoid breach of privacy and to allow for creative freedom in the storytelling.

As the author of *Wastra,* my intention was to create a captivating and immersive narrative that would transport readers to Bombay's underworld. The story explores the power struggles and complex relationships that exist in this shadowy realm and the ways in which these relationships are influenced by broader historical events.

At the same time, I wanted to delve into the psychology of the characters in the story and explore their motivations and desires. At the heart of this tale of violence, betrayal and death is Wastra, a mysterious and enigmatic figure, and the story is as much about the search for the truth about this presence as it is about the events that take place.

As I wrote this book, I was motivated by a desire to shed light on a world that is often hidden from view, and to give readers a glimpse into the complex realities of life in Bombay's underworld. I also wanted to create a work of fiction that would be both entertaining and thought-provoking, and that would encourage readers to think deeply about the ways in which power and violence shape our world.

I drew on a wide range of sources, including historical accounts of Mumbai's underworld, personal interviews with people who had lived through the events depicted in the story, and my own experiences of living and working in Mumbai. I was fortunate to grow up in a time of colourful characters who shaped my youth. Many of them are no longer in this world and I have endeavoured to give them a measure of immortality through my words. I also drew on my background as a writer and a storyteller, using the tools of fiction to create a world that is both vividly real and imaginatively rich.

Ultimately, my hope is that *Wastra* provides a compelling and immersive reading experience that will take readers on a journey into a world that is both fascinating and terrifying.

I hope that the story will challenge readers to think deeply about the nature of power, violence, and human relationships and that it will inspire them to look beyond the surface to uncover the deeper truths that lie beneath.

ONE

WHO IS WASTRA?

He heard them coming down the tracks. His ears, finely tuned to the sounds of the night, picked up their footfalls as they made their way from Churchgate Station towards Marine Lines.

It was two in the morning, and the last train to Virar had just gone by, carrying a thousand broken souls back from their mediocre jobs to their miserable rat-holes in the far suburb they called home.

Bombay, the city of broken dreams and false illusions of grandeur, with its Marine Drive skyline ablaze with the lights of the high-rise buildings inhabited by the chosen few, slept for now.

He listened carefully. These were not some drunken office-goers who had missed the last train. Their footsteps were measured, their soft tread barely flicking a pebble as they headed towards Babu, who was huddled in the garbage about a hundred meters from Marine Lines Station. He put out the fire that he had started hoping for a quick fix, stored the needles and the brown sugar in a rubbish pile nearby, covered himself with some newspapers, pretended to sleep, and hoped the strangers would pass him by. They were almost upon him now. There are nights when people pass you by and leave you to get on with whatever it is you were doing. This was not going to be one of those nights, as the sharp kick to his side informed him. It wasn't designed to hurt, just to jog him awake, and that type of control gave him a sick feeling in his stomach because these men knew what they were doing.

He rolled over on his back as though waking from a deep sleep and sat up, taking in the strangers through hooded eyes. There were twelve of them in a semi-circle around him - lean, dark, and silent. The one with an air of authority in the centre, quite obviously the leader, stood closest to him, a slightly mocking smile on his face. He had ripped muscles, not like a bodybuilder but like an athlete or a fighter.

Now, Babu wasn't expecting anyone from any athletic commission and, by the simple principle of exclusion, came to the unpleasant conclusion that the gentleman was some kind of fighter. Upon further covert examination, he came to another similar and equally unpleasant conclusion that the rest of the group were also all fighters. The third unpleasant conclusion he reached was that their intentions were not honourable.

This brought about the next unpleasant question: What were they doing on the railway tracks near Marine Lines kicking him awake?

His brain started shifting gears, and he decided to try the time-tested druggie method of ass-kissing. It might get him a few more kicks, but hopefully, they would realise their mistake and be on their way, and Babu, too, could go about his business of getting high.

Still sitting down, he raised both hands in the *namaste* gesture.

"Salaam Saab. How can I help you? If you are looking for something to smoke, Shantabai, further down the tracks, has a very good *maal*. She will also put you in touch with Gopi, who has the best girls in the whole area, Saab. *Kawla maal*! Very young, almost untouched; you will really enjoy. Just tell her that Babu sent you. She'll take good care of you," Babu winked conspiratorially and smiled in an ingratiating manner.

The mocking smile widened, and the leader shook his head, waggling his right forefinger at Babu, saying a name he had not heard in many years and had almost forgotten.

"*MANZAR ALAM*," said the man.

Oh god! They knew!

The sinking feeling in his stomach got worse. He had a bad feeling that things were going to go south very shortly, and he didn't see himself walking away from this situation that had arrived at his doorstep.

However, a small voice inside his head told him that there was still time. There was always time. He had to try and talk his way out and escape. If he could get out of this arc of death that had hemmed him in he could make a run for the gap in the fence. This gap was located about a hundred meters to the north from the direction of Marine Lines Station, and it opened out onto Charni Road. Most passengers getting off the trains used that exit to cross the road instead of the overbridge to save time.

You had to be a regular to know the existence of the gap in the fence, and Babu wasn't just a regular. This was his home. Once he was through the gap, he knew they would never be able to catch him. He knew each and every street and by-lane like the palm of his hand. He knew a hundred hiding places. They could pass by him and still not know that he was there. Babu had to try and make a break for it. He slowly got to his feet, but the leader noticed and began to speak. What he asked then made Babu sure that he was going to die on these railway tracks, which had been his home for years.

"Where is Wastra?"

Babu was a creature of the streets and knew how to roll with the proverbial punch. He was shaken to his core but did not let his consternation show.

With an ingratiating smile, mixed with a large dose of bewilderment, Babu answered the question with a question, "Saab, who is Wastra? I don't know this person. I am just a poor *gardulla*. My name is Babu. Ask anyone, and you will know. Everyone around here knows me."

The ripped leader of the killers laughed out loud, a pleasant sound that was at odds with the prevailing situation, and shook his index finger again.

"No, no-no. Let me introduce myself. I am Suleiman Khan, and you are Manzar Alam. At one time, you were the bodyguard and confidante of Wastra. Tell me where he is, and I promise I will send you to Allah quickly and painlessly. Otherwise ..." he took a pause, pointing to his group, "These men are from beyond the Hindu Kush, and their talent lies in making you feel pain like you have never felt before. They will make you talk anyway, and then you will die."

As if acting on an unseen signal, the man to the left of Babu lashed out with a near-perfect *mawashi-geri*. Babu took the roundhouse kick to the face, felt a couple of teeth splinter, tasted the familiar metallic flavour of his blood in his mouth, and went down like a house of cards. The semi-circle tightened as Babu got up, spitting out blood and tooth fragments from his mouth.

He knew about these men from beyond the Hindu Kush. In another life, he had fought against them and won. He knew them to be fearsome warriors, devoid of the quality of mercy, and the only thing worse than them were their women.

The British found that out the hard way during their campaign in Afghanistan in the nineteenth century. He had heard of a writer called Rudyard Kipling, who had written a gruesome short poem about them, but Babu couldn't remember it for the life of him. He knew that all British soldiers had been told that if they were wounded during the battle and found themselves left behind, it was highly recommended that they keep one bullet for themselves and use it without hesitation if they saw any Afghan women approaching them.

These women would take their time with the wounded enemy soldiers, skinning them and then emasculating them before finally burning them alive, if that was what you could call those torn and broken bodies. It was a slow and extremely brutal process; the screams of the tortured ones could be heard across the mountains for days.

Eventually, the British decided that Afghanistan was not for them and returned to India, where they could make Indian troops kill their own countrymen. Babu had been part of a group that had defeated these dreaded warriors a long time ago. But here on the railway tracks, he was all alone, and he knew there was no help coming. He knew that he had run out of time.

There was no use pretending. They knew who he was, and Babu knew this type of killer. He had been one himself in what seemed another life, and in a kind of sick and twisted way, he felt a kindred spirit with these dealers of death. He remembered his training camp in the jungles where an Israeli instructor named Shlomo had thrown him into a deep muddy pool that had been constructed specifically for fear control. He was weighted and held down with heavy leg weights tied around his thighs and ankles and had been tasked with staying underwater for five minutes.

After ninety seconds, the oxygen deprivation started to kick in; his brain reacted by telling him to get to the surface. The instructor, who had also got in but with an oxygen tank, held him down firmly as he began to struggle, and let him suck on some oxygen for five seconds. This time Babu held on for one or two minutes.

Eventually, after two weeks of intensive, gut-wrenching underwater training, he could stay submerged for eight minutes straight without feeling the need to swim to the surface. That was a lifetime ago, but he felt the training return, took a deep breath, and let it out slowly. He relaxed his muscles like he had been taught to and prepared to sell his life dearly.

In all fairness to the killers, Babu, in his tattered, smelly clothes, tall, skinny with his broken and discoloured teeth, didn't look like much; so, it came as a great surprise to all when he pivoted like a ballet dancer around the man to his left clasping the man's face in the palms of his hands and snapping his neck like a twig. Using the falling body as his support, Babu swivelled and caught the next man in the semi-circle with a spinning back kick, breaking his neck not with power but precision. Still swivelling, he got behind another of the killers and lifted him off the ground in a perfect suplex. Babu's shoulders and the other man's neck broke their respective falls.

The speed and ferocity of the counter-attack took the killers by surprise, and the semi-circle widened considerably as everyone went for their weapons. Babu rolled over and came up with a revolver in his hand, which he had taken from the waistband of one of the men he had killed.

One more killer went down with a bullet in the chest, but the leader showed professionalism right there in the middle of the evolving chaos. He stood his ground, drawing his Walther .38. As Babu prepared to fire again, he shot Babu expertly in his right kneecap, shattering the bone. Babu screamed with indescribable pain. Dropping his gun, he fell back to the ground, holding his shattered knee, vomiting all over himself.

Suleiman moved closer, his eyes gleaming with controlled rage, kicking the gun away from Babu, "That was good, my friend, very, very good. This is as far as you can go, but we are just beginning and can do this all night. Let me end your suffering now before it gets worse."

The tone was one of concern, caring even, but the truth was that Suleiman had no intention of letting Babu die easily, not after he had killed four of his men. He mentally kicked himself for not briefing his men and taking adequate precautions against exactly this kind of attack. The man they were hunting was a hunter-killer himself or had been, once, a long time ago. But the information he had received was that the junkie had one foot in the grave and would pose no threat. In retrospect, it might have been prudent to run his own checks, but that was always the case with hindsight. Everyone was always smarter after the fact.

***

Babu just lay in the dirt, writhing and moaning, trying to nurse his shattered knee. He may have been in agony, but he showed no sign of being communicative. Suleiman stepped on his shattered kneecap, trying to persuade him to see the light, and Babu screamed again.

"We can go all night long, my friend. Just tell us where Wastra is. My men know how to extend life while extending the pain. You will want to die after a while," Suleiman continued, "In fact, you will beg for it. But it will be denied to you, my friend. I cannot let you live, I have my orders, and I am a soldier like you. All this can be avoided. I promise you an honourable end. Just answer my question. Where is Wastra?"

Babu knew the torture was about to start as he tried to go to another place. Through the cool dark air, he heard, "Everybody dies."

It was Paul, but he knew that was impossible. Paul was dead, shot by the Williams gang.

"What a stupid way to go," thought Babu. Paul had been like General Custer, in love with his own legend, blinded by his ego, and he had paid the price, shot down like a dog at Fort. They had driven the Toyota Landcruiser over him a few times to make sure he was completely and absolutely dead because Paul had displayed an uncanny knack in the past, of cheating the Reaper just when everyone had written him off. He saw

Rasul, tough like a bull, with his thick neck and bulging muscles, chillum in hand.

"Be strong, bro," said Rasul, but as Babu tried to talk to him, he kept getting interrupted by these terrible screams. It seemed to come from the very depths of hell, and as he tried to look around to see who it was, he realised the screams were coming from him.

The soles of his feet had been sliced open, and one of the gang members had sprayed lighter fuel into the gaping gashes on his soles and set him on fire. It was a slow burn. Essentially, Babu was being roasted alive on a slow fire. Babu screamed again, both in agony and at the horror of it all.

Suleiman bent down and said conversationally, "All night long, my friend, like the Lionel Richie song. I used to like that song so much. You can stop this," Suleiman bent down and put his hand on Babu's shoulder.

"Let me end this for you. You have done more than can be expected. You are an honourable man and deserve an honourable death. I will give it to you. Just tell me where your leader is. Please, my brother," Suleiman sounded the most concerned. Babu kept screaming. Suleiman sighed, looked up to his left, and nodded.

"Now, we are going to do the same thing to your palms. By the time we have finished, you will be well done," this brought about a round of savage laughter. They held Babu's skinny hands down, palms facing upward, and smoothly sliced both open. Babu convulsed briefly and then stiffened. Suleiman bent down and felt for a pulse. "Defib," said Suleiman sharply, and a portable defibrillator was placed on the ground.

The killers had come well prepared.

TWO

THE UNEXPECTED DEATH

Sub-Inspector Subash Thakre was on night duty and was not thrilled about it at all. As the officer on duty at Marine Lines Police Station, he had the unenviable responsibility of conducting the night patrol of the area under Marines Lines jurisdiction with four constables, one driving the jeep and three in the back. The conversation was stilted as the five policemen drove slowly through the dark streets, hoping they would not come across a crime in progress.

Subash wanted to return to his new bride and her soft, warm body. His wedding had been arranged, but he had the opportunity to meet with his prospective bride before they married, and had fallen in love with her. She was smart, educated, beautiful, and although a virgin, which Subash was not, she learned quickly and was extremely malleable in bed. Hence, there was a great desire within him to be with her at that time, instead of these stupid *hawaldars* and their mundane conversations.

They were skirting Marine Lines Station in the direction of Churchgate when they heard the screams. Subash Thakre had been a boxer in Khalsa College, had won the Intercollegiate Middle Weight title, and had also proved to be pretty adept in the firing range. But his relative inexperience with hands-on crime and the thought of confronting evil in the early hours of the morning made him sweat a bit. His grandmother had always been very superstitious about the magnification of the power of evil spirits between one and four in the morning.

Although he would never admit it, his grandmother's superstitions had passed on pretty much undiluted to young Subash. He felt the droplets of fear start to roll down his cheeks, and the back of his khaki uniform shirt began feeling damp. Still, he was in charge of this motley crew and didn't want to lose face. He gave a curt order to the white-faced constables, and all five of them got out and crept down the road, following the direction of the screams.

By the time they hit ground zero, Babu had passed out, and Suleiman and his fighters were in the process of reviving him with the defibrillator. All the cops could see through the darkness were numerous shadowy figures where no one was supposed to be. Subash Thakre took out his .45 Colt, checked the chambers, and signalled his crouching, shivering team to get ready. The constables raised their antique Lee Enfield .303 rifles from the World War II era and woefully inadequate for modern-day urban warfare to their shoulders, shaking with fear as they prepared to confront what they were sure were demons or some gathering of evil spirits. Summoning all his courage, Subash Thakre shouted at the figures in the darkness to freeze.

Suleiman and his team were taken aback by the arrival of a police contingent. They had been reliably informed that there would be no interference and that they would be free to work their charms on the druggie. Realising that they were caught in the open with no cover, Suleiman cursed in Pashto, snapped a curt order to his team, and loosed off a shot in the direction of the police. It winged past a terrified constable who hit the pavement, the face first, his rifle flying out of his hands as he began to pray loudly to Lord Ganesha. Then the rest of Suleiman's team opened up, and bullets flew like angry hornets all around the constables, who hit the dirt and stayed there. They had absolutely no desire to engage with the shadowy, obviously well-armed figures on the tracks.

On the other hand, Sub-Inspector Subash Thakre discovered, much to his own surprise, that he was made of sterner stuff and didn't cringe for cover like his colleagues; instead, he gave constable Khade a hard kick and yelled at him to be silent. Now that he had figured out that there were no evil spirits involved, he took aim and fired four rounds in quick succession into what he hoped was the centre of the group.

Suleiman took one in the chest and was dead before he hit the ground. His team opened up again in the direction of the police party, scattering the police patrol behind the parked cars on the main road with the exception of Sub-Inspector Thakre, who seemed numb to the hail of bullets and the imminent danger to his life and had taken cover behind a lamppost while continuing to fire. He then dropped to his knees as he clicked on an empty chamber, reloaded, and resumed firing in the direction of the muzzle flashes. He was rewarded by the painful screams of another one of the shadowy figures.

Shaken by the death of their leader and the surprising resistance of the police, the remaining assassins melted into the darkness of the tracks, leaving behind their fallen comrades. One of the constables who had crawled back to the jeep during the shootout had the presence of mind to set off the siren. Emboldened by the arrival of their trusted enforcers of law and order, someone from the Hindu Gymkhana building on the side of the tracks towards Marine Drive started shouting. Lights flickered on in various buildings as people rediscovered courage. Subash raced back to the jeep and called for backup, and what followed would resurrect the dead from their slumber and send a reporter on the story of a lifetime.

THREE

THE NEW HIGH-PROFILE CASE

Shalini Shanmugam cursed silently but viciously as she swayed from side to side in the back seat of the *dukkar taxi.* The Bihari driver was driving at breakneck speed, executing death-defying manoeuvres as he negotiated the traffic from Kemp's Corner to Nariman Point, talking and smoking his disgusting-smelling *beedi,* all at the same time. The rush hour was over, but the traffic was still dense as they hit Marine Drive.

The 'Queen's Necklace,' as it was also known, lay resplendent before them, bathed in the morning light, and sunbeams danced off the Arabian Sea like a million little jewels. In the distance, Shalini could see a couple of fishing boats with their white sails painted into the blue horizon, getting back after an all-nighter. There were a few windsurfers closer to the shore, taking advantage of the strong winds as they sped towards the Oberoi Towers. A couple of kites were up in the air, dancing erratically and painting colourful designs high over the sea.

All in all, it was quite a breath-taking sight, even for the hungover Shalini. Still, it was lost on the taxi driver who was complaining about the Pragati Bharat Party (PBP), a political party run by the son of a former deceased politician. The older man had created the party with very radical right-wing intentions in the early '70s. He immediately targeted the migrant population from the south of India, who were predominantly Tamil, for persecution. Now the average Tamil is rather non-aggressive, very hardworking, and is more preoccupied with matters of finance rather than politics. However, one should be aware that one must attempt to corner a Tamilian at his own peril.

The PBP leader obviously hadn't received the memo, so when the sevaks, as they were called, were thrashed in successive street battles, he was forced to bring an end to the hostilities as the membership began to dwindle. Nothing makes a person rethink their political ideology more than a good beating from a bunch of guys labelled by their party leaders as useless 'dosa-eaters.' For a long time after that, the party had stayed more or less in the political wilderness, preferring slogan-shouting to any confrontationist activities. Then the party experienced a change in fortune in the '80s when it had secured a few seats in the state legislature; its political strength had grown due to smart alliances.

But the untimely death of the old man in the late '90s had seen the mantle pass on to the son. He had rekindled militant fires that had been dormant for a decade and had fixed the party's sights primarily on the poor migrants from the northern state of Bihar, who had come to Bombay in search of a better life. The PBP had started voicing their demand - that all non-Marathas leave Maharashtra. It was completely absurd, and everyone knew it, but it was a political gambit. Their leader was playing to the local masses, hoping to win enough seats to form a government unencumbered by political alliances. There had been a few isolated incidents of violence against the Biharis, which had gone unpunished by the largely ineffective law and order machine prevalent in the city, but on the whole, Bombay was cosmopolitan in its outlook; the only break in normalcy coming in the early '90s race wars, where Hindus and Muslims had slaughtered each other in the names of their gods.

"Just see, madam, every day they are beating us and telling us to leave.

Who will clean the streets, deliver your dabbas of lunch, and drive the taxis if we go? We are doing the jobs that no one else wants. Still, they are beating and threatening and telling us to leave. I have brought my wife and two sons to Bombay.

My wife works as a *kaamwali* and cleans twenty houses a day, while my two sons run a tea stall. We are making just about enough money, and maybe one day, I can have my own taxi service and get a contract with some Bollywood company. Then my life and my family's life will be secure.

"But until then, we all have to struggle to survive, from day to day, and now we also have to deal with all this nonsense. It is too much, madam," Shalini nodded her agreement, and the jerking motion made her want to throw up.

It was a Thursday morning, and the weekend was almost upon her, but Wednesday night had been a ladies' night at The

Ghetto, which had meant free drinks and lots of single guys. At five feet and eight inches, her slender body, with her highlighted black hair and hazel eyes in startling contrast to her dusky skin tone, was a magnet to all men within a hundred mile radius.

And while she enjoyed the male and sometimes female attention, the one who broke her heart still weighed deep in her soul, and contrary to how she portrayed herself, she wasn't a one-night stand type of girl. So, she had a few tequila shots, washed them down with a couple of whiskies, and got a bit drunk; she sang along loudly to Aerosmith's 'Living on The Edge' and other similar retro songs that Joel, the in-house DJ, was so famous for churning out, and flirted with the fast and the furious of Bombay's very fickle society. She fended off several offers, some of which were rather tempting, but rather than waking up the next morning feeling like the bottom of a bird cage, she gave Thomas Cheriyan, the affable Bar owner, a hug, waved goodbye to Joel before hailing down a passing cab and going back home to sleep alone.

Of course, she was crazy late for work the next morning, and it came as no surprise to her when her Samsung hummed. She knew who it was even before she answered it. Shantanu Sukul, the editor of the *Navi Bombay Times,* was a stickler for punctuality and mostly everything else. He ran a tight ship, and if Shalini hadn't been the exceptional reporter she was, she would have been sent packing a long time ago. Still, Shalini had to grudgingly admit that he didn't ask his team to do anything he wasn't willing to do first.

"Obviously, a few too many last night," snapped her boss, startlingly on point.

"I'm sorry, Shantanu, but the alarm didn't go off," was her lame reply.

"Hard to hear an alarm when you're semi-comatose."

Shalini felt her blood pressure rise. "I'll be there in fifteen minutes, sir," she said in a very controlled tone. She didn't want the hangover to get the better of her and make her say something that might be misunderstood as rudeness.

"No need. You've missed the morning meeting anyway. I need you to go to St. George's Hospital and check out a case for me. A junkie got killed last night."

"What's so special about that? They are dropping like flies all over the town. In fact, there are some people who might say that a good junkie is..." she let the last bit trail off.

"Yes, yes, I know, a dead one. But this case is different," said Shantanu.

"In what way, sir?" she asked. She wasn't questioning Shantanu's judgement. She knew him too well for that and knew he was not given to flights of fancy. She was genuinely curious to know what had caught Shantanu's attention.

"Well, for one, before the junkie got his ticket stamped, he killed several obviously highly-trained assassins, including Salil Seth. All this took place late last night somewhere near Churchgate Station. It looks like they initiated the whole fracas themselves, and from what I hear, the junkie was only defending himself."

Shalini perked up, "You mean Salil Seth, the Chief Minister's personal bodyguard? But that guy has 'Z' class training. He wasn't a very nice guy, but he was tough as nails. Anyway, you don't get paid to be nice in his business. He always came across as bulletproof."

"Exactly my point. I want you to get to the bottom of this story. Something doesn't feel right. The initial reports seem to indicate that the attackers weren't even *desi* boys, which begs the question as to what the hell was the Chief Minister's personal bodyguard doing, hanging out with foreign hitmen, attacking some broken-down junkie, and how is it possible that he got himself killed in the process, along with some of his associates? I find it impossible to believe that one man was able to do so much damage, but at the same time, the bodies in the morgue at George's beg to differ. Use your legendary charm and get some useful information."

"I'm on it, boss. Get back to you with an update," she affirmed then realised that he had already cut the call. She let out a deep sigh of frustration, shook her head, and then tapped the taxi driver's shoulder. He was now singing one of the latest Bollywood hit songs completely off-key, but with great enthusiasm.

Shalini gave him the new coordinates.

FOUR

WORTH THE WEIGHT OF GOLD

St. George's Hospital was situated in the Fort area of Bombay. A large colonial structure of beautiful red stone with carved columns and tastefully designed balconies, it was known as the European General Hospital during the British era, catering only to European clientele until the British were booted out. Now it was a government hospital providing free care to the poor, although it also provided advanced treatment and post-operative care for those who could pay. All corpses, by law, had to be brought to George's for post-mortem and had to be certified that they had either died of natural or unnatural causes before they could begin their final journey to the grave or the cremation grounds.

The large courtyard was quiet, with most of the craziness always seeming to happen during the hour of the night. Shalini saw an old couple sitting in the far corner, under a tree. They looked defeated and worn out, and Shalini hoped that they were not waiting to claim the body of a loved one.

They were old and poor and most likely would be waiting for quite a while before anyone would deign to look at them. This, Shalini thought, was the real India, where the poor just got poorer, where dignity in old age or death was a luxury, not a right.

A couple of orderlies were going about their work, pushing some trolleys through the hospital entrance, their wheels clattering on the cobbled floor, but nothing untoward seemed to be happening as far as she could see.

Then Shalini saw Billimoria and ducked behind an ambulance. Inspector Billimoria was a tall, burly brute of a man. He was a Faruzi, an oddity among the cops because he was the only one of his race serving in the police force. He had been a widely respected officer until Shalini had uncovered a story about a ring of police officers moonlighting as hitmen for the rich and famous, cleaning up their messes and eliminating their rivals, all run by Billimoria.

This, coupled with his *lathi* charge on a women's activist group's protest outside the Chief Minister's home, had put his career on hold. While he had survived the axe primarily due to the disappearance of a couple of key witnesses, the word was out, and he had been demoted back to the inspector from DCP, with no station under his charge. Several of his henchmen had not been so lucky and sentenced to many long years in jail. Two had already been found dead in their sleep. Gangland does not forget.

But if Billimoria was here at George's, Shalini realised a few things. One, his apparent fall from grace was exactly that - apparent. It was evident that the higher authorities still valued his services. Two, if he was here, it had to do with the junkie, and so Shantanu's tip, that something smelt terrible, had been bang on the money. Three, Billimoria knew it was Shalini, who had broken the story about him, and while Shalini was not afraid of the Faruzi inspector, she knew that she could expect no help from him or his goon squad. She also didn't want to tip him off that she was on the dead junkie case until she had all the relevant details. Billimoria was famous for making evidence disappear.

So, she waited until he went back inside the hospital, then departed hastily from the courtyard of George's Hospital and took refuge in the nearby restaurant, New Light of Asia, and scrolled through her contact list until Moti Singh's name popped up.

***

Moti Singh worked in George's Hospital as an orderly. His father, Nahar Singh, was a security guard in a building named Ferena in Colaba. He was a hardworking and extremely honest Nepali who had come with his young bride to Bombay in the early 1970s, looking for better prospects. Being uneducated, his options had been limited, and he had been lucky to get a job as a watchman.

It had initially been a temporary gig until he caught a couple of carjackers red-handed one night, trying to have their way with a Ford Zephyr belonging to Dr Hakim, who lived on the fifth floor. He had tackled both the thieves on his own and got stabbed in the gut for his efforts, but he prevented the robbers from getting away. Dr Hakim had been the president of the Owners' Association then and had got the terms of Nahar Singh's employment changed to permanent.

Furthermore, Nahar Singh had been given the small room on the terrace as his flat, where Moti Singh was born. Unlike his father, Moti went to school, got a decent education, and helped his father with the building maintenance, so it came to pass that Dr Hakim could secure a job for him in the hospital. It guaranteed job security and a reasonable salary, and eventually, the plan was to have him as Security Chief for the hospital. But Moti was not content with wheeling patients in and out and change their bedpans. He made a note of newsworthy cases that arrived in the hospital and sold the stories under the condition of anonymity to discerning reporters. He had earned a lot of money from his side business and had recently made the down payment for a house in Borivali.

Some years earlier, he provided crucial information that enabled Shalini to uncover a paedophile ring run by certain Catholic priests. It rocked the foundations of the Catholic Church in India. The pompous Archbishop was prosecuted and jailed. It made a national hit in the *Navi Bombay Times,* cementing Shalini's reputation as a star reporter. She had maintained Moti's anonymity and nurtured their relationship with gifts and money; in return, he had always provided her with juicy, actionable intelligence.

She watched his chubby Nepali framework work its way across the crowded restaurant to her, with a genuine smile of pleasure on his face. A waiter placed two cutting *chais* along with two *pavs* in front of them, and they exchanged pleasantries while sipping on the sugary tea and talking about the weather, the political climate, and Moti's parents. It wasn't a song and dance routine. Shalini found that Moti was one of the few people with whom she could have a meaningful conversation.

As she broke off a piece of the tasty warm bread, preparing to get down to business, Moti pre-empted her.

"Madam, I know why you called me."

"Really?"

"Yes. It's about the gardulla they brought in last night, right?"

Shalini knew she shouldn't be surprised because Moti was anything but dense.

"Yes, Moti. I got the call today from my boss, who seems to think something shady is going on." She did not talk about seeing Billimoria around.

"Madam Shalini, it was complete chaos last night. Inspector Thakre brought in the gardulla and five more dead bodies, one of which was Salil Seth. You know who he is?"

Shalini nodded, "The Chief Minister's head of security. 'Z' class training very tough, a complete asshole. Yes, I know him. How was he killed?"

Moti continued, "His neck had been snapped. I overheard that the rest of the dead men were not Indian, maybe Afghani. Two of them had been killed by Inspector Thakre. The bullets matched his gun. But the rest had been killed by close contact strikes to their throats and necks. It was extremely professional, and although I can't believe it, it seems that the junkie killed them."

Shalini sipped her tea and tried to make sense of this unbelievable story.

"So, the junkie killed four or five trained killers? How is that possible? What could have gone down that resulted in this body count?"

And as she said the words, she began to see an outline, a possible sequence of events that had resulted in the gaggle of corpses in the morgue.

"Moti, tell me if I'm seeing this wrong. These guys, these killers, went looking for this junkie, specifically. He was their target. They knew exactly where to find him, meaning someone had provided them with the intel. The presence of our esteemed Chief Minister's bodyguard at the battle zone makes for a pretty strong case. These killers wanted something from our junkie friend. I don't know what they expected, but they got a surprise. The junkie went all black cat ninja, killing a couple of them before they brought him down."

Moti nodded excitedly, "He had been shot in the left kneecap. Most likely, that was what stopped him."

"There you go!" exclaimed Shalini, "So they get him down and start beating him up."

"No, madam, not just beating. They were torturing him. They had burnt the soles of his feet, and his palms were sliced open to the bone."

"That wonderful custom is from the North-West Frontier Province, so you are probably correct about them being Afghans. But then, as they are in the middle of their entertainment, they get interrupted by the cops. They probably weren't expecting guests at their party, and they go for it with the police; a full-scale gun battle ensues, and they lose a few more of their company. Now, this wasn't the easy picking they were expecting, so before things spiralled further out of control, the rest of the guys disappeared, leaving many dead bodies in their wake.

"All of them were dead on arrival except for the junkie."

Shalini choked on her tea. Spluttering, she exclaimed, "What? The junkie is alive? Oh my God, Moti! Why didn't you tell me this right at the start?" Moti smiled triumphantly, and Shalini continued agitatedly, "You pirate! Okay, okay, you get a bonus for this. But tell me all, and don't leave out anything obscure you think it might be. I need to know everything, Moti. And I need you to get me inside to talk to this guy."

"Madam Shalini, I will tell you everything I know, but getting inside for an interview is impossible. Billimoria and his goons are guarding him. They came in the right after the bodies were brought in. Billimoria was shocked that the junkie was still alive and ordered all hospital staff out, but Dr Hakim refused to leave. There was a huge argument, and phone calls were made. The Dean came down on Dr Hakim's side, but Billimoria got the green light to guard the entire ward. No one comes in or out without his approval. Dr Hakim has ordered a doctor and an orderly to be present at all times in four-hour shifts. If I didn't know better, madam, I would swear they wanted to encounter the gardulla."

Shalini was familiar with the encounters of the Bombay police. Let's say they had someone in custody who was a suspect but against whom they couldn't get a conviction. Once the cops got the go-ahead from their superiors, they took the suspect out for a drive. They would stop at a quiet place where they wouldn't be disturbed before putting a couple of bullets into the suspect and writing it up as self-defence, claiming that the suspect tried to flee and the poor police had no choice but to shoot him dead.

Or let's say they caught a wanted criminal. Before they formally arrested him and went through all the unnecessary paperwork required by law, which would result in him having his day in court, they just killed him. They wrote that they were minding their own business when this crazy guy just opened up on them with a gun, and they had no choice but to put him down like a sick dog. It was cold-blooded murder and human rights violation at its worst, but they had been getting away with it for a while now, all in the name of national security.

Quite a few of the people killed in 'self-defence' were pretty disreputable and probably deserved the end that they got, but it didn't justify the vigilante justice being meted out by the cops. It was often said that the police were the most dangerous criminals on the streets. It was best to neither make friends nor enemies out of them.

"But why encounter the gardulla? What could they possibly hope to gain? They must have got their orders from somewhere higher up in the food chain," Shalini thought aloud.

Moti placed a photograph on the table. It was old but well-maintained and showed five men in their early twenties. The one in the centre was the leader, evident by the protective flanking of the rest of the group.

Moti pointed to the figure on the extreme right, "That could be him, the gardulla, but he looks healthy there. Now, he's just skin, bones, and bad teeth."

Shalini nodded, "Drugs will do that to you."

Moti continued, "I don't know these guys, but I know where it was taken. That shop in the background is 'Janta Stores.' It's in Colaba. My father works in a building close to that shop. It's owned by some people from Vaarnis clan. They do photocopying and stuff like that. It might not be too bad of an idea to go there and ask around. I can't guarantee you any answers. They tend to be a close-mouthed bunch. Still, shaking the branches and seeing what falls out wouldn't hurt. Just my opinion, of course, Madam Shalini."

Shalini put her hand on Moti's chubby one and said, "You're worth your weight in gold. You will go very far. Just remember that I predicted it first."

Moti glowed, "Thank you, madam; anything for you, Madam Shalini."

FIVE

CHE UNGLI

A crow hacked a dry cough as Shalini got out of her cab and took in the dreary exterior of Mistry Chambers. The building was six floors of a dirty green colour that matched the slimy trails left by the leaking pipes stretching from the ground floor all the way to the top. It was quite evident that a major maintenance operation was long overdue.

But Shalini was not fooled by the decrepit structure. She knew the price per square foot in Colaba. A crappy little two-bedroom apartment would cost you an arm and a leg in Mistry Chambers. But just having the necessary change wasn't enough.

You needed to contend with the building society chairperson and the board, suck up to them, make a sizable donation, and then maybe, just maybe, you would get the keys to a dark, dank, musty flat for which you would have to show your gratitude eternally. Given the pitfalls described above, it would be logical to assume that no sane person would be inclined to begin preliminary purchase preparations. However, such an assumption would be extremely wrong. The waiting list for potential buyers was normally about ten years, and such was the craze of owning a flat in Colaba and Cuffe Parade.

The entrance to the dark and uninviting corridor, which ended at a ramshackle elevator from a bygone era, divided the Janta Stores into two sections. The section on the left sold stationery, sweets, cheap fake jewellery, and other commodities catering to the lower-income clientele and contributing to the bulk of the purchases. It was the other part, the one that did the photocopying, that Shalini was most interested in. She recognised it as the background of the photograph.

Moti had been spot on! She realised that he had grown up in that area which explained how he had immediately recognised the backdrop of the photograph.

Che Ungli Mama sat at the counter at the entrance, taking in his surroundings and all the people in it with a distinct lack of interest. It wasn't that he was unaware he just gave the impression to the idle onlooker that he didn't care. Shalini had been briefed about him by Moti, who had described him as being extremely bright, with a charitable twist to his personality that he kept hidden from all except the chosen few, quite in contrast to the rest of his vegetarian Marwari creed who worshipped money and would sell their collective mothers for an extra rupee. He was called 'Che Ungli' or six fingers because he had an extra pinkie on his right hand. The Vaarnis were a tightly knit clan that married only within their own community, primarily intending to keep the money in-house. They were not known for their martial temperament but had the proverbial Midas touch and could make money in any business they started. Judging by the number of customers present, Shalini did not doubt that the photocopying business was making a handsome profit.

She had thought about it and had decided on a full-frontal assault. Moti knew about Che Ungli and had briefed her that she probably wouldn't be too successful in getting any information from anyone in the shop. Another trait of the Vaarnis was the lack of loose talk, even amongst themselves. So, she strode into the shop, shouldering her way past some angry customers, who turned with marked irritation on their faces. Still, any harsh rebukes were stilled by the unusual attractiveness of the dusky lady who had unceremoniously pushed them aside.

She stood before Che Ungli, put the photograph down on the counter in front of him, and stared at him, matching his expressionless gaze with hers. They were locked like this for a very long thirty seconds or so, black on hazel, then Che Ungli blinked and looked down at the photograph, involuntarily jerking back ever so slightly. He recovered his poise admirably and returned to his original disinterested self, but only not quite. The photograph had caught him by surprise, and there was no doubt in Shalini's mind that she saw the flash of recognition across Che Ungli's face. She knew that he knew, and as he looked at her, Che Ungli knew that she knew that he knew.

Continuing with the full frontal, Shalini said, "I'm not looking to photocopy, photograph, anything or make an international phone call. I want you to tell me about the boys in this photo."

One of the assistants, a weak-looking, short guy in a typical Vaarnis white vest, went by, looked down at the photo, almost collapsed with shock, and got a sharp rap behind his ear for that from Che Ungli. He continued with his work, looking behind him as though he had seen a ghost or, in this case, a group of them.

The reaction of his colleague seemed to put Che Ungli on edge. He lost his air of nonchalance and started to scribble something on the paper pad that was reposed on a wooden attachment below the counter where he sat. He seemed very busy and studiously avoided Shalini's gaze that remained on him unwaveringly.

"I'm not looking for any trouble. I'm just looking for some clarity regarding the antecedents of this photograph. I would be most grateful for any information you might be kind enough to share with me."

Che Ungli stopped scribbling and suddenly gripped Shalini's palms that faced down on the counter. She glowered at the slightly built Vaarnis. In a voice heavily laced with tension, he said, "We don't know anything about any photograph. We are a respectable business establishment. Please leave and don't come back."

Shalini left without a word, exited Janta Stores, and took a right past Strand Cinema towards Radio Club. Once clear of prying eyes, she unclenched her fist, unfolded the piece of paper Che Ungli pressed into her hand, and read the word that would change her life.

SHINDE.

SIX

SHINDE

"Now there's a name that's risen from the dead," Shantanu was his usual brisk, all-business self.

"You mean you know this person?" Shalini asked incredulously.

"He's a bit of an urban legend, you know? Funny that you haven't heard of him. He's a creature of the night. At least, that's the way the story goes. He's the man who talks to ghosts and knows their secrets. But he's been off the grid for a while," Shantanu said.

"The first problem is finding out exactly where he is right now. No one I know has an address, so a house visit's out of the question. He's known to frequent the not-so-trendy bars, euphemistically speaking. Finding him is only the first part of the problem. Getting him to talk is the next. Neither one will be easy, and I'll have to ask around. He's known to have an insight into things that are not immediately apparent, but a procedure needs to be followed to get him to talk. You remember 'The Plumber'?"

The Plumber was the name given to a serial killer who had killed nineteen homemakers in a span of two years. He'd never been caught.

"So, from what I've heard...," Shantanu continued, "Sanjay Sipla from Radiant TV was covering the story for his channel and ran into Shinde in some Bar. Now here's the deal with Shinde. First, he needs to like you, then you need to buy him endless amounts of beer, and then he'll tell you a story. Most likely, it will shock the pants off you. He told Sipla about a serial killer killing homemakers in South Bombay.

"According to Shinde, The Plumber was a shopkeeper who owned a shop selling household goods like sugar, cooking oil, vegetables, fresh milk, etc. He knew when the wives were alone because he provided free home delivery and set his killing schedule accordingly. This tiny detail was unknown to the police, who initially dismissed the killings as unrelated. Still, after the fourth or fifth murder, it became apparent to everyone in town that a serial killer was on the loose. He was christened The Plumber based on the rumour that he strangled his victims and left a plumber's wrench near the crime scene.

The Home Minister descended upon the Commissioner like a ton of bricks, who in turn summoned his Deputy and additional commissioners in charge of various police stations and districts and gave them all a reaming, ordering them to have a suspect in custody within a week. Now let me tell you, there are some brilliant policemen in the Bombay Police, but they are few and far between. The vast majority of the rank and file are not known for their brilliance in forensic and detective work. They followed what they felt to be a tried and tested method, rounded up known criminals and troublemakers, and began to conduct their inquiries."

Shalini knew precisely what that entailed, having interviewed many such detainees interrogated by Bombay's finest. Shantanu continued, "The interrogations involved a sound thrashing with big thick leather belts and telephone directories. After a session of such tender, loving care, the recipients would confess to anything and everything as long as it would stop the relentless beating. So, of course, the police got many confessions and tips out of them, which were all false, and ended up chasing their own tails. All the while, the killing spree continued unabated. They even arrested a waiter from Mezban Restaurant. They were sure they had captured the killer based on information gleaned from Panna, a street photographer who hung around Gateway of India, fleecing the unsuspecting tourists. However, the next day after the arrest, another housewife living in Third Pasta Lane was found strangled with a plumbing wrench near her lifeless body. It had understandably acted as a damper on the celebrations at Colaba Police Station. After a very intense interrogation, it turned out that Panna was just using the cops to settle a score with a rival. Panna never really walked very upright again. Getting kicked in the gonads repeatedly will do that to you. All in all, the ground reality was that the police had no clue as to the identity of the plumber.

Based on Shinde's story, Sanjay Sipla got permission from his employers and began covert surveillance of certain shopkeepers in the Colaba and Cuffe Parade area. It wasn't long before he had narrowed it down to three main players because the establishments in question were the only ones offering free home delivery. Sanjay battled for and was approved the hiring of the Globe Detective Agency to help with the surveillance. The detectives from Globe were pretty good at their jobs and began to run round-the-clock surveillance of the delivery boys. Twenty of them worked six-hour shifts, and they followed the delivery boys all day, trying to piece together a profile. But before he could get any further, Paresh Nerurkar, owner of Swabal stores, one of the stores under surveillance, was shot dead.

"Further investigation of his Cuffe Parade residence yielded several items of jewellery and clothing hidden in a crawl space in his bedroom that were identified as belonging to many victims. Paresh's killer was never caught. Due to the police's inability to find any corroborating DNA evidence linking Paresh to the murders, it was never proven that Paresh was The Plumber. However, since his demise, there hasn't been a killing."

Shantanu said, "There is no doubt that Shinde has sources that no one else has, and if the six-fingered Xerox guy gave you Shinde's name, then that's the road you must follow. Let me see what I can rustle up. I'll call you back."

SEVEN

CORRIDORS OF THE PAST

Shalini went across the street from Janta Stores, sat down in Strand Coffee House, and ordered a tea and *maska* pav. Strand Coffee House was a classic Irani restaurant, unchanged from the sixties, with batwing doors and wooden furniture surprisingly well-maintained and polished to a dull sheen, not the plastic nonsense that adorned the cafes strewn all over Bombay. An old Parsi gentleman with a rude face, also from the sixties, sat at the cash counter at the entrance to the restaurant. The tea arrived piping hot, and as Shalini chewed on the delicious bread and butter, she contemplated the day's events. She could see Che Ungli from where she sat, but he couldn't see her. He was still sitting at the cash counter but wasn't looking very nonchalant anymore. He answered the phone several times, speaking animatedly into the mouthpiece.

Shalini wondered who it was that he was talking to and had no doubt it all had to do with her visit to his establishment. She had gotten used to the reactions she evoked in people when she was on a case, asking the wrong questions, hitting the odd nerve centre. She had learned through hands-on experience that people's reactions to questions often provided more accurate answers than their actual replies.

She had learned to spot the involuntary tick or the twitch of the shoulder, the tendency of the person being questioned to look to the left when telling a porky pie, and getting aggressive and tunnel-visioned when Shalini hit the nail on the head.

Her thoughts shifted to her family. Her parents lived in Chennai now, but before his retirement, her father had been the Vice President of a multi-national company. He was now enjoying stock option payouts and other sensible and timely investments. Her brother had a degree in business administration from Bajaj and had joined the young professional programme with the World Bank and now lived in Brussels. He was a source of pride and joy to his parents, and the siblings had a close bond.

At twenty-seven, unmarried, living independently, and doing a job that didn't reel in big bucks made her feel like the black sheep, although she had to admit she was lucky with her family. They were extremely supportive, and her father partly funded the rent for Shalini's Nepean Sea Road apartment. She wished she wasn't such a wild card, but you can't change who you are, and she loved her job and lived for the action. She knew that her profession and the dangers that came with it gave her parents sleepless nights, but she had no intention of settling for a mundane nine-to-five job, doing fashion reporting or some other mediocre crap. She was a crime reporter and was damn good at it.

And then her thoughts suddenly drifted towards Rahul, and her combative mood changed; she felt the initial twinges of depression darkening her sky. He had been her knight in shining armour and had turned out to be her Trojan horse. She had met him in Goa while doing an undercover piece about the Russian mafia and its growing dominance in the nightlife in Goa. The Russians even had their own enclave called Russia Town, and Indians weren't allowed inside without an invitation. It was done with the blessings of the politicians who were the beneficiaries of loads of Russian drug money. She had gotten an invitation to Russia Town and checked herself into a small bed and breakfast, ostensibly to party, sniff, and snort. Her real goal was to try and identify the connections between the Russians and the Indians.

Rahul was a well-to-do America returned student with an MBA from Cornell and with big prospects in Citibank. She had been smitten with his bronzed looks and quick wit. They had begun a relationship, and she was soon head over heels in love. She didn't care that he had a bit of a bad habit. She just put it down to him going a little wild before settling into corporate life. Her story in Goa didn't pan out as she had thought it would, and she had to leave quickly since the Russians found out who she really was. Even after returning to Bombay, Rahul continued his drug habit, progressing from recreational to full-on deep throat.

She struggled to make him kick his habit, and her dogged determination and total commitment to him brought Rahul back from beyond the edge. A few months later, once he'd secured his Citibank gig, Rahul gave Shalini her real reward for her unflinching sacrifice. He told her at dinner at Khyber - the ageless restaurant at Kala Ghoda that his mother had found a bride for him from their own community.

Too late, she discovered that the Indian male is always a mama's boy and never cuts the umbilical cord. What stunned her was his assumption that she was so weak that she would accept his proposal to continue their relationship, even after he got married. More than the revelation of his upcoming nuptials, the option he presented to her, the fact that he thought she had no willpower or dignity was what devastated her. She'd chucked a glass of water on his face and walked out, never looking back again. But her heart would never be the same again. There had been a couple of casual affairs after that, but nothing that gripped her torn soul. She found solace in the *Navi Mumbai Times* and her job as its crime reporter.

* * *

Shalini's phone rang, disturbing her dark thoughts.

"I spoke to Sanjay," Shantanu said and continued, "He was pretty tight-lipped and wasn't too keen on sharing information, but I worked my incredible charm on him that works on members of both sexes, I'll have you know. Eventually, he succumbed and gave me a location. You got a piece of paper?"

Shalini was sure it wasn't Shantanu's charm or lack thereof that had yielded his success. He was the proverbial wheeler-dealer, and she wondered what quid pro quo deal he had struck in return for the information.

"Yes," she lied.

"Sujatha Bar in Colaba Market. That's where he is nowadays. That can't be too far away from where you are. I'm sure it's not 'The Ghetto', but this happens when you do what you love, isn't it?"

The humour was lost on Shalini. She asked for directions to Sujatha Bar as she paid her bill at the counter on her way out. The elderly Parsi gentleman at the counter pointed towards the market area with a disapproving look.

Shalini wasn't in the mood for judgemental looks from some person who didn't know her, had no idea what she did for a living, but was immediately able to jump to a negative conclusion. It was so typical of this yesteryear crowd.

She brought her face forward conspiratorially and told the dumbfounded Parsi gentleman, "It's the alcohol. I'm a slave to the bottle."

As she got out and proceeded towards Colaba Market, she felt Che Ungli's eyes on her.

EIGHT

HADLEY CHASE

If you go south on Colaba Causeway, take a left at the Hanuman Mandir and then take a right, you will come to Strand Road, named after the famous Strand Cinema Theatre. The building was a broken, uninhabited dump, but in its heydays of the '80s and early '90s, the glitterati of Bombay had graced its auditorium repeatedly. Black marketeers had made their fortunes selling tickets of the sold-out shows to the movie-crazed public that thronged the streets around Strand Cinema in droves, ready to pay twice or thrice the actual price for a chance to see their favourite actor or actress in action. Hookers had made a more-than-decent living after the late-night shows. The arrival of the internet signalled the end of the 'Housefull' sign, and the fortunes of Strand Cinema steadily declined until it was finally shut down for good.

It was rumoured that Ranjit, the pimp to the stars, had started his illustrious career as a black marketeer in Strand. Of course, now one called him a pimp at significant risk to one's life. He wanted everyone to know him as a respectable real estate mogul, but it was common knowledge where he'd got his start-up capital from. Now the building that was once Strand Cinema no longer blazed bright and was used by the homeless to escape from the night patrols of the police and by hookers, who still plied their trade. However, the customer quality had deteriorated rather drastically.

After Strand Cinema, you come to Mistry Chambers and Janta Stores, Mohini Mansion, and Strand Coffee House on the right of Strand Road. If you continue further down, passing Telephone Bhavan on the left, you hit a long T-junction that is Colaba Market.

Vendors of all flavours plied their trade here, putting their vocal cords to the test against their neighbours, even if they were not selling the same product. Vegetables, spices, clothes, cheap electronics, meat, fish, and a horde of other products competed against each other, creating the perfect cacophony. The air smelled of jasmine, cinnamon, salt, and something else Shalini could not identify, but it was not unpleasant.

On the far side of the T-junction to the left was a row of chawls, the centre building looking to be in a much better state than its neighbours. She found Sujatha Bar on the ground floor of that building. She had imagined it to be the proverbial hole in the wall. As she stooped slightly to enter through the low arch of the entrance, she was greeted by a dark, dingy, smoke-filled interior. It was eleven in the morning, but there were already a few customers who, by the looks and smell, had been there for a while. A grouchy-looking middle-aged man sat at the cash counter on the right and did not look surprised to see Shalini. He just took her presence in his establishment rather calmly and pointed to the back of the bar.

Shalini shrugged, "Looks like I'm expected, or maybe I'm not the first girl to grace these hallowed halls."

She found Shinde sitting in the darkness at the back of the bar. He had a wheatish complexion, was clean-shaven, of indeterminate age, and had a half-drunk mug of beer and a packet of Gold Flake cigarettes on the table before him. He was reading a book, which in itself seemed to be a miracle, considering so many things, not the least the lighting.

Following the full-frontal assault principle, she stood before Shinde and placed the photograph on the table right under his face, waiting for a reaction. Shinde looked up from his book. Intelligent, light-brown eyes took in the tall slim figure. They moved from top to bottom, taking in the wild hair, the amber that was her eyes, and the well-proportioned breasts. The gaze was not lustful, just academic, objective, analytical even, and she felt an illogical rush of gratitude. It was refreshing to know that she wouldn't interact with the usual lecherous Indian male that this demographic tended to produce.

What was shocking was that the worst of them were the older men in their fifties and sixties, the ones most likely with grown-up kids of their own. Shinde gestured to the seat before him, and Shalini slid in. She put her tote bag on the seat next to her and rummaged about inside, taking out a small digital recorder. It was state of the art and could run for twelve hours on a single charge. Not to forget the standard triple-A battery backup.

"You've been expecting me. Who was it? The Janta Stores guy or the reporter?" Shinde smiled as he looked at her recorder and understood that this girl had come with certain goals in mind, and chances were she didn't intend to leave without achieving most of them.

"Both."

Would you like a beer?" Shinde looked meaningfully at the grubby little waiter with a dirty towel over his left shoulder hovering expectantly.

Shalini recalled her conversation with Shantanu, *"This Shinde is something like that character from the Chase novels—Barney the beach bum," he had said.*

"Who is Chase?" Shalini had asked, blissfully ignorant. She had read Grisham, Lee Child, Forsyth, and a few Indian authors like Amitav Ghosh and Adiga, but she hadn't heard of Chase.

"You mean you've never heard of James Hadley Chase? Unbelievable! One of the greatest writers of our age. The Mozart of authors. Versatility and creativity at its best. But your generation rarely reads. And it's not your fault. The market is flooded with hacks who pass off as writers today. Take that Jhiyush Pha, for example.

"It's unbelievable that his drivel has gotten published. It's stilted, disjointed, fragmented, and completely lacks originality. Unreadable trash! He speaks of Bombay as though he knows the city, but someone should tell the fool that drinking some chai in an Irani restaurant doesn't make you an expert on Bombay."

Actually, Shalini had the same impression of Jhiyush Pha. She had tried to read a book he had written, some sort of a crime novel based in Bombay, and had given up halfway, unable to reconcile with the lukewarm, insipid writing. After trying to read the nonsense he was passing off as literature, she had gotten the impression of superficiality and lack of character. But she hadn't come to discuss the failings of Indian authors. There were a lot of fantastic Indian writers, and Pha wasn't one of them, but that was not her concern today. Shantanu had gotten back on track with a little effort.

"In some of the Chase novels, a beach bum called Barney loves his beer. He's exactly what you'd imagine a California beach bum to be like. Floral shorts, a white vest covering an enormous beer belly, hanging around all day near a well-known beach bar. Now, this guy wasn't anything to look at, but if you brought him enough beer, he would tell you a story that would most likely knock your socks off. He had his ear to the ground and knew everything that went down in his city. This Shinde is like that, apparently. Just start a tab when he asks whether you would like a beer. Let's see if he has any leads on the photograph.

"The stand-off between the hospital staff, Billimoria, and his goon squad is worsening. Someone powerful wants the druggie dead, yet he seems to be protected by someone equally powerful. I would love to know what the hell is going on, and this alcoholic might hold the answer to it."

So Shalini nodded at the waiter, who produced a big jug of beer and glass seemingly out of nowhere.

It was around eleven in the morning, but Shalini figured it was seven in the evening somewhere on the planet, and she said, "Don't mind if I do."

NINE

THE TRUTH DICTATED BY THE POWERFUL

Shinde looked at the photograph, took a large swig of his beer, and lit a Gold Flake, offering one to Shalini, who declined. As he smoked, he looked at his visitor and found that she was looking straight back at him with an unwavering gaze.

Brown eyes locked horns with hazel ones, and Shinde liked what he saw. He nodded almost imperceptibly.

"May I ask where you obtained this photograph from?"

"From the ICU of St. George's Hospital, out of the pockets of a druggie who is supposed to be dead but is not. And not for lack of trying on behalf of the Bombay Police."

Shinde shook his head and laughed, "That damned Manzar Alam. He was always so underrated. You're saying he's still alive?"

So, Shinde already knew about the incident at the railway tracks but more importantly, she finally had a name. Shalini felt the excitement bubbling over, but her professionalism and training kept her in check, and she asked in a fairly calm voice, "You know who I'm talking about? The guy at the Xerox place said he had no idea, although I thought that was not altogether true." In keeping with her policy of protecting her sources, she didn't share that Che Ungli had given her his name, although Shinde had already confirmed that Janta Stores had pre-announced her visit.

"You're asking about the wrong person, Miss."

Shalini knew he was talking about the guy in the centre, the one the rest of the group was flanking—more like a protective detail than just friends posing for the camera. She pointed to him in the photograph, and Shinde nodded.

He took out a cigarette from the packet of Gold Flakes lying on the table, lit it up, and said, "In the early 90s, a new power had taken over South Bombay, almost magically. His name was Wastra. Everyone spoke his name in hushed tones, and every warlord south of the Mahim Creek swore allegiance to him. The undisciplined street gangs had suddenly been regimented overnight. They displayed almost military discipline as they patrolled the myriad streets from the Opera House and Museum to RC Church, protecting the kingdom of South Bombay. Tight, well-knit formations of six or seven fighters each, backed up by shadows in jeeps, brought a certain order to the streets that had never been seen before. The night patrols of the police learned to avoid the 'Warriors,' as they were known. But this did not happen immediately."

Shinde poured a glass of beer from the half-empty pitcher before him and continued, "Initially, there had been altercations between the cops and the street fighters, and the resulting stand-offs had seen some fighters being taken into custody. As per their orders, which they followed rather unwillingly, they had not resisted, although all of them fairly salivated at the prospect of sharing their newly acquired combat skills with their erstwhile oppressors. Everyone found out, some sooner than others, that Wastra always had a plan, was always at least two steps ahead of everyone, and there was always a reason behind everything he did. In this case, the reason became abundantly clear as the arrested Warriors were out a couple of hours into their internment after the chief inspectors of the police stations concerned came hurtling in at full speed, yelling obscenities at the arresting officers. of It was important that the rank and file in the police stations, the constables and sub-inspectors, knew that they were powerless, that they amounted to nothing in the grand scheme of things."

Shinde blew a near-perfect smoke ring, "They never even saw the bus that should have taken them to court. Shortly after that, the cops involved were transferred, most of them sent to the outskirts of the state, where the robber barons ruled with impunity, and the local police lived in fear for their lives. A couple of ambushes later, when some police lives were lost, the message was loud and clear: it was best to leave the Warriors alone or be ready to dance with the devil. The stand-offs came to an abrupt end. The obliging chief inspectors and the deputy commissioners received an infusion in their finances through well-stocked briefcases and gunny bags delivered to their doorsteps. After their wives were seen driving cars and shopping at establishments entirely out of their husband's pay grade, it became obvious that it was way more profitable to at least not interfere with these citizens of the night, as they carried out their orders from a higher power.

"You must understand," said Shinde as he emptied his glass, "the areas of South Bombay, from Colaba up to Opera House, from Kamathipura to Worli, were gold mines of business during daytime.

"Shopkeepers, pawnbrokers, jewellers, and gas stations all paid the Warriors a hefty protection fee, but the real money was made at night. At any given time, more than 1500 hotels served as boarding houses for the thousands of foreigners and locals who thronged the streets of South Bombay, looking for cheap booze and easily available drugs. There were over five thousand dance bars and a phalanx of drug dealers, all plying their respective illegal but highly profitable trades. Pimps used many of these 'guest houses' to conduct business, and local peddlers blocked rooms by the month, making money hand over fist, dishing out their various poisons at hefty profits. They were allowed to deal with no fear of repercussions, but they paid the price for their sins, which was hefty. In effect, there was, for lack of a better term, a corporate entity controlling every single aspect of business, both legal and illegal and everyone paid homage to its faceless king."

Shinde continued, looking meaningfully at the empty pitcher, as a mildly irritated Shalini nodded impatiently to the waiter, who produced a keg of beer out of what seemed thin air, and half of it disappeared equally magically down Shinde's unresisting throat, "To the untrained eye it would seem that all the night patrols were the wanderings of thugs bent on mindless violence. But it was anything but mindless, and violence was used only as a last resort. All the areas under the new organisation were mapped into grids. Each grid was the responsibility of a warlord. His job was to ensure that every drug dealer, pimp, gambling den owner, dance bar proprietor, and other entrepreneur of the night paid their daily and weekly dues. No mercy or latitude was shown to these dealers and dens of iniquity. But hookers and the poor street vendors did not have to pay a *hafta*, and although the boys sometimes got themselves a free blowjob or shag behind a taxi, which was normally given quite willingly, rape was not permitted at any cost. Initial resistance to this rule was met with straightforward executions and fizzled out rapidly."

Shalini nodded, "Perfect governance. I get that, but what about the guys who disagreed with this new rule? There must have been a lot of gangs that would not have been ready to toe the line or just give up their territory to an invading force without a fight?"

Shinde smiled as he replenished his mug, "Take Hanif Kuttha, for example. He was known as *kuttha* or dog because he tended to go off the rails like a rabid dog when he felt his authority or fragile ego challenged. He led a tough gang and ruled the Null Bazaar area. Null Bazaar was, and is still, famous for its export houses and illegal or *hawala* currency dealers. Hanif Kuttha protected all of them and collected a handsome fee in return. Khadpa Naresh was sent as an emissary to invite him to join the Wastra umbrella. A fearsome warrior in his own right, he was a part of the inner circle and was widely respected. Hanif Kuttha invited him for drinks at the local *adda* or drinking joint, and everything seemed to be on track until, acting on an unseen signal, Akbar Pathan, a shooter who worked for Hanif, came up from behind and took a swipe at Khadpa's neck with a sword. Now it was just sheer luck that Khadpa leaned down at that exact moment to pick up a cigarette that he had dropped, and the sword missed him by the whisker of a kitten.

"Khadpa felt the swish of the blade, rolled off the chair to his left, came off the roll to a crouch on one knee, and threw two knives, which he had expertly released from sheaths in the back of his neck, in quick succession at Akbar. As the daggers buried themselves deep in Akbar's chest, sending him to the great beyond, Khadpa rolled again and came up behind a chair, which he broke on Hanif Kuttha's head. The four dark-skinned fighters, sent along as bodyguards waiting outside, heard the commotion, killed Kuttha's guards who were waiting with them, and then went inside, opening fire with their Kalashnikovs and killing everyone in sight. It was absolute carnage. The air was filled with gun smoke, and the floor was slick with blood and shattered bodies. When the police arrived much later, they found Hanif Kuttha's head greeting them, strategically placed on a table. Finding his torso from among the dead bodies took a while," Shalini exhaled softly through pursed lips as she poured herself a glass of beer.

Shinde continued, "There were a few more encounters, but none as prolific as the destruction of Hanif Kuttha, and after that incident, most gang leaders, in relatively quick succession, bowed to the might of the King of the South."

Shinde took a drag of his Gold Flake, "Do you know that the Nazis started disappearing Jews right from their homes in broad daylight? These German citizens who had lived in these homes for generations were well-known to all their neighbours and the general community. Yet no one questioned their disappearance. In the same way, some dissenting warlords just vanished overnight, never to be heard from again, and no one questioned their disappearance. I believe it's just human nature to accept things prima facie. In any case, a certain law and order situation began to prevail shortly after that and suited the vast majority just fine; business was good, so why upset the apple cart? Humans are, by a huge majority, flocks of sheep."

Shalini nodded. "As I said, it was perfect governance. But where is it now? Elvis has left the building. Just look at the city today. It's a disaster zone. Open and rampant corruption, unchecked police brutality, weak, ineffective politicians, and let's not talk about the news and media. Free press! What a joke! All the newspapers and channels have sold their principles to their economic and political masters. The common man reads and hears the doctored version of the truth. And what really is the truth but the story decided by the powerful? Social media is the only thing that's still free, which is also on its last legs. If you say the wrong thing, you're branded as a traitor, so everyone keeps quiet, and those in power enact their diktats with impunity—with no fear of the law. How can you fear the law when you control it?" Shalini scoffed derogatorily.

Shinde smiled and said, "Well, not all. The *Navi Bombay* is still independent and free of any shackles, political or otherwise. At least that's what I've heard."

Shalini raised her glass in a toast, and Shinde raised his.

"Oh yes! We are the last of the Mohicans. But I digress. Where is this organisation now?" asked Shalini.

Shinde replied, "Even the best-laid plans are vulnerable to the free radicals. The unintended consequence of an unconnected occurrence. In this case, it was a tragedy that should have gone unnoticed but didn't."

"And that being?" Shalini pushed for an answer and continued, "And who was this Wastra anyway?"

Shinde took a large swig of his beer and said, "The tragedy was the sad demise of Lesley in the summer of '95. And as to the question of Wastra.... well....Ms Shalini, allow me to answer your question with one of my own."

Shinde lit a cigarette and asked, "If you were a tree, where would you hide?"

TEN

REAR-VIEW MIRROR OF LIFE

Shinde took an enormous sip of his beer, looked meaningfully at Shalini, and then at the hovering waiter. She was amazed at how the contents of the pitcher had evaporated. A barely imperceptible nod from her resulted in the almost magical appearance of another pitcher of beer and the equally magical disappearance of almost half of it barely seconds after it was put on the table, it seemed. Shalini was forced to admit that the stories about Shinde's beer-drinking abilities had been largely underplayed by Shantanu. The man had an unquenchable thirst, and he did not seem to be affected by the amount of alcohol he could put away. He chatted away about the prevailing state of affairs in the state and the country.

"Democracy does not have any place in India. Before India became the country that we know it as now, it was a collection of princely states. The rulers of these princely states were petty, selfish, and myopic. So, when the Mughals and then the British invaded, they were able to easily conquer the whole subcontinent by playing one ruler against the other. In their desire to see their neighbour fall, the rulers failed to see the bigger threat and eventually succumbed to the more organized and disciplined invaders. This is the way that India was completely conquered. The British didn't have the numbers to rule India, so you know what they did?" asked Shinde.

Shalini nodded. She knew the history that so many people were trying to forget, but even if you deleted it from the books, the truth was impossible to erase.

Shinde continued, "They used Indian troops to quell the Indian rebellions and Indian courts to convict Indian freedom fighters. And do you know who hanged the Indians or executed them by firing squads?"

"Other Indians," answered Shalini, and Shinde nodded as he lit another cigarette.

"The point I'm trying to make is that this culture of divisiveness and racism has plagued our country for years, and democracy is a failed venture in a country like ours. If we want to move forward, progress, and compete with the industrial powerhouses of the planet, then we need someone who has the vision to see beyond the petty religious and cultural divides, someone who will go beyond the four principal pointers of the compass and erase the evil of racism that has plagued this country of ours for a millennium. There can be no opposition on the road to progress because you will find that when you cut to the chase, the opposition to reforms will be based on religion, culture, or just personal greed," said Shinde.

Shalini didn't necessarily share this viewpoint, "What you're suggesting is a dictatorship—unfettered power in the hands of one man. That isn't a formula for success," she said.

"Isn't it? The uneducated masses, which form over ninety per cent of the population, have no idea what to do with their so-called freedom of choice. Before giving them such a dangerous weapon, they need to be educated about what to do with it. Otherwise, as we have seen in the past, what will prevail is anarchy, careful manipulation of the uneducated by ruthless politicians, and vested business interests for personal profit. In my opinion, the corrupt politicians and business families of the last fifty years have looted India more than the Mughals, and the British put together in the last thousand years. What is needed is a man who will rise above the rest and brook no opposition in his plan to move our country into a powerful future."

Shalini shook her head vehemently, "It will just give rise to another form of corruption, that's all," she said.

Shinde laughed pleasantly and said, "Please don't take my words seriously. Although, many true words are spoken in jest. I just enjoy a good debate. It's not often I have someone of substance with whom I can have a healthy discussion. I could also have easily argued for a democratic India and the plague of dictatorships that are rising all over the world under the guise of democracy."

Shalini realised that while it was good to have a political discourse, she and Shinde may have gone off track a bit. In an attempt to bring Shinde back on course, she said, "Lesley."

"Ah yes, Lesley," Shinde took a sip, refocused, and carried on, "Indians are very colour-conscious, Ms Shanmugam;

perhaps the most colour-conscious bunch of people on the planet. Fairness creams and treatments are a hand-over-fist business here. It's beyond their understanding that the rest of the world views all Indians as brown. We are, without a doubt, the most racist towards our own. I'm sure you may have experienced some of that yourself growing up in Bombay, going to that famous school at Fort, which some say has an affiliation to Eaton and Harrow in England."

* * *

More than being offended or irritated, Shalini was curious about how Shinde knew about her school life. It wasn't as though they had known each other for a long time. Yet he seemed well informed about her all the way back to her school days, which meant that from the time she was making her enquiries to her entering Sujatha Bar, someone had sent him something akin to a dossier on her, most probably to his phone, which meant that this alcoholic sitting in this dingy bar had a tight network of reliable informers.

Shalini wondered who had sent the dossier, what was in it, and how far back it went. There wasn't anything earth-shattering or compromising in her past as far as she could remember, but one could never tell, and she remembered an old saying about how everyone had something that they hoped no one would ever find out. But she had to admit that Shinde was damn perceptive because what he said was uncomfortably true, and his analysis of the average Indian was spot on. It hadn't been easy being dark-skinned in a very racist school. Even the fucking teachers had been racist.

She remembered being singled out for taunts by certain students, with the teachers looking the other way. Never being invited for birthday parties or class get-togethers, and the unforgettable moment when that bitch Gina Mathai had left her stranded in Juhu because, according to her, Shalini's hair was too oily and would damage the car seats. She had had to wait for her mother to come and pick her up and suffice it to say, everyone was in a foul mood on the way back. Her parents' complaints fell on deaf racist ears.

But they all hadn't been like that. She remembered the Vice Principal, Mrs Patruni, who had told her that the boys mistreating her now would be the same young men who would pursue her later in life. She remembered Mrs Isaacs fondly, who had seen her inner strength. There had been a few good moments, but mostly it had been terrible, and she had breathed a sigh of relief when her last day of school was over. Shalini realised that the alcoholic sitting in front of her was a lot more than he let on, and she wondered what had happened in his life that had led him to the bottle and this place. But she didn't want to get off track. She wasn't here to debate politics or her traumatic school life. That was in the past.

As if reading her mind, Shinde said, "We should learn to leave the past where it should remain—in the rear-view mirror of our lives. We should learn from it, never allow the bad things to happen again, and move on."

Shalini quickly asserted, "I absolutely agree, Shinde, but I would appreciate it if we could stay on point. I need to know about the photograph and this Manzar Alam and what the event from last night has to do with events that occurred twenty years back."

Shinde continued, "I understand that you have many questions and that you are under pressure to come up with answers, but the fruits of patience always taste sweeter. The dots will connect themselves; you have to trust me."

He leaned forward over his glass and looked Shalini directly in her eyes as if to impress upon her the need for her to be patient, then leaned back and lit up yet another Gold Flake and continued, "So, in a city obsessed with fair skin, Lesley was a stark contrast. Dusky, blessed with a fantastic bone structure and a body that stimulated the fantasy glands of every man she passed by, had the most beautiful green eyes that seemed to flash emerald fire. She was, it seemed, destined for fame and fortune. They say even the great Dev Anand sat outside her house for hours on end, hoping to be able to sign her up for a movie."

"Really? Then what happened?"

"The unfortunate reality was that Lesley was totally uninterested in fame or fortune. She was, it seemed, unaware of the reaction she elicited from men. She had known only one man in her life, and that was her boyfriend, Greg. She was a simple girl and, as most men found out, could not be bought with gifts or promises. She was absolutely non-materialistic. She just wanted to have a family with Greg, always be close to her brother Mario, and live the simple life, you know?"

"Yes, I get the whole 'house with a picket fence and a dog named Spot' concept. That's just so admirable, but what I don't understand is what all this has to do with the photograph and who is Wastra?" Shalini was a girl who felt that she was rooted in the grim reality of the present, and she wasn't able to relate to the portrait of Lesley that Shinde was painting. She was a product of capitalism, and although she knew it was an incorrect assumption, she instinctively connected money with happiness. She had never met Lesley, only had this alcoholic's word that she had ever existed, and yet Shalini felt mildly envious of this girl from the past, but not because Shinde had praised her beauty. Shalini was confident in her head-turning capabilities. What made her incomprehensibly defensive was this lack of ambition and absence of greed. She knew that she was afflicted with both, though her greed was not pecuniary—it was more for recognition.

Shinde shook his head and smiled slightly as he drained his glass and refilled it to the brim as if he was mildly amused by Shalin's cynicism.

"Before I tell you about Wastra, let me ask you, do you know what a Wastra is?" asked Shinde.

Shalini shook her head, "Absolutely no idea!"

"It is the razor that street barbers use to shave. Originally known as *ustara,* it got modified over the years, as many words have and became a uniquely Bombay street slang. It was the traditional, masculine way to get the bristles removed from your face until Gillette took it all away. The whole process was almost like the Japanese tea ceremony, but like that age-old tradition, the street barber and the *wastra* are slowly disappearing from the fabric of our society," said Shinde.

Shalini liked the name, the masculinity it portrayed, and of course, the danger. She wondered how the title had come about and was sure there was a story there.

Shinde continued, "It was in May of 1995, at a meeting of the warlords, that the news of Lesley's death reached Wastra. These meetings were held once a fortnight, and the purpose wasn't only financial discussions. The warlords brought news from the streets. There were impressive networks of spies in place that brought news of dissent, police interference, and potential threats from non-affiliated gangs operating from beyond Mahim Creek, which was the unofficial border. For example, there was a motorcycle gang called the Hudson Gang that operated outside Bandra. They were mostly Goan, ran drugs in the northern districts, and controlled the highways that connected Goa and Bombay. They were well-armed and had the blessings of the North Bombay politicians, who got a hefty cut. After a while, they decided to expand their operations into South Bombay, where everyone knew the real money was and began discreet negotiations with Hajeed Ahmad, a well-known warlord who had his headquarters in the slums of Dharavi. Hajeed figured that he could use his connections to penetrate Agripada and use it as a launching pad for their operations. Krishna Nagral was an enforcer in the Hudson gang and was entrusted with liaising with Hajeed Ahmad. Now Krish, as he was fondly known in his gang, was a tall, well-built, well-spoken man whose smooth veneer hid a maniacal disposition to extreme violence. After consultations with Hajeed Ahmad and his advisers, it was decided that Krish, along with five armed members of the Hudson Gang and backed up by fighters from the Hajeed

Ahmad Gang, would break up the Leopold Cafe, which was a well-known and respected bar on Colaba Causeway, just as an initial show of strength. It was necessary that everyone concerned knew that there was a new sheriff in town and that he had some great products to share. The operation was planned for a Saturday night when the bar would be brimming over with tourists and the local party crowd."

Shinde drained his glass, pointed to Shalini's glass, and she nodded her head. Shinde topped them both up, and the waiter appeared again, seemingly out of thin air, whisking away the empty jug and replacing it with a full one. They both had a sip, Shinde's being significantly larger than Shalini's, and then Shalini reached for Shinde's packet of Gold Flakes and helped herself. She leaned forward, Shinde lit her up and continued, "It was a sunny Friday afternoon when Krishna Nagral awoke, slightly hungover. He rolled himself a joint and yelled at his housekeeper, an elderly Nepali called Bhim Singh, to make him some coffee and get some food prepared. He heard the kettle come on and got up, and went to the toilet. Bhim Singh was an excellent cook, and as Krish relieved himself, he wondered what he could expect by way of lunch. He went over his day and the things he needed to get done. There was a drop-off of cocaine at a famous Bollywood star's home. There would be some sharing and caring, and later on, he had a meeting with a member of parliament to make a pay-off. This was the oil that greased the wheels of the Hudson Gang business. He thought about the next night as he washed his hands and sluiced some icy cold water over his face. There was a day-old stubble that gave him a dangerous look that the girls loved. He wondered about the extent of the damage he would inflict on Leopold as he came back into his bedroom. There were four men standing in his room, and the first thing that stood out to Krish was that the guy in the centre was a good six inches taller than his six-feet-four-inch frame. The other three were much shorter, dark-skinned, and had Kalashnikovs in their hands. The last thought that went through Krish's mind before a well-placed axe strike from the giant separated his head from his body was that lunch might be delayed a bit. Almost at the same time, in Dharavi, at his secure and well-protected flat, Haji was surprised to see that his regular afternoon masseuse, Rekha, had been replaced by a stunning, voluptuous Kashmiri who answered Alia.

"They made some pleasant small talk, and once Alia understood and happily agreed to the concept of the happy ending, Haji stripped down and lay on his bed and prepared himself for what he was sure was going to be a pleasurable afternoon, which would be followed by *naan* and chicken *tikkas*. An hour later, Alia left, leaving instructions to the bodyguards that the boss had asked not to be disturbed for an hour. The bodyguards looked at Alia and understood that the massage must have been exhausting and laughed loudly.

It was about three hours later that they realised something was not right and burst into Haji's room and found him with his genitals stuffed into his mouth, extremely dead. Later that evening, a contingent of Hudson Gang bikers, escorting a truck carrying two hundred keys of coke, was hit on the highway into Bombay from Goa. There were no survivors, and they lost the merchandise. That was rather inconvenient because the Silver Crescent Triads needed their money, and the Hudson

Gang wasn't able to pay. They began to drop like flies all over Bombay, and after their leader Pankaj Mehta, an ugly pig of a man, was found in a 'gunny bag' chopped to little bits, the gang more or less ceased to exist." Shalini found that her glass was empty and hadn't even realised that she had been drinking, so caught up, she was in the story. Shinde refilled both their glasses and continued, "Information is power. The fact that there were meetings going on between the Hudson Gang and the Hajeed Ahmad boys had been passed on to Wastra by the rag-pickers who deposited their goods regularly at Dharavi. They were on the payroll of Madhya, one of the inner circle warlords of Wastra, as were the eunuch bodyguards who provided protection to Hajeed Ahmad. From the moment they began their clandestine get-togethers, Wastra had ordered that he get regular updates and had begun his own counters to stop the potential threat in its tracks and to send a message to any other gangs that might have had similar thoughts of glory. It will suffice to say that the message was received loud and clear."

Shinde lit a Gold Flake and began.

"So, it was at such a meeting and just in passing that Rasul, warlord and overseer of the Museum and Lion Gate areas, mentioned Lesley and her demise."

"Arey Bhai, you remember Lesley? Mario's sister?' Rasul said. 'The pathaka, firecracker? She died two weeks back. They found her body decomposed in the Army & Navy Building. She was living in a sadela flat in that sadela Army & Navy building with that gardulla brother of hers. The neighbours called the police about a bad smell coming from her flat. When the cops broke into the flat, they found her dead. According to the coroner, she had been dead for four days. Mario was also there, stoned out of his mind. He must have gone in and out of the flat many times, but he was so junked out that he never realised his sister was dead. The police put him in the lock-up, thinking he had killed her, but after the autopsy showed a brown sugar overdose, they let that chutiya go.'

"Wastra was curious, 'How did that happen?' Wastra asked. 'From what I remember, she was quite a healthy girl with no vices. I've seen her around, along with Mario and Greg. They didn't mix around a lot with people, kept mostly to themselves, but they were happy, and I never heard anything about substance abuse.'

"Arey boss, I have no idea how or when that happened, but you know the story? Once you check in, there's no checking out. It's a one-way street to death. Only Allah can help you to beat that demon. But you are right, boss. Now that you mention it, that group didn't ever do any bad stuff. Maybe some daaru, but that's it. But the sad fact is that she had become a gardulla, a junkie bitch. And Mario was selling her for brown to anyone for a hundred or two hundred rupees. What a shame, boss! She was an asli maal," he exclaimed.

"What about the boyfriend? He was a shippie, wasn't he?" asked Wastra.

"That fucker died about two years ago. From what I hear, he also died of a drug overdose. That boyfriend and brother made that beauty a junkie and a whore. Boss, you cannot believe how she looked at the end. I saw her standing near Khyber restaurant one night, looking for customers. All her teeth were brown, and some had fallen off. She was skin and bones, and her tits had disappeared somewhere, I don't know. Only her eyes, boss—those eyes were still alive. I recognized her only because of her eyes. Very sad, Bhai!' he sighed. Rasul's grief was contrived.

"Junkies were overdosing all over the city. And for every junkie dying, four more were popping up. They were just the by-products of business, and business was good." Rasul didn't give a shit about Lesley or Mario or any druggie as long as he made the weekly targets. Rasul would have liked to get it on with Lesley, given half a chance, but now that she was dead, it was que sera sera in Rasul's book."

After the meeting was concluded, Wastra spoke to Richard, "Who runs the drugs out of Museum?"

"Santosh Saukar, boss. Why?" Richard replied curiously.

"Wastra had just shrugged and shook his head, 'Nothing really," he said, "just curious."

"He's a good guy, boss. Always makes his payments on time. No problems with him," Richard affirmed. Wastra had nodded his head thoughtfully and moved on to the impending party plans. Murali Sheora, a local MLA, had won the national parliamentary elections and was going to be a part of the ruling government at the centre. It was a matter of great pride for all of Colaba, and preparations were underway for a grand celebration to honour this great achievement. But Richard noticed his eyes. He had seen that look before in a young pilot's eyes. Blood and death had followed just after."

"Later that evening, the Everest Bar & Restaurant was bustling with customers. It had recently been taken over by Arjun, who was a pilot for Indian Airlines, and his good friend Vasu. Arjun sat at the cash counter near the entrance, and Vasu patrolled the floor, chatting with customers and making sure that the waiters were not slacking off. He wasn't in a good mood, and that was large because of the 'entourage.'

"They were, for want of a better word, Arjun's go-to guys—his bodyguards, if you will. Vasu didn't really like them very much. He could not understand the friendship and considered them to be useless drug-using alcoholics who were just draining the establishment of booze and money," said Shinde. "The 'entourage' consisted of Prasanjit, Dharvesh, Amjad, and Manzar. The youngest was Amjad, or 'pretty boy' as he was known for his good looks. He was seventeen. Then came Dharvesh and Manzar, both lean and wiry twenty years old. And finally, the oldest, Prasanjit—built like a bull, was twenty-one. They were an odd bunch, and what made things even odder was that they had made themselves at home at the Everest bar and had the blessings of the owner."

Shinde nodded to the waiter, who produced a pitcher of beer and set it on the table. He topped off Shinde's glass, but Shalini stopped him from topping off hers. She was trying to pace herself. "How they came to be recruited was a mystery to everyone, but just like that" — Shinde clicked his fingers—"they were suddenly there."

"It wasn't that they were unknown. It was quite the contrary. They were street denizen: flitting between gangs, struggling and clawing for the scraps Colaba offered. Then, without warning to anyone, including the inner circle warlords, they were elevated to the position of the 'entourage' as they came to be known. They were Arjun's guard dogs who had been given very long leashes. When they were around, which was mostly all the time, no one, except for Vasu and Richard, could get close to Arjun without first being thoroughly frisked.

"It caused a lot of friction with the rank and file on the streets, who were understandably upset at the promotion, but as I said, they were given free rein by Arjun, who refused to admonish them for any of their perceived transgressions. The senior gang leaders gave them a certain amount of respect, so while most did not understand, after a while, they also grudgingly accepted the elevation. For a while, the entourage had disappeared, most likely doing drugs in Goa. They had come back recently, much to the disappointment of Vasu, who had been thinking in terms of good riddance and bad rubbish."

Shinde finished his beer, topped himself off, and continued, "There had been a lot of commotion before they left, you know? They took umbrage at just about anything and didn't hesitate to let their fists fly. There was some grumbling about payback, but mostly everyone left Arjun and his friends alone because the shoot-out was still fresh in everyone's mind, and it was well known that although he was a *raees*, you know, living in a flat, Arjun was as dangerous as the worst of the street fighters, and he always had his entourage backing him up. They functioned like a well-oiled machine in a fight.

"The bouncers at Malini Bar found that out the hard way one night. Funnily enough, though, when the entourage returned from their sojourn, they seemed to be more disciplined, for lack of a better word. They seemed to have grown up and were given control of the bar's security. Vasu didn't like it, but even he had to admit that the four took care of the problematic issues that arose very professionally and with a minimum amount of violence, which was surprising given their well-known penchant for breaking faces and taking names.

"The thing is that the entourage hadn't been there at the shoot-out," said Shinde, "so people couldn't make the connection. Not that it mattered. They received a wide berth from everyone, including the gang lords. They were exclusive to Arjun."

Shalini interrupted the monologue, "I'm completely lost. One minute you are talking about this 'Wastra' who is in the photo and who quite obviously ran the protection rackets, and the next minute you are talking about a bar owner called Arjun and his four lackeys.

What is the connection? And what shoot-out are you talking about? Did I mention that I was completely lost?"

ELEVEN

ARJUN

"Ah yes! The shootout!", said Shinde, as took a big swig of his beer, and lit a Gold Flake.

He continued, "On New Year's Day of 1992, early in the morning, Arjun came back home with his friends to celebrate his birthday with his parents, as it had been a custom for a few years. This was all before he became a bar owner and a first officer in Indian Airlines. Instead of birthday greetings, he was met by police in his apartment and the sight of his parents' beaten-up faces. They had been waylaid right outside Strand Cinema, on their way back from a party, by a gang of rich, tough, drunken boys, and had been beaten within an inch of their lives."

"My God! How awful!" exclaimed Shalini.

Shinde kept going. "This changed everything in Arjun"s life. Events unfolded, and spiralled out of control, and nothing would ever be the same.'

Très dramatique, thought Shalini, as she helped herself to a Gold Flake, but Shinde had the floor, and it was his story.

Shinde continued, "It didn't take long for Arjun to find out the identities of the attackers: the leader of the pack who did most of the hitting was Ravi Satyamurthy; the son of a jeweller living in Cuffe Parade, Kumar Vaswani; and Prakash Shetty, the scion of the Shetty underworld and son of don Sharad Shetty."

"Oh, I remember that name. He was one of the original dons of Bombay, wasn't he?" asked Shalini, getting into the story in spite of herself.

Shinde continued, "Yes, that is correct. Sharad Shetty was one of the 'famous three' mafia dons of Bombay's ruthless underworld who rose to power in the '70s. The other two were Aadil Sheikh and Amin Lala. They were the original smugglers, supplying foreign goods like electronics, food, and clothes which were banned by the government of India for normal import into the country, without the payment of exorbitant taxes, to the crazed Western population in India. They made incredible fortunes supplying cheap labour to the Middle East, to countries like Saudi Arabia, Kuwait, and the UAE, exercising iron control over that business by ruthlessly eliminating all players who tried to get in on the game. Then they branched out into drugs and prostitution and allied businesses. For more than two decades, they were the untouchables.

"Once Arjun found out the identities of the perpetrators of this crime, he knew he was up against a wall. There was no way any action would be taken against the violators, as was evident by Inspector Billimoria's lack of enthusiasm. Furthermore, it was well known that Billimoria only took the side of the wealthy and while Arjun's parents weren't exactly paupers, the underworld don's son and his friends were in another league. After two weeks of running around, his parents gave up hope of justice being served.

"That's when Arjun did something that would change Strand's history and create the stuff of legends."

Shalini lit a Gold Flake and waited. Shinde topped his glass, took a big swig, and continued, "He went to Richard, the boss of Strand, and asked him to help him kill Prakash Shetty and the other attackers of his parents." Shalini was silent as Shinde contemplated lighting up a Gold Flake, then decided against it. He continued, "Standing at an even six feet in height, Richard was from Mangalore and functioned under the blessings of Subash Raut, a powerful overlord with fingers in a few pies across South Bombay and the head of Subash Raut's umbrella, which had a few small-time warlords and a couple of petty politicians under his control."

"Hang on, hang on!" protested Shalini. "I'm getting completely lost."

Shinde stretched his legs under the table as he took a big swig of his beer and said, "Well, you did say what shoot-out. And to understand Wastra, you have to know Arjun. It's a deep and very complicated relationship. You came for a story, and you will get one, Ms Shalini, and it will be worth your time and money, but it is a dark past, and as you can see, it doesn't seem to be over."

"You mean to tell me that all these events that purportedly occurred way back then are connected to the druggie in the hospital?" asked Shalini.

"Yes. All is not what it seems, Ms Shalini. You have a reporter's nose and can smell bullshit a mile away. I know you have your doubts, but I also know you feel them. The possibilities of a great and jaw-dropping story, if it's the truth. You wouldn't be here otherwise," replied Shinde.

Shalini chewed on her lower lip as she looked across at Shinde. That damn alcoholic was correct, as usual. There was a story here. She could feel it, but how much of it was the truth and how much of all this were the meanderings of a drunken mind was something she wasn't completely sure about. She would have to separate the chaff from the wheat later. She nodded her head and said, "I'm pretty invested in the story now to back off. Please carry on."

Shinde took a deep breath before exhaling softly through pursed lips, took a swig of beer, and continued, "Nobody would ever understand why Richard decided to help Arjun. I mean, there was nothing to gain from it but trouble, and the assailants of Arjun's parents were connected and absolutely untouchable. There would definitely be a heavy price to pay. A few months earlier, Prakash Shetty had been on his way to see his favourite whore, had stopped near Colaba Post Office and ordered a bouquet of roses."

Shalini laughed, "I think she may not have been into the red roses and chocolate thing, but then again, I could be wrong."

Shinde smiled and said, "Prakash Shetty had a romantic streak about him, but it was replaced with a red rage when the florist asked him to pay. It's not that Prakash Shetty wanted cash; he just felt affronted that the florist had not been polite enough by his standards. So, he took out the Mauser that had been recently gifted to him by his father and shot the flower seller dead right there on the street, in broad daylight, in front of several bystanders."

Shinde lit another Gold Flake, took a deep drag, and continued, "Of course, no one had the guts to give witness evidence to the hostile police, but what was even more galling was that there had neither been an apology from the Shetty family, nor blood money paid to the family of the flower seller. It had been cold-blooded murder, it had happened in the territory under the purview of Richard and Strand Company, and Richard had been hamstrung by his boss Subash Raut's orders not to react. Richard had given a lot of his own money to the victim's wife and two sons from his own pocket.

Maybe it was the anger Richard felt, or maybe the deep sympathy for the young man in front of him, but to the obvious dismay of his counsellors, he got up, hugged Arjun, and said, "Your war is my war, but baba, you will fire the first shot."

Arjun looked at him grim-faced and nodded his acceptance. Richard continued in a sober tone, 'Don't rush into this, baba. It is one thing to hit someone, but killing somebody in cold blood is a completely different thing. Taking a life willingly will change you forever. You will lose your soul and may never find it again."

Arjun looked unwaveringly into the gang boss' eyes and said, "Don't worry about my soul. Have no doubt that I will open up the party. Make sure your fighters don't falter."

"In hindsight, some present at this meeting would have cause to remember this entire conversation and realise the charade that was meant to galvanise the Strand warriors to battle."

Shinde laughed, "Open up the party! And a party it was. A once-in-a-lifetime, never-to-be-forgotten party," Shinde fell silent, and he seemed to be reminiscing.

Shalini didn't want this drunk to get lost down memory lane at her expense, so to speak, so she tried to bring him back, "You were talking about the shoot-out?" she asked delicately.

"Ah, yes! Sorry. I got lost for a bit," Shinde took a deep breath, then a deep swig, and continued,

"Richard put out the word on the streets for news of the Shetty gang. For two weeks, there were scattered reports of sightings, but the gang never stayed too long in one place. Arjun went on leave from his airline, and the days and nights were spent in Richard's house in the Mohini Mansion building or in the Sundernagari fisher village while he waited for news that would send him to war.

"Finally, one Friday night in February, they got actionable intelligence about the gang. The street vendors working at the Gateway of India sent news of a bunch of rich kids in cars parked across the Taj, drinking and creating a lot of trouble. Namdeo, from the fisher village, was sent to confirm their identities and to make a phone call on Richard's landline from a payphone close to the Taj to put to rest any doubts. In those days, there were no cell phones, but you were probably just a baby," said Shinde smiling. He had an infectious smile, and Shalini found herself smiling back.

"Probably," she said.

"They had practised for weeks preparing for this night, and everyone knew what they had to do. Ryan, the famous Anglo-Chinese fighter, possibly the only foreigner to fight on the streets in Bombay, had schooled the unskilled in the fine art of close-up killing."

"A foreigner in the street gangs?" asked Shalini.

"His mother was British, and his father was Chinese, doing stunts in Hindi films. Ryan was notorious as a break-in specialist, but he was also a skilled knife fighter and very handy with automatic weapons. In the village of Sundernagari, they practised, first with rubber knives and blanks, then moving to the real thing. There were more than a few injuries, but after two weeks, the list of the front-line fighters was finalized."

Shinde continued, "They had swords, axes, and handguns. The men were divided into groups of ten, with one squadron leader per group. Each squadron leader was given either a Makarov or a Glock 9mm, and the soldiers under them were given country revolvers. These were made by manufacturers in Bihar and were on sale to dacoits and other nefarious elements that operated in the Chambal Valley and other such areas. They were known as '*kattas*' which made a big bang and were notorious for their tendency to backfire and take out the shooters' hands and eyes. It was an art form to be able to use these 'countries,' as they were known."

"Wonderful," murmured Shalini under her breath.

"Arjun had displayed a knack for strategy from the outset, and the plan had been to get the gang in a pincer grip, from which they could not escape. *There can be no survivors,* he had said, and although it seemed strange to the Strand fighters that a perfectly decent kid like Arjun could talk about death with such ease, they understood the logic of 'no plaintiff, no case."

"What does that mean?" asked Shalini.

"It means that they planned to leave no survivors so that no one could identify them. No plaintiff, no case. Do you see what I mean?" asked Shinde and Shalini nodded.

"They knew the fight would take place on the streets, but they just didn't know where. To that end, they practised in different, controlled environments, simulating crowded areas, heavy rains, and police interference. In a very short period of time, they morphed into a cohesive fighting unit.

"The Gateway Road provided the ideal conditions for the planned pincer attack. One group, consisting of fighters from Dhanraj Mahal led by Najeeb, approached the gang from the north. They blended in with the throngs of evening visitors to the Taj and the Gateway of India, street vendors, and such. Arjun, flanked by the toughest and most loyal fighters of Colaba, approached from the south—from the radio club side. James, Richard, Ryan, Ghaniya, and a platoon of extremely tried-and-tested fighters were with him. Kalidas, one of Arjun's most loyal friends from the fisher village, led a group of fighters from the west, cutting off the route to Colaba Causeway."

Shalini found her pulse rate quickening. If nothing else, this drunk was able to spin a good story. His tone and inflexion varied as they set the mood. Here, in this dingy bar, with the grubby waiters and dull lighting, everything took on a slightly unreal feel with the telling of the story, and suddenly anything seemed possible.

"Prakash Shetty and all his merry men had gathered on the promenade at the end of the Taj Mahal hotel structure, with a clear view down to Colaba Causeway. They had four cars with drivers sitting in them parked on both sides of Gateway Road, facing both directions. The job of the drivers was that if they were to spot any potential trouble, they would honk three times and start shooting, giving time to Prakash Shetty and his guys to get their guns out. These boys were rich, but they were not stupid or careless, although they gave the impression of being like this to the casual observer," explained Shinde.

"These were men who had killed with no compunction in the past and were ready to take lives at the drop of a hat. Arjun knew that his parents had been lucky, and the thought brought a cold rage upon him. There would be no mercy from either side," said Shinde.

Shalini found herself drinking faster than usual. She was already on her third mug of beer but found herself holding out pretty well, all things considered.

Shinde lit a Gold Flake and continued, "Several things happened almost simultaneously. Rasul, chatting with a couple of guys, approached one of the cars parked near the Taj building. He bent down as if to ask the driver of the car a question and slit the driver's throat from ear to ear. There was a red spray, and the driver collapsed head-first onto the horn of his car. The line of sight of the minders was blocked by the arrival of a bunch of young men who, it seemed, had placed themselves by sheer chance between the dead driver's car and the rest of the lookouts. As Prakash Shetty turned to see what the disturbance was, he found himself looking straight at Arjun, who seemed to have magically appeared. A millisecond passed, and as Prakash Shetty went for his Mauser, which was tucked in the back of his extremely expensive Guess jeans, Arjun shot him. The hollow point bullet went into his chest, shattering the sternum, bounced around inside the chest cavity, and exploded. Prakash Shetty died with a shocked look on his face. With incredible dexterity, Shyam Tandel, Namdeo, and Bhagya, like they had practised a thousand times, ice-picked the ears of the remaining drivers, killing them instantaneously."

Shalini found that she was smoking one of Shinde's Gold Flakes, her hand shaking a bit.

"Kumar Vaswani, who had been particularly brutal while punching Arjun's mother over and over again in her face, turned to run and found himself facing the open sea. He flipped over the low wall and fell fifty feet into the water. It was low tide, and the rocks broke his fall and his back. He survived but would never walk again. He suffered severe skull fractures, and this rendered him incapable of speech. He would be a vegetable for the rest of his life. The rest of the gang scattered, but they were caught in the grip of death, as all paths of escape were cut off. And then the massacre began. The Strand warriors used their guns and were not averse to wet work at close quarters, but the fisherfolk were old school and used only their knives and swords. This would change in future battles. Pandemonium gripped the area as sightseers screamed and ran helter-skelter in all directions. There was absolute chaos," Shinde took a deep breath and continued with his narration, "At the end, not one of the nineteen gang members survived. The air reeked of blood and gunpowder. The screams of the mortally wounded blended in with the panic-stricken screams of the stampeding crowd like a symphony from hell."

Shalini gulped down her beer as Shinde continued, "Ravi Satyamurthy was dying. He had been stabbed several times, and his right arm lay next to him; it had been partially hacked off by Lhoncha just above the elbow and was swinging grotesquely, connected to his broken body by a sliver of skin as blood pumped out in spurts. In the days after the beating, his father, the jeweller, had sent his apologies and a gold mangal sutra through inspector Deshpande of the Colaba Police Station, which had been summarily rejected by the Srinivasan household.

A word from Arjun and Lhoncha stopped mid-strike. Although he was dying, Ravi Satyamurthy still felt a stab of fear as Arjun stepped towards him. In retrospect, he realised that he had not taken the young pilot seriously enough. His lieutenants had run a check on the possibilities of a comeback, and their evaluation had been that there was no threat. Boy, had they been wrong! Arjun bent down and looked Ravi in the eyes. His face was flecked with red, and his blue shirt, drenched with blood, had turned dull black. When he spoke, it was with a surprisingly calm and controlled voice, which was completely at odds with the surrounding chaos.

"Look at you. All fucked up. And take a look at your hired dog," he said as he grabbed a chunk of Ravi's hair, lifting his head, and made him look at Aslam Qureshi, the feared shooter of the Shetty gang. Legend had it that Aslam could shoot the eye of a sparrow from a hundred yards. Ghaniya and Namdeo had strung him up against a lamppost.

Lhoncha walked up to Qureshi, who was flopping around weakly on the lamppost like fish on a hook. Arjun examined the Mauser that had fallen from Prakash Shetty's dead hands and said, "Nice piece. Tell your friend I will put it to good use when you meet him."

Arjun nodded, and the gutting knife in Lhoncha's right hand moved in one fluid upward arc as he sliced Aslam Qureshi open from the stomach to the sternum. His intestines spilt out and lay steaming on the pavement, still connected to the body like a glistening snake, and the stench was overwhelming.

"Arjun lifted Ravi Satyamurthy by his hair until he was sitting up. There was a swish, and Nagaiya swung his sword, separating his head from his body."

Shinde took a long swig of his beer and continued, "Although it seemed longer, the entire battle lasted only about ten minutes. The Warriors had been well-prepared and had executed their plan to perfection, but no one was under any doubt about who was to be credited with the success."

"If this Arjun was just a normal, average, everyday guy, how was he able to plan and execute such an operation?" asked Shalini.

TWELVE

THE CHANCE FACTOR

Shinde took a break from his narrative and poured himself a glass of beer, replenished Shalini's glass before she could say no, and lit a cigarette, suitably impressed that this young reporter was always ahead of the curve.

He continued, "It was not a question that anyone thought about at the time, even as the shock waves of the shoot-out reverberated through the halls of power, both legitimate and the not-so-legitimate. Never before had such an operation been carried out on the streets of Bombay. The coroner's office spent all night scooping up body parts, and it took almost another day to clean up the promenade where the slaughter had occurred. The fire brigade was called in, and they used their high-powered hoses to clean away the blood and remaining pieces of dried flesh and bone that had fused to the ground. It may have been psychological, but most police and other personnel involved in the clean-up could swear that they smelled dried blood everywhere, even in their sleep, for days after the cleaning operation was completed. And do you want to know the best thing?"

"What?" asked Shalini.

Shinde laughed and said, "A devastating attack had been carried out that had left nineteen dead bodies, but no one had a clue as to who had carried out the operation."

"After the 'Shoot-out at Gateway,' as it came to be known, the fisherfolk retreated to the safety of their village, and the Strand warriors went underground in the various streets and back alleys of Colaba, hunkering down as they prepared for a retaliatory strike that they were sure would come. Defensive perimeters were set up along Colaba Causeway in a very unobtrusive manner, using the numerous street shops as storage facilities for weapons. Many shopkeepers on Colaba Causeway suddenly had a lot of hired help.

"At night, when the shops were shut and the crowds had thinned to a trickle, sharpshooters were placed on the top of the buildings along the Causeway in ten-hour rotations, looking for attackers from the north. If the attack came at night, the plan was to create a kill box at the crossroads where Colaba Police Station, electric house, Sheela Garment store, and the 'light of Asia' restaurant formed four points of a square and inflict maximum casualty damage on the attackers. The south was a veritable fortress with fisherfolk and Strand Warriors monitoring all the entry points so that there were no gaps in the defensive lines in case the enemy was able to bypass the watchers, make it down the road to Cuffe Parade, and attempt perimeter breaches via Badhwar Park and other soft spots all the way down to RC Church. Najeeb and the Dhanraj Mahal fighters took care of the roads into the gateway area and Lions gate to stop them." Shinde explained further.

Shalini was no military expert, but she realised the magnitude of the planning that had gone into setting up a successful outcome in the incident at Gateway. However, the logistical requirements to set up a defensive perimeter post-shoot-out over such a vast area and set up the communication lines between the various outposts were enormous.

Then there was the issue of keeping this enormous defensive operation under the radar and making sure that the details were not leaked to the wrong ears. This demanded intense loyalty from the key commanders, who would be in charge of enforcing strict discipline amongst the foot soldiers, which meant that there had to be an organisational hierarchy, not unlike that of a regular army. The Vietnamese had transformed themselves into the formidable fighting force that was the NVA, but that was with the help of the Russians.

Who were the military advisers here? Shinde, however, was an unstoppable train and forged on, disregarding the questions that were written all over Shalini's face and continued.

"However, nothing happened, and although there were the occasional alarms, they turned out to be damp squibs. This was because even though the police had conducted frantic investigations in the aftermath, they had turned up no leads, and this was due to the lack of any credible witnesses. The attack had produced a hundred per cent kill rate, and the circle had been kept so tight that there were no leaks. The usual police informers had mysteriously disappeared, some never to be seen again, and the ones that did resurface were vehement in their affirmations that they hadn't the foggiest idea as to identities of the perpetrators of the violent massacre. No number of threats or bribes were able to shake their testimonies."

Shinde was well into his fifth pitcher when Shalini returned after a trip to the restroom. The one at the Sujatha Bar was less than ideal for a lady, and Shinde had organised for her to use the facilities at one of the flats in the chawl above the bar, where Karate Vilas, the local *shaka pramukh*, had a western-style toilet. Nevertheless, Shalini semi-squatted over the bowl. She was not too happy with the general hygiene conditions, but when you have to go, you have to go, so she had gone. Shinde waited for her to settle in as he lit a Gold Flake and then continued, "For the Shettys, this was not computing at any level. Not only had they lost the scion to their empire along with some of the top shooters out in the open, in front of what should have been multiple eyewitnesses, but in spite of all their efforts, they were unable to unearth a single lead that could give them an insight as to the identities of the attackers. The stories were conflicting, ranging from some saying that it was a group of men, while others were certain they saw women wielding weapons, and then were some real crazies who kept talking about a giant. Most of the witnesses were innocent civilians who had been out for an evening walk, taking in the majesty of the iconic Gateway structure, the beauty of the Taj Hotel, and the cool evening sea breeze.

"Some were locals living in the nearby buildings and were regulars, while some had come from as far as Bhayandar. Some were guests at the Taj and other hotels, and some were from out of town, from places like Ahmedabad and Surat, who were on a tour of Bombay. The confidential informants of the police had all disappeared en masse overnight, frustrating the police and not giving a chance for the Shetty enforcers to work their charms. Then there were some who had resurfaced and were handed over to the same Shetty enforcers after being unsuccessfully questioned by the police."

Shinde took a large sip of his beer, took a drag of his Gold Flake, and continued, "The enforcers decided to use the back rooms of the Colaba Police Station, where they could conduct their questioning without the subsequent screams being heard. Their leader was a short, squat man called Devi Prasad Shetty. Like many Indian males, he sported a moustache, hoping to add some machismo to an otherwise unremarkable face. He had a typical brutal face that men with low intelligence quotients with a fondness for violence possess."

Shinde lit up a Gold Flake, took a deep drag, and continued, "No one really knew what happened in the night, but the four Shetty enforcers were found dead in the very same rooms they had decided to use for their tender questioning. It wasn't that they were dead that scared the cops at Colaba Police Station. It was how they were found that terrified the pants off everyone, and even Billimoria felt a chill run down his back."

Shalini felt a similar shiver run down her spine and said, "What are you trying to say? Were these thugs hit inside the police station? But that would mean ... ?" She left the question hanging in the air.

Shinde answered her question, "It was obvious to all concerned that there were elements in the police force whose loyalties lay somewhere else and that they were working with these invisible hitmen and had given them the required information that had resulted in the slaughter right inside Colaba Police Station. But what sent a wave of superstitious dread was that they were found decapitated, and their heads were placed in a row on a table in such a way that it was the first thing everyone saw when they broke into the room. There was no sign of the torsos. Just four grimacing heads with no bodies. Of course, the informants who were to be recipients of the interrogations were never seen again.

"Sharad Shetty vacillated between extreme sorrow and raging fits, but the hard truth was that there was just no news. Furthermore, it was obvious that they were up against a very organised enemy that was hidden in the shadows. As the days went by, the don sank into madness that only extreme sorrow could trigger as it became more apparent that the chance of a break in the case was slim to none. The fact was that the operation had gone off better than anticipated. All holes had been plugged, all information sources eliminated, and unknown to the Shettys, Arjun's fighters were in the position to fight a highly successful defensive war if required. It was a work of genius," Shinde took a big swig of his beer and continued, "It was Billimoria who put it all together. And it wasn't because of some great detective work or sleuthing skills on the part of the Parsi inspector. As with all great cases that get solved, the answer just fell into Billimoria's lap by chance."

"I get it. The chance factor. What happened?" asked Shalini as she allowed Shinde to top her off.

"You see, Ms Shalini, on the night of the shoot-out, the president of Portugal was on an official visit, staying at the Taj. There was intense security, not like today, of course. Now you can't even walk near the Taj Hotel without being frisked. Those terrorists really did a number on everyone. I promise you, madam, they would not have made it past the fisher village alive if Wastra was still there. I've been given to understand that the Taj terrorists came off rubber dinghies and walked through the fisher villages near Cuffe Parade without anyone even raising a basic alarm. I can assure you that if Wastra was still in control, these dogs would have been taken care of with minimum fuss, and their bodies would have been dumped back into the sea where they came from," said Shinde.

Shinde lit a Gold Flake, took a large swig of his beer, and continued, "In the aftermath of the Bombay tragedy of 26/11, a lot of questions went unanswered and have remained like that till today."

Shalini took a sip of her beer and said, "Okay, I'll bite. Not exactly what I came here for, but go ahead."

Shinde said, "So one of the terrorists was captured alive; he was paraded on national television, making a mockery of our judicial process, before he was eventually executed. But I'm given to understand that more than ninety per cent of the terrorists escaped, and no one has thought to ask how that happened and where did they all disappear to?"

Shalini said, "I'm not sure that is entirely accurate."

Shinde laughed, "You shouldn't believe everything you hear on the news. These guys attacked multiple targets in a coordinated strike that spoke of precise planning, and none of them was ever caught. Take, for example, the attack at VT station."

Shalini took a sip of her beer and said, "It's called Chhatrapati Shivaji terminus now, in case you didn't know, and yes, I have to admit that there are some questions."

Shinde nodded as he took a swig and emptied his glass. "Almost all of them escaped. What does that tell you?"

Shalini said, "That they had help?"

Shinde nodded approvingly, "Exactly. This is what I've heard. In fact, most of the terrorists who attacked the Taj had checked in as guests a few days earlier. They didn't have any weapons on them. So how were they able to procure such a large number of sophisticated weapons and ammunition?"

Shalini's interest was piqued, and she said, "It would mean that they had help from inside the Taj. At least that's what I think you are getting at."

Shinde nodded vigorously as he lit another Gold Flake, "I heard some shopkeepers received containers of goods a couple of weeks ahead. They were paid handsomely not to ask any questions. Most likely, they thought it was gold bullion from Dubai. In fact, rumour has it that one of the stores was, and is still, owned by a socialite, who may or may not own a leather store, and the jury is still out as to whether he had actual knowledge of the contents of the boxes that were stored in his shop."

Shinde shrugged and said, "Of course, he hides behind a veneer of respectability, and chances are that his standing in the elitist social circles of Bombay will place him above the law, so we will never really know the truth."

Shalini felt that there was another story there, but not the one she had come in search of, and said, "Conspiracy theories normally flourish like weeds in the wake of catastrophes. It's difficult to glean the truth, and I'm sure it's lying there waiting to be discovered, but I'm here about the photograph."

Shinde topped off his glass and continued, "You are right, of course, Ms Shalini. That is a story for another day. Let me return to the aftermath of the shoot-out at Gateway. The security had been tight, but only inside the hotel and the immediate periphery. The shooting happened on the far side of the road, opposite the Taj, where there was no security at all, and the chaos triggered an immediate counter-response by the 'Z' class commandos assigned to the president's detail, who first rushed to secure the Taj building from any possible attack. By the time they figured out that there was no threat to the President, more than fifteen minutes had passed.

"As per their training, they then turned their attention to securing the surrounding areas but were hampered by the stampeding crowds. In the prevailing chaos, and apart from the sure fact of gunfire, they were unable to determine what was going on. But their training was top-notch, and they were able to establish a perimeter around the scene of the action. Arjun and some of his warriors got trapped in the net. But rather than shooting their way out, they threw their weapons into the sea and blended in with the panic-stricken throngs, generously contributing to the screams with matching ones of their own.

The fisherfolk retrieved the weapons under cover of the night, approaching the Taj shoreline from the Sundernagari village using rubber dinghies. Everyone was concentrated on the bloodbath outside the Taj, and no one thought to take one look at the sea," Shinde laughed shortly.

Shalini glanced at the hovering waiter and said, "So what you're saying is that shortly after the incident, the security commandos had the killers in their net but did not realise they had them.

Shinde nodded enthusiastically as he gulped down his beer and lit a Gold Flake, "There were almost two hundred people caught inside the perimeter, and they were all herded into police vans and taken to Colaba police station. By the time it came to questioning Arjun, the commissioner of Bombay Police had received a call from a very prominent politician, and at 4 am, he and two DIGs had rolled into Colaba police station, screamed obscenities at the harassed inspector-in-charge Ashok Tawde, and with many apologies, Arjun had been released. His fighters were released about an hour later after it was determined that they were just innocent passers-by who had come for an evening stroll to take in the magnificence of the Gateway of India and the Taj Mahal hotel and bask in the refreshing sea breeze but had innocently gotten caught in the crossfire. In fact, no one present even made a connection between Arjun and the various fighters who were released. It was beautiful, a work of art."

Shinde took a swig of his beer and lit a Gold Flake. It was incredible that he was still as lucid as a judge. Shalini could not help but feel a grudging respect for this alcoholic and his imbibing skills.

"But Billimoria made the connection. How?" asked Shalini.

"As I said, Ms Shalini, it was by chance. You know how sometimes a problem arises that seems to have no solution in spite of all your efforts, and when you've given up, the solution just drops into your lap? Like a tune that flutters on the borders of your consciousness and dances on the tip of your tongue, just out of reach, and when you've given up, you suddenly remember the name of the song? It was like that for Billimoria. He had taken a lot of flak from the Shettys over the shoot-out and his inability to have produced any results, but he knew the answer was out there. He felt sick in his stomach that he could not find out the identities of the members of the hit squad—and it wasn't for the lack of trying."

Shinde emptied his glass, leaned back and lit a Gold Flake before continuing.

"Billimoria, like several of his colleagues, was corrupt, but he was diligent, and once he got his teeth into something, he was like a dog with a bone. His tenacity had always been rewarded with results. But this operation had been so tightly guarded, and the fighters hand-picked so carefully that no snitch was able to provide any information whatsoever. Like I said earlier, the ones that could have provided an insight had just vanished into thin air, and the ones that did return had bouts of amnesia regarding the night in question. It was a veritable trick. And then there was the very discouraging night of the four heads."

Shalini laughed as she tried to imagine the looks on the faces of the cops when they entered the room and were greeted by four heads without bodies, all neatly placed in a row. Shinde continued, "Billimoria realised that he was at least two steps behind and that there were men on the police force working against him, but he had no idea who they were for the love of money. And when you live in a glasshouse, you better be careful about the stones, if you know what I mean? Billimoria may have had his suspicions, but he dared not air them because he wasn't exactly pure as the driven snow. But six months later, when he had given up hope of ever finding out anything about the hit squad of that fateful night, the answer just fell into his lap. At first, he couldn't believe it. Could it be that it had been staring him in the face all this time? Billimoria felt like he'd taken a violent blow to the liver. They say that the stupidest farmer finds the biggest potatoes, and Billimoria, by the same sheer dumb luck, found out the perpetrators of the shoot-out."

"It's quite often like that, isn't it? You try to find the answer to a question with absolutely no success, and then when you've given up, the universe opens its doors to you," said Shalini, checking to see if her digital recorder was still rolling. She looked up to see Shinde pouring himself another glass of beer.

"Six months had passed after the shoot-out," said Shinde. He was off on another tangent but continued, "Arjun went back to flying, had a few hours under his belt, and the takeover of the Everest Bar passed by almost unnoticed because there was a hot and new topic on the streets. The talk of the town was the rise of Wastra. Not long after the shoot-out, while everyone looked for answers that weren't there, a new king took control of the streets of South Bombay: omnipotent, controlling everything from behind a mantle of invisibility. No one knew who he was, but his power was supreme. His will was being done through the various war chiefs who spoke of Wastra in hushed whispers. No one had seen Wastra, but everyone knew someone who had met someone who had met Wastra. The legend of Wastra took on gigantic proportions in a very short period of time."

"You see," said Shinde as he drained his mug and continued, "there was a lot of confusion and chaos prevailing among the crime families following the shoot-out, and the resulting power vacuum was deftly and adroitly filled by Wastra. Before anyone realised it, the new king had ascended the throne, and everyone in the south bowed to his crown."

Shinde looked at the waiter reproachfully, and another pitcher arrived. Shalini lit up another of Shinde's Gold Flakes and took a sip of her beer. She didn't want to visit Karate Vilas' home unless absolutely necessary. Shinde watched her light up, took a swig of his beer, and continued his tale.

"There is lot of mass migration taking place around the world, as people flee from poverty and war to safer havens. Everyone is acting like it's something new, but actually it's been happening since the dawn of time.' Shinde switched gears, "The Faruz of India are concentrated in Bombay. Did you know that?" Shalini looked confused, then realised that they were off on yet another tangent, and there was nothing that she could do but just go with the flow, and she nodded as Shinde continued,

"I met a man once who told me about them, and also clarified that it was his point of view. According to him, they were one of the original refugees to India. They fled Persia eons ago to avoid religious persecution and were given refuge in Gujarat by the ruling king of that time. Eventually, a vast majority migrated to the regions that became Bombay. They were allowed to practice their religion in peace without fear of persecution and were given a lot of latitude, but they never attempted to integrate with the locals, whom they looked down upon with benign arrogance. As the centuries went by, they forgot about their flight from Persia and their refugee status and began to believe that they were a superior race."

"Even to this day, they mostly marry amongst themselves, which has led to a seriously weakened gene pool. It is rumoured that every Faruz family has at least one mentally or physically handicapped member. There are definitely very many talented Faruz and, of course, very rich ones too, but most of them are lower middle class or impoverished. But even the poorest of them still think that he or she is superior to the other Indians, even though they don't have a rupee to their name and live on handouts provided by the rich members of their community and live in gated communities paid for by the affluent from their community. There are rumours that some of the big Faruz business houses made their fortunes by bringing in drugs from China at the turn of the twentieth century, during the opium wars, so in the strictest of terms, you could say that they were the original drug cartels of India. Of course, they have gone completely legitimate now, and with the passing of the decades and the changing of the guard, they have deliberately chosen to forget about their not-so-legitimate beginnings and entry into the corridors of wealth and power."

Shalini was thoroughly confused by now. And she was almost certain that some of the statements of Shinde were dubious. To say the least, she said, "I'm not sure all that you're saying is true, but even if it was, I don't see the connection."

Shinde guffawed, "Oh, there is a small connection. And I was just presenting some facts."

"Well, those facts could get you sued for slander," said Shalini with a smile.

"What happens or is said in Sujatha Bar stays in Sujatha Bar," said Shinde.

Shalini bowed her head in mock acquiescence and replied, "Of course."

Shinde continued, "Not everyone followed the Wastra line immediately. There was resistance, but the repercussions were so brutal and violent that in a very, very short time, all dissenters came around with resounding alacrity. Take, for example, Sammy Khajotia; he was a Faruzi who ran a gambling den at Mereweather Road, hence my earlier observations of the Faruzi community in Bombay. He paid his bribe money to Billimoria, another Faruzi, and after a while, Sammy Khajotia thought he was a priest and his den of iniquity a temple. He forgot that he was almost illiterate and at one time impoverished, as he rough shod his customers, sold watered-down alcohol for exorbitant prices, fixed the tables so that the house almost always won, and got away with murder, which happened when some drunk customers couldn't or wouldn't pay, as he gave the in-house bouncers' to do as they saw fit. In a short while, his arrogance grew in leaps and bounds since having Billimoria's blessings, and protection made him virtually untouchable. One day, Homi Contractor, a young Faruzi architecture student, stopped by the gambling den and asked to speak to Sammy. Since he was a Faruzi, Sammy deigned to meet him. To Sammy's surprise and rage, Homi told him that from the following week, Sammy did not have to pay Billimoria anymore and that he, Homi, would come along to collect the weekly contribution on behalf of Wastra."

"Sammy's fair skin contused with rage, and he yelled for his bouncers, who came in, smacked Homi around, and threw him out. They would have killed him, but he escaped because he was a Faruzi, and as Sammy picked him up and slapped him a couple of more times, he was told to remember that there would be no latitude shown to him the next time. Two nights later, Lhoncha, Namdeo and twenty fighters visited Sammy's gambling den.

"Using swords, axes and whips made of eel skin, which opened the flesh to the bone and maximized the bloodletting, they butchered the bouncers. The ones that made it to the streets found themselves face to face with Kalashnikov-toting, dark-skinned men who mowed them down where they stood. Inside the bar, Lhoncha and his crew turned their attention to Sammy's two children, Ronnie and Shirley."

Shinde lit a Gold Flake, drained half his glass in one savage gulp and continued, "Ronnie and Shirley Khojotia were an extremely tough sibling pair, having trained under Parvez Mistry, the legendary karate black-belt guru, and were famous for being able to handle themselves against superior numbers with minimum effort. In fact, Shirley was a lot more vicious than her brother and had sent many unsuspecting guys to the hospital with life- threatening injuries. But they were not prepared for the violence that visited their establishment that fateful night. Lhoncha tore open Ronnie's face with a flick of his whip, forever scarring the relatively handsome face beyond repair. Namdeo ducked under.

Shirley's spin kicked, lifting her twirling body and slamming it into the floor. He broke her right leg at the knee, which made a loud crack as it met the flat end of his sword. He broke her jaw with an efficient heel stamp at the junction of her left jaw bone and skull. They dragged the siblings out into the streets, and their fists pounded them viciously till their broken faces were masks of blood. Then they turned their attention to Sammy, who had been restrained by two of Lhoncha's fighters so that he could witness the destruction being meted out to his hired help and children. They dragged Sammy out onto the road, where his children lay unconscious and his bodyguards lay dead. Then they proceeded to re-adjust his jaw with a hammer and then used the same hammer to break both his legs."

Shinde took a swig of his beer and continued, "No one ever heard of what happened to Ronnie and Shirley, but rumour has it that they were sent away to the US to stay with relatives. Another rumour was that they were sent away to Dubai. Regardless, they were never seen in Bombay ever again. It took six months before Sammy could walk again and even longer before he could chew solid food. He never told anyone, especially Billimoria, what had actually transpired, but he categorically informed Billimoria that there would be no more weekly pay-offs. Enraged, Billimoria began a fruitless manhunt for six Nigerians armed with automatics. The fear of seeing your loved ones under the gun trumps anything else.

"Sammy had seen the vicious pounding of his offspring and was under no illusion as to what would happen if he decided to go the distance with Wastra. He was certain that Billimoria was a mere beginner when compared to the giant and his comrades who had destroyed his bar. Homi was treated like an honoured guest every week when he came to collect. And just like that, all across south Bombay, pockets of resistance were rooted out and extinguished. No one dared to challenge the might of Wastra. He very successfully employed the carrot-and-stick method at all levels. It was not always violence, I might add. Take, for example, Puranchand Joshi. He was a popular Vaarnis jeweller who was not excessively greedy, and he loaned money at reasonable rates. Ghaniya visited him one morning at his Colaba Causeway store and played a video for Puran, who immediately accepted Wastra's terms. Later on, he made a successful bid for the local municipal council and served as municipal councillor for five years."

Shalini couldn't contain herself and asked the obvious question, "What was in the video that was played to this Puranchand jeweller?"

Shinde smiled and said, "I'm glad you asked. The video showed the beating of Sammy and his kids. Now, Puran had been personally beaten black and blue by Shirley on Gateway road one evening when he had innocently tried to chat her up. So, you can understand he wasn't too upset by what he saw. He was forced to watch the entire video to the bloody end, and he wasn't made of stern stuff and almost threw up. But what he saw right at the end helped him with his decision."

Shinde stopped to refill his glass and light a Gold Flake before continuing. Shalini almost yelled in exasperation, "Oh, come on, Shinde! Don't stop now mid-sentence."

Shinde smiled and said, "I guess you want to know what was in the video right at the end, which helped Puran with his decision. Am I correct?"

"Of course, yes!" Shalini blurted.

Shinde continued, "Right at the end of the video, after the visual experience of the Sammy Khajotia incident, expertly edited in was a personal message to Puran from Wastra himself. And it wasn't just the message that rocked Puran's world. It was then that Puran became aware of the identity of Wastra, and to say that he was surprised is like saying Siberia is cold in winter. His shock was mixed with fear as he realised that this knowledge was a double- edged sword. He knew he was being made privy to a most closely-guarded secret, and his next move would decide his fate. He could either sink, which he was pretty certain would happen rather violently when he least expected it, or he could ride the tides of fate, swear loyalty to the king and see where that took him."

Shalini laughed and said, "I guess it's a pretty fair assumption that he decided in favour of keeping the faith."

Shinde nodded and continued, "He turned out to be extremely loyal and trustworthy. He was rewarded with success in business, and his humble political aspirations came to fruition. He was a trusted confidante, provided timely information over the years, no one ever knew his affiliation to Wastra, and he was loyal to the end."

Shinde took a sip of his beer, looked across the bar behind Shalini at some customers coming in, and continued, "Yes, there were the obvious questions from so many people from both sides of the law. Mostly everyone wanted to prostrate themselves at the feet of the great one, but apart from the chosen few, most were always given the run around by the gatekeepers. There were some attempts to intimidate the inner circle gang lords. These attempts were met by the pen, in the form of high-priced lawyers, and the sword, which is self-explanatory, and after a while, these attempts ceased. It also became clear that there were police officers who were aware of Wastra's identity and were being nurtured by the king of the south, but it was impossible for anyone to know who or how high up the food chain they were, and this served as an extreme deterrent to all the threats to the throne."

Shinde sighed as he poured himself a glass of beer, and Shalini lit a Gold Flake Shinde continued, "But even the most carefully laid plans are prey to the chance factor, the unfactored variable, and one fine September morning, it reared its ugly head and handed Billimoria the answers he had been searching for."

THIRTEEN

LEGENDS AND LEGENDARY FIGURES

"One Monday morning, about six months or so following the Gateway incident, after a long night of total lethargy at the police station largely due to the general peace prevailing all over his jurisdiction, Inspector Billimoria went on a final round of inspection of Colaba before calling it a day.

"Now, normally, a keeper of law and order should have felt happy basking in the peaches-and-cream environment that had gripped Colaba in an inexorable grip, but that could not have been further from the truth. It was around seven in the morning, and he was frustrated because this morning, like every morning over the last six months, had been totally and completely incident-free."

A new jug had arrived, filled to the brim with beer, and Shinde ordered another packet of Gold Flakes. He poured Shalini a glass, topped off his own, took a large swig and continued, "Not one criminal case had been registered, and not one arrest had been made. The Colaba look-up, once a source of pride due to the famous inmates who had graced the drab and dreary cement cells and, more importantly, a source of income, now housed a few homeless drunks. Billimoria, like several of his colleagues, supplemented their meagre government salaries with incomes earned from arrests and the subsequent bribe money from the affected individuals to suppress or delay criminal charges from being filed. The money came from either their families, desperate to get them out, or from the organisations they worked for.

"Sometimes, the cases were too severe to be swept under the table, and there was even more money to be earned by providing protection to the accused while they languished in jail, awaiting a trial date. The worst thing about being in police lock-up is the absolute and total lack of anything to do."

Shinde offered Shalini a Gold Flake, but she declined, and he continued, "The real prisoner is the mind, and so, for a few dollars, one could arrange for alcohol to be provided so that one could put oneself into a coma until bail was granted. For a few more, one could enjoy the privilege of a conjugal visit at one of the interrogation rooms, and top-dollar got you an acquittal due to lack of witnesses, misplaced documentation, and so forth. It was most profitable, but these cases were short in supply, given that no criminal cases had been filed for over six months. He had tried to shake down a few bar owners, pimps, and other flowers of the night, hoping for some easy money, but the arrival of some very tough lawyers every time had put paid to those aspirations pretty damn fast.

"Furthermore, several complaints of harassment had been filed against Colaba Police Station with the Police Commissioner's office, and Billimoria found himself being called in for tea and biscuits one morning, which wasn't a part of his grand retirement plan. It may have been his imagination, but at the meeting, after seeing the expensive gold Rolex on his wrist, he felt that PKB Suryavanshi, the Director-General of Police, had to be on someone's payroll because there was no way he could afford that watch on a Commissioner's salary. Now it wasn't any of the underworld families because he would have known about it, so there was quite a chance that this top cop was on Wastra's payroll.

"But Billimoria didn't want his career or his life to come to an abrupt halt, so he decided to keep his suspicions with the only person he trusted—himself. He knew that his stay at Colaba would come to a swift and violent end if he tried to get too smart, ambitious, or greedy. He wondered why he hadn't been targeted by Wastra yet, silently crossed his fingers and toes, and left it alone."

Shinde was well into his sixth pitcher. Shalini had to visit Karate Vilas' home again. She knew it was getting late, but there was no rushing Shinde, and she needed to let her boss know how she was progressing. She made a phone call to Shantanu while in the loo, who listened to her update and told her to stick with Shinde.

"I've been trying to do research on your alcoholic friend, but there's not too much information out there about him. Can't find any information on his parents, siblings, or relatives. He's known to hang out at a few bars, although the one he's in right now has been his regular watering hole for quite a while. No idea how he supports his thirst, but he doesn't seem to be wanting for money."

"I agree," said Shalini, "He's not badly dressed, from whatever I can see, and he's well- groomed and well-spoken. So, what he's doing here in this part of town is something I can't understand. A broken heart, maybe?"

"I'll check," said Shantanu, "but keep the pressure on. I'll get back to you if I get any useful information."

"Let me know if you come up with anything useful. Send me a text, and I'll call you. But this guy is no fool, he cannot be pushed around, and boy, can he drink! He's on his sixth pitcher. And let's not get started on the smoking."

"With some able assistance from you, no doubt."

"You have to take one for the team," said Shalini with a smirk.

She returned to her seat, and Shinde started without waiting for her to settle in.

"Billimoria was cruising down Mereweather Road when he saw Homi walking ahead. He accelerated so he could say hello when Homi turned right and went into Sammy Khajotia's gambling club. Homi was a budding architect and the pride of Faruzi community so Billimoria was curious, to say the least, about the fact that Homi was visiting Sammy's den of iniquity. What was even more curious was that Homi was accompanied by Mangesh, a dreaded shooter of Strand Company. Billimoria would have liked to encounter hell out of Mangesh, but suddenly this well-known criminal had become untouchable. His request to proceed with an encounter with Mangesh had met a stone wall.

"Not only that, he had been summoned by PKB Suryavanshi and had been told, very categorically, to never even look wrongly at Mangesh, and consequently, he had followed his orders to the letter. But now, his interest piqued, Billimoria went up ahead and parked just out of sight.

"About fifteen minutes later, Homi came out carrying a duffel bag. A vein pulsed on Billimoria's forehead. He knew what that bag contained, having been the recipient of several such bags in the past until Sammy had just stopped one day, and no amount of threats or coercion had been successful in changing Sammy's mind. Now Billimoria knew why.

"He sent one of his plain-clothed constables in pursuit of the duo after giving him orders to stay at a safe distance and to report to him immediately once he had ascertained the destination of the duffel bag. So, Billimoria was absolutely dumbfounded when the constable reported that Homi had entered the Everest Bar, and when he left, it was without the package. He could not get around the connection between Homi and the Everest Bar. He had guessed as much, but now it was confirmed that Sammy Khajotia was paying Wastra. Homi was obviously one of the several bag-men that the police force was not aware of, and one of the drop-off points was the Everest Bar. If a highly respected professional like Homi was working for Wastra. Billimoria wondered who else was."

Shinde lit a Gold Flake and, leaning forward, said, "It was only after Billimoria found out who the owners of the bar were that the proverbial penny dropped. Like I've said, Billimoria was many things, mostly all bad, but he wasn't stupid. He got on to Gateway road, flagged down a *chaiwala* under the shade of Oliver Guest House, lit a cigarette, and began to try and piece the puzzle together.

"He knew that Homi and Arjun had been friends since childhood. They lived in neighbouring buildings, and Billimoria had often seen the two together on their way to school and to the tennis courts, where Arjun used to practice. He was well aware of the assault on Arjun's parents, having been the one that had stonewalled all attempts by Arjun's parents to have a criminal case registered against Prakash Shetty and the rest of the now-deceased gang. He also remembered that Arjun had been in the lock-up after he had been scooped up by the 'Z' class commandos immediately after the shoot-out, and he remembered the uproar it had caused and how Arjun had been released. He checked the records and found that Vasu had also been in the lock-up and also had been let go.

"Suddenly, Billimoria found that his hands were trembling as the picture began to unveil itself to him like a shy bride. He just could not believe it! Could it be that the entire upper structure of the Shetty family had been dismantled by this pilot? He was nothing, or was he? How had he gone from being a pilot to a bar owner? How had it slipped everyone's notice? He obviously couldn't have pulled off such an operation all by himself.

"So, it was obvious that he had the blessings of Wastra. And one did not have to be a soothsayer to know that once he took his suspicions to Sharad Shetty, and if they proved to be correct, then there would be a war coming soon. Billimoria knew he would have to play his cards very carefully if he wanted to avoid ending up on the casualty list."

Shinde shook his head, looking past Shalini, lost in thought.

"What happened after that?" asked Shalini, trying to push the pace, hoping that Shinde wouldn't collapse into an alcoholic stupor before finishing his story.

Shinde took a large swig of his beer, gestured to the hovering waiter and continued,

"Billimoria was a good dog. Like most cops who were on the payroll of one of the underworld clans and, as I had mentioned earlier, Billimoria owed his loyalties to the Shettys. It was because of them that he had been able to buy the expensive Cuffe Parade flat, afford his high-maintenance mistress, and enjoy a rather comfortable existence. Billimoria knew that he was a small cog in a machine larger than he could imagine because one can rarely see the big picture when one is right in the middle of the frame."

Shinde continued, "Rather than take his suspicions to his superiors within the police force, Billimoria, like the loyal dog that he was, presented his facts to Sharad Shetty. In a country where it was of paramount importance to have a son, the loss of his firstborn had taken a terrible toll on the don. He had aged twenty years overnight and barely slept for two or three hours anymore, vacillating between fits of rage and tears as all his efforts to trace the killers of his son came to nought.

"He looked at Irfan Pathan, the tall, burly, Nagpada fighter who had taken over as the war chief for the Shettys after Aslam Qureshi's departure from service.

"Boss, I find it hard to believe, but let me check it out,' he said.

"'Sir, nothing is carved in stone, and maybe I'm wrong, but I'm just presenting the facts, and they don't lie. This needs to be checked out. Would you like me to take care of it?' said Billimoria.

Irfan Pathan laughed derisively, and Sharad Shetty held up his hand before saying, "Billimoria, thank you for the news. We will take it from here."

He spoke to Irfan, "There will be no action taken in haste. Send in Yeda and Kalia. Let them shake the branches, and let's see what falls out. I want their assessment of this pilot-cum- bar owner. If he killed my son, then I will wipe his family and him from the face of the earth with my own hands and fuck this Wastra, whoever he is. I fear no one; my death is forewritten, and it's timing cannot be charged by any man. But we must be sure before acting. His parents were already beaten up by our boys, and if he is innocent, then I don't want to be responsible for any more unnecessary deaths."

Shinde lit a Gold Flake, drained his glass, and continued, "And thus entered Yeda Hussein and Kalia Sunil into this canvas of blood. Hussein was known as 'Yeda', or crazy, because he was supposed to be fearless in the face of death. He had faced down twenty killers at Elphinstone College and had walked away unscathed, leaving six dead in his wake.

"Or at least that's how the story went. In the underworld, stories often got embellished with every retelling. But there was no doubt that Hussein was a legend, at the very least in his own mind."

Shalini laughed into her glass, "Isn't that almost always the case with most legends and legendary figures? A reinvention of memories to suit the mood of the time?"

Shinde nodded as he topped off his glass, "Yes, but in this case, there was no doubt about Yeda's ferocity. He had a lean and hungry look about him, and with his long hair and craggy features, he was not entirely a bad-looking man. But his proclivity for unfettered violence and his inability to connect with members of the opposite sex left him relatively free of female company, as I'm sure you can understand."

Shalini laughed into her mug and nodded her agreement, and said, "Girls like bad boys, but we need to be able to have a conversation before jumping into bed. There are a few girls I know who like it rough, you know? But violence is a complete turn-off. Well, at least for most of us," she said with a hint of sarcasm.

Shinde smiled and continued, "Kalia Sunil was a bestial-looking dark man who was Yeda's constant partner. Rumour had it that the relationship between the two was a little more than just a professional friendship. The general talk about town was that they also shared the same bed."

"Oh my! Were they gay? And out in the open? That could explain the lack of women. Maybe they just needed each other," said Shalini, and both she and Shinde laughed loudly.

Shinde said, "Being gay has never been taboo on the streets. For example, if you were in the lock-up and you were connected, it was perfectly normal to enjoy the company of a guy or male prostitute or the period of your incarceration. In fact, some noted underworld figures were openly gay."

"No kidding? One would think that they were flush with women?" said Shalini.

"Ms Shalini, that's exactly the reason. It's all about supply and demand. Thomas Keynes 101."

Shinde smiled, took a swig, and continued, "Not withstanding their orientations, Yeda Hussein and Kalia Sunil were expert confrontationists. They knew how to spark a conflagration and burn it all to the ground when required. They were skilled in hand-to-hand combat and were quite comfortable with guns and swords. When they heard that the owner of the bar they had to break up was Arjun, Yeda was rather relaxed. You see, he had known Arjun from the Elphinstone College days and hadn't been too impressed with him. Further, he had no doubt about the awe he, 'the crazy one', generated. He was absolutely one hundred per cent certain that this would be a walk in the park.

"Backed up by Mobin and Tufael from Dongri, they arrived at the Everest Bar around 10 pm. The bouncer manning the entrance was from Third Pasta Lane and recognised the group as potential troublemakers; he asked them politely to wait while he sent for backup. When he turned back to face the belligerent group, Yeda broke a bottle on his head for his troubles. Other bouncers rushed in to assist their overwhelmed colleague, but Hussein's head-butted one of the bouncers in the face while Mobin expertly swivel-kicked another. The group spilt out onto the pavement. Hussein had whipped out his signature Iranian army regulation assault knife, and Sunil had himself a small .22 pistol, useless for anything beyond ten feet but deadly at close quarters. The two groups squared off against each other, weapons drawn. But before there was any further escalation in violence, there was a terse command, and Arjun pushed his way through to stand before Hussein with a pleasant smile on his face and said, "Hussein Bhai, namaste! Sorry for the behaviour of my security guards. They did not recognize you."

"Arey, so you're the owner of this chutiya bar? I remember you from Elphie. You used to hang around with that pawli Brian and that other chooth, Timpy."

Hussein was unable to control the derision in his tone. But as he spoke, a warning bell went off in his brain. There was something about that group in college he had forgotten, but before he could get any further with his thoughts, Kalia Sunil joined in with a few more choice insults.

"Since when did someone like you become a bar owner? Who did you lend your ass to? I heard it belongs to this fucking Wastra? Maybe you like a mystery fuck?" Hussein and Sunil laughed uncontrollably. Arjun raised a hand, and the growling amongst his bouncers stopped.

Hussein had been in the killing fields of Kermanshah and Ahvaz. He saw the gesture and the immediate obedience it received, and once again, something about that group from Elphonstone College, the one this bar owner used to be a part of, knocked on the periphery of his memory banks. He wasn't seeing something, and he had a feeling he was missing something important, but with all this cacophony and impending violence, coupled with a few lines of coke he had snorted, he just couldn't concentrate. He mentally shrugged and dismissed the black feeling that was creeping up on him. He had his orders, and he intended to follow through with them, regardless of the feeling of foreboding that was all around him like a wet blanket.

Far from being scared, Hussein found himself aroused. It would be amazing to kill this guy, to see the life go out of his eyes. It was almost sexual, and he felt a warm glow wash over him. Kalia Sunil was less refined. He had seen four young faces in the background. He was looking at the entourage.

He looked beyond Arjun at Amjad. "What a pretty boy," he rasped. "I'll fuck you till you're pregnant. Come, come," he gestured with his brass knuckles towards Amjad, who just stared back with a neutral look that showed absolutely no fear. Again, a warning bell went off in Hussein's head. If he didn't know better, he could have sworn that the kid had military training. He had a feeling that the four young bucks hanging around in the background were a lot more trouble than the bodybuilders who were blocking his way into the bar.

Arjun's smile never wavered, "Guys! I don't understand what has happened. This is all one big misunderstanding. Come in, and let me buy you both a drink. In fact, please drink as much as you want."

Arjun went over, arm outstretched for a handshake. Instinctively, Hussein returned the gesture. As they shook hands, Arjun leaned over and said in a low tone, "Hussein Bhai, please enjoy the hospitality of the Everest Bar. All on the house. I have some work that I have to take care of. I'll be back in a couple of hours. Please stay, I would like to talk to you regarding a business venture, and I could really use your help and advice. I'll make it worth your while just to listen to Bhai, please."

Suddenly, the clouds of trouble and the premonition of doom vanished, and Yeda Hussein and Kalia Sunil shared a mental sneer as they pushed past the bouncers and shouldered their way into the bar. There was no way Arjun was capable of anything violent. There was an obvious answer as to how he had become the owner of this bar, but it definitely wasn't anything earth-shattering like that fool, Billimoria was insinuating. This Arjun hadn't been much in college, and he had obviously not changed. Sharad Bhai was wrong. Hussein chugged down a large Black Label and signalled for another. But a vague misgiving still lingered, one that stubbornly refused to go. Then two beautiful women walked into the bar, one of them a famous model, and surprisingly started lavishing their attention on the two bravados and their friends, who just couldn't believe their luck. Then the alcohol kicked in, and before they knew it, Hussein and Sunil were enjoying their rock-star status in the bar, the free booze, and forgot all about Arjun."

FOURTEEN

THE WARRIORS

Shinde continued, "The Shetty stronghold, 'Lhotse', lay in a cul-de-sac at the end of Minoo Desai Marg in Lower Parel. It was a plush four-storey building encompassed by high walls and a huge gate that was electronically operated. High-resolution CCTVs, strategically placed, monitored all movement in and out of Lhotse and also the surrounding areas. The command and control centre, located in the basement, had state-of-the-art LED screens connected to the CCTVs, which were operated by a two-man team on a six-hour rotation. The command-and-control centre also housed the heavy weapons cache of the Shetty army. High-intensity searchlights came on at sunset and switched off automatically at 6 am. There were six guard units at all times, patrolling the compound in four-hour shifts.

The building complex itself had several luxury apartments for the Shetty family and the thirty soldiers who lived there. There was a state-of-the-art gym, swimming pool, sauna, Jacuzzi, and an additional arsenal room on the first floor. There was underground parking for at least twenty of the fanciest cars that money could buy. It could be said that the Shettys lived well. Sharad Shetty had a penthouse on the top floor where he lived with his wife and two kids— now reduced by one since the shoot-out.

The Warriors came out of the darkness like wraiths from a mist. There was a power outage in Lhotse, and in the thirty seconds it took for the generators to kick in, they had breached the perimeter walls. The guards were mowed down by machine pistols fitted with silencers and crossbow bolts. No one could understand why the guards at the control centre in the basement hadn't set off the alarms like they were trained to do, but the police found them all slaughtered at their posts.

Sharad Shetty's wife was in her hometown of Udipi, visiting her parents, so it was only Sharad and his son, Manav, in the penthouse having a drink, waiting for news from Colaba when the door exploded off its hinges, the shockwave rupturing their eardrums and flinging them off their chairs. Sharad Shetty, completely disoriented by the ringing in his ears, instinctively looked for his son in the smoke and debris. Manav Shetty was eighteen years old and, unlike his older brother, was academically proficient and had been shielded from the family business. Sharad Shetty had wanted his son to go to Harvard, but as he looked at the lifeless body of his younger, beloved son, he knew that yet another one of his dreams would be unfulfilled.

The don choked back his emotions. There would be time to grieve later. His training was kicking in already as he stood up on shaky legs and looked for his guns. They were under attack, he had understood, but what he could not understand was the lack of retaliation from his security teams. Then, through the acrid smoke, he saw Viju Shetty, his nephew, step through the door and felt a stab of relief. Irfan had summoned Viju from the Shetty homeland along with his shock troops in preparation for war against Strand. There were very few people who were feared as much as Viju was. But his relief turned to confused consternation as Viju lifted the head of Irfan Pathan in his right hand.

Behind Viju, another figure stepped in. Sharad did not recognize the dusky lean young man or the army of lean dark fighters who filled the room. They were not Annas from Antop Hill but could have been, except for the military ease with which they handled the silenced Kalashnikovs that hung around their necks. The don was completely confused about these strangers, but his heart sank into his expensive Gucci shoes as he realized there would be no help coming from Viju that evening.

The leader spoke, "Sharad Anna, I am Arjun," and the don then knew he had grievously underestimated the threat from the south.

"Your sons are dead, and I am to blame for that, but I did not start this, and none of it has brought me any pleasure, but your journey is at an end. There is no worse failure for a father than to fail his children, and in life, you have failed your two sons in every possible way. Maybe it will be different in the afterlife, if there is one."

Sharad Shetty had lived by the sword and had known that one day the chances were brought that he would die by one. As a volley of bullets sent him to join his children, he died with a curse on his lips, spitting venom at his killers.

* * *

Back at the Everest Bar, Yeda Hussein and Kalia Sunil were completely intoxicated, and Mobin and Tufael were not too far behind. The music had been exceptional, the DJ playing all their requests, while the two attractive ladies had been their constant companions. Sunil had even copped a feel of some of the waiters' backsides, so, all in all, it was a great evening. If they hadn't been so drunk, they would have been aware that most of the patrons had left, leaving behind only the bouncers who, extremely unobtrusively, had cordoned off all avenues of escape.

The music suddenly stopped, and Yeda turned around to shout at the DJ, only to find himself facing Arjun. Yeda knew it was time to fight and went for his weapons, but they were no longer on him. Those damned women! Then Yeda saw Lhoncha and almost had a cardiac arrest. The stories had not been exaggerated. There really was a giant in the Strand army! Hussein saw the axe in the giant's right hand and knew what was going to follow.

"Listen, Bhai!" said Yeda Hussein, looking calmly at Arjun, " There is no need for further violence. We will forget this happened. Give us our weapons, and let us go. You dogs can continue running this piss hole you call a bar," Hussein hoped he would, as he had in the past, be able to bluster his way out of what he realised was a very dangerous predicament. But he had done it before by playing it cool, and he was confident he could do it again. All he needed was to get out of this mess and report back to the don that Billimoria was right. It was clear as day that this fucking bar owner was the leader of the kill squad that had taken out the Shetty firstborn. They needed Viju and his shock troops, and then they would return and take care of this upstart and his fucking giant.

"Your boss is dead. Irfan Pathan, Ejhaz Khan, Asif Ismail, all gone," the eyes that delivered the devastating message were as expressionless as the tone of voice. For all practical purposes, Arjun could have been talking about the weather—only he wasn't. He was talking about a catastrophic event, which he had obviously engineered with great panache.

It was at that precise moment Hussein, like many before him, realized too late that his people had been behind the curve all the time. He had no clue how but the pilot had been aware of all their moves. While he and Sunil were kept distracted at the bar, this motherfucker had gone and attacked Sharad Bhai in Lhotse. Hussein realised the enormity of the subterfuge, and the air went out of his lungs. He checked his watch and realised that this pilot had completed an impossible task in less than two hours. He wondered how they had gotten past Viju and his shock troops. It was impossible, he knew, but this bar owner seemed to be blessed by the devil himself and had somehow pulled it off. The audacity of this operation left him stunned and impressed in equal parts. But he also knew that there was no escape now. He realised he would not be able to bluster his way out this time. He could expect no mercy.

Yeda sighed. So, this was the end of the road. After surviving countless skirmishes in the back alleys of Tehran against the royalist pigs and then on the battlefront against Saddam

Hussein's American-funded dogs, Bombay had been a holiday paradise where everyone was terrified of him. It was ironic that he was going to die here, in what he had thought was a vacation gig, and it was very clear that his journey to meet Allah was about to begin. Yeda had no lack of steel in his blood; he looked Arjun straight in the eye and did not flinch as Lhoncha decapitated him. As his body collapsed, his head flew in the air, smacked against the wall, and fell onto one of the tables, knocking over a few glasses that crashed on the floor. Kalia Sunil was not made of sterner stuff and soiled himself, whimpering like a wounded puppy.

Amjad put a bullet in his head and ended his misery. Mobin and Tufael followed their bosses into the great beyond with a lot more dignity than Kalia Sunil. Arjun watched dispassionately as they all collapsed like rag dolls. All he said was, "As far as Yeda and Kalia are concerned, well, now we know who was on top." There was grim laughter in the bar as the clean-up started. An hour later, the bodies had disappeared, the broken glass had been cleared away, and the bar was pristine once again. You could have eaten off the floor.

Shinde looked at Shalini's empty glass and said, "Talking about eating, may I suggest some food? The *jhingha masala* and *surmai* fry are to die for, and I think you could do with some sustenance."

Shalini let out a long breath and nodded gratefully as Shinde signalled to the waiter nearby.

FIFTEEN

MONEY, POWER AND LOVE

There was a short silence after Shinde placed the order for food, and Shalini digested the story so far, trying to find her bearings mentally.

"So, who is this Viju Shetty? Obviously, he's the guy who brought the Shetty house down, so to speak. From what you have told me, he was the head of the Shettys shock troops. I'm not entirely sure what that means, but hazarding a guess, it would mean that they were the heavy-duty artillery that was sent in when things threatened to go out of control. As the head of such a critical arm of the Shetty forces, it meant that this Viju Shetty was a high-value soldier, highly trusted, and supposedly blindly loyal. But he was also the inside man for Arjun. How could it be that Arjun was able to turn him?"

Shinde nodded encouragingly, and Shalini continued, "That's very interesting. I thought these gangland boys were very tight. Thicker than blood and all that stuff?" She took a drag of a

Gold Flake. Between Shinde and her, they had polished off his cigarettes and had ordered a new packet.

"That's a fallacy, Ms Shalini. Gangland is extremely greedy, and greed makes for two things."

Shalini laughed and said, "I'm not going to ask what they are because I'm sure you're going to tell me anyway."

"You're absolutely correct. I am going to do exactly that. Firstly, a greedy person, in his desire to accumulate, becomes corrupted, and when I say corrupted, I mean that person can be controlled either by money or by information."

"I get the money part, but what do you mean by information?" asked Shalini.

Shinde opened the new pack of Gold Flakes and lit one. The cook, a young man in his twenties, a *banyan* and *lungi* that had both seen better days, interrupted them, asking Shinde how spicy the cook should make the food. Shalini was no slouch with the chilli, but Shinde asked for the spiciness to be kept medium.

"You see, Ms Shalini, if the food is too spicy, you will miss out on the taste. And then you end up drinking too much beer."

Considering the amount of beer that had been guzzled by Shinde, Shalini wondered exactly what he meant by "too much beer".

Shinde continued, "Take, for example, the Kaskar gang. They operated out of Dahisar, running drugs and prostitution. Iqbal Kaskar, their leader, was ruthless, and he ran a tight ship, dealing with suspected informants and traitors with his trademark manner of burning them alive. Ramesh Sanil, his second-in-command, started doing some side business, neglecting to tell his boss about the additional income and definitely forgetting to share. Lacking the operational skills of his boss, he made one mistake too many and got snagged in the net of the Goonda Branch of the Bombay Police. But rather than arrest him, which meant he would be most certainly dead much before the case came to trial, Inspector Sadashiv Hedge offered the rat a deal. His deeds would not be made public as long as he made regular reports on his gang's activities and provided the police with a detailed list of the gang's suppliers and customers. Sanil Shetty, as Ramesh Sanil liked to call himself, went above and beyond the call of duty and turned out to be a gold mine of information. In six months, the invincible Kaskar gang was brought to its knees as their operations got steadily crippled by police raids on their godowns and their key fighters were either arrested or encountered by the ruthless Goonda Branch.

"Iqbal Kaskar executed several suspected traitors, but the crackdown just kept increasing in intensity. Finally, Iqbal Kaskar and several of his trusted lieutenants were lured out of hiding by false information provided by Ramesh Sanil and killed in an ambush at Vashi, where he thought he was meeting with a new service provider who could turn around his run of extremely bad luck. That turned out to be inspector Sadashiv and some members of the anti-terrorist squad. Ramesh Sanil miraculously escaped, but like all rats, he finally met his end in a ditch on the Bombay-Pune highway, burnt to a crisp.

"Someone always talks, and gangland never forgets," said Shalini, "I see what you mean about information, the power to control and how greed makes a man weak."

Shinde nodded his head as he took a large swig of his beer, "However, to be honest, in the case of the Shettys, it was different. All critical positions were held by men who were related by blood to Sharad Anna, so the chances of betrayal were slim to none. Viju Shetty was the head of the shock troops for the Shettys. He was called in when the normal fighters were not able to handle a situation. As you correctly surmised, his shock troops were the heavy artillery. But they were also like a nuclear deterrent. For example ... " Shinde smiled as he saw Shalini's reaction to yet another tale, " ... there was a high-ranking politician with 'Z' category protection who was not toeing the Shetty line. He was demanding exorbitant rates from Sharad Shetty and was not providing any service commensurate with his monetary demands. Sharad Anna tried to reason with him at his Mantralaya office and was unceremoniously ejected from the premises. Then the Don sent for Viju."

Shinde took a large swig that emptied his glass. He did a quick refill, all the way to the top, and signalled to the waiter.

"Viju arrived from the Shetty heartland with twelve of his highly trained fighters and began to shadow the minister, getting a feel of his daily schedule, trying to find a soft spot they could exploit. After a month of non-stop, round-the-clock surveillance, they found that the minister's weakness was his monthly retreat at Lonavala, where he hosted a number of Bollywood personalities for a weekend of debauchery.

"Naturally, there were no 'Z' class commandos present because this was an off-the-books type of affair, if you know what I mean?"

Shalini lit a Gold Flake, took a drag, blew out an elegant trail of smoke, and replied wryly, "Of course I do. I'm well aware of the proclivities of several key members of our state government."

Shinde continued, "At these monthly get-togethers, the minister used the services of a private security firm that provided protection to several big business houses and celebrities. Normally, the Lonavala celebrations would be preceded by a request from the minister's aide to the security company about five days before. Using an extremely high-priced hooker to seduce the minister's aide, Viju got the proposed date for the celebrations that month. After that, it all just sort of fell into place. Viju and his fighters waited in the darkness until the party was at its peak.

"The bungalow was an eight-bedroom, two-storied structure built in the old colonial style, with tiled roofs and wooden pillars. They decimated the guards in the two jeeps that were parked at the entrance of the long driveway. Viju's fighters killed all the security personnel with minimum fuss. Once the all-clear was given, Viju strode into the party, lashing out at random people who were unfortunate enough to get in his way to the minister, who had stopped lavishing his attention on a young upcoming starlet and was screaming hysterically for his guards. He didn't touch the minister or threaten him in any way. He stood for a while, staring expressionlessly at the minister while his men wrecked the beautiful bungalow.

"Thirty minutes later, he turned around abruptly and left. There were no words exchanged, but there was a marked improvement in the quality of service provided by the minister in question, and no demands for payment were ever made. It took all of the minister's influence to keep the deaths of sixteen-armed, private security personnel under wraps."

* * *

Shalini filled her empty glass to the brim, took a sip, wiped away the foam moustache from her lips, and said, "I see what you meant by nuclear deterrent."

Shinde nodded as he took a drag of his Gold Flake, "Viju was a dark, rugged bull of a man, well-known for his ferocity, and his very name normally shut down any potential resistance, both from within and from outside the clan. You know about the betrayal because you're following the story. But for Sharad Shetty Yeda Hussein, Kaila Sunil, and the rest of the Shetty clan who were guarding the compound, the attack on their citadel and the ease with which the enemy had penetrated the compound was a mystery, and they went to the next world completely confused."

"You see, Ms Shalini, a man will commit an act of betrayal for three things: power, love, and money. You can virtually hold a man hostage with love or get him to do the unthinkable. Money is a pretty good motivator, but love tops money."

"With power at the top of the pyramid. Your words," said Shalini, wagging her index finger at Shinde good-naturedly.

Unfazed, Shinde continued, "In Viju Shetty's case, it was a little bit of everything and a lot to do with love."

"As you now know, Prakash Shetty was the eldest son of Sharad Shetty and the heir to the throne. He was, beyond doubt, most beloved by his warrior father and had displayed a knack for the family business from a very young age, having organised the killing of Narasimha, a business rival of his father, when he was sixteen."

Shinde emptied his glass before he refilled his and Shalini's, lit up a Gold Flake and continued, "Narsimha was also from Karnataka, but he wasn't from the Bunt caste of the Shettys. He was sort of looked down upon by Sharad Shetty who considered him to be inconsequential and not really an equal. After he had opened his first bar near Metro Cinema, he began to expand his business to the surrounding areas and, in a very short while, he was the owner of six bar-cum-restaurants, turning over high profits. It was only natural that he was expected to pay a tithe to Sharad Anna. Narsimha, however, had other ideas and surrounded himself with loyal fighters from his hometown. He was a good paymaster, and that attracted local talent. He created a formidable fighting force that met the Shettys head-on and refused to pay any form of tax.

"One afternoon, Narsimha was sitting at his bar, the first one that he had started and his favourite, sipping on some piping hot masala chai, when he heard a commotion outside on the street. He went out to see what the problem was and saw a bunch of twelve-year-olds having a heated argument. Seeing that this was not a serious issue, Narsimha walked up to the youngsters with a big smile on his face and attempted to defuse the fracas by inviting the warring youngsters to join him for a cup of tea. All of a sudden, two of the boys whipped out knives."

Shinde took a deep drag, "The coroner counted seventy-one stab wounds on Narsimha's body during the autopsy. None of the kids was ever caught, but later on, it was rumoured, though never proven, that they had been brought in from out of state by Prakash Shetty. The death of Narsimha brought about a quick end to his organisation, and the businesses were scooped up in quick double time by the Shetty company. This cemented Prakash Shetty's reputation as a formidable force, and his accession to the throne was guaranteed.

"Now, although Prakash Shetty wasn't exactly lacking in the women's department, he had a bad habit of helping himself to his soldiers' women from time to time. Some were coerced, but quite a few went willingly. Better to fuck the heir-apparent than the hired help."

"Oh yes, the BBD syndrome," said Shalini, "The bigger, better deal. Though it doesn't always have a happy ending." Shinde nodded in agreement and continued, "The fear that he generated amongst the soldiers was such that no one dared to complain for fear of ending up dead in some ditch. Not to forget that Aslam Qureshi had been assigned to him as a personal bodyguard, and no one had the gonads to invoke his wrath. Prakash Shetty saw Sonali at Cafe Mondegar and was smitten at first sight. Discreet enquiries revealed the unfortunate fact that she was Viju's girlfriend. Now Viju Shetty was bonded to Sharad Shetty through family ties, and although he was a commander in the Shetty army and came from royal stock, he was, in the strictest sense, an employee."

"Which meant she was fair game," Shalini completed the sentence with a look of disgust, "What a pig!"

Shinde nodded and continued, "Sonali wasn't one of the gold diggers like the rest of the Shetty 'WAGS'. She came from an independently wealthy family and laughed in Prakash Shetty's face when he approached her at Sydenham College during a music festival and asked her out on a date, rejecting him point-blank in front of his bodyguards."

"Good for her," said Shalini. She knew that WAGS stood for wives and girlfriends. Shinde, obviously, also followed football.

"Prakash Shetty was used to getting his way with any woman he desired, and he didn't take the rejection very well. He grabbed Sonali by her long black hair, dragged her out onto the street, and slapped her around while his bodyguards stood around, daring anyone to interfere," said Shinde.

"I see this beating up of defenceless people started early in life for that asshole," said Shalini, wrinkling her nose.

Shinde refilled his glass, signalled for another pitcher and continued, "Viju Shetty had gone wild with rage, and had forced his way past the security at Lhotse, looking to chat with Prakash. He had five of his soldiers with him, weapons drawn, and a disaster of mammoth proportions was prevented by the interference of the don himself, who promised that he would take care of the matter."

Shinde lit a Gold Flake and continued, "However, eventually, nothing was done to Prakash. He was, after all, the heir apparent, the proverbial apple of his father's eye, and therefore beyond Viju's reach, on pain of death. It was made very clear that any punitive action against Prakash Shetty would be considered treason and dealt with accordingly and that all his family back home would also suffer the consequences of his actions.

"But Sharad Shetty knew Viju and his popularity with the rank and file. Rather than have a potential civil war brewing in his backyard, he decided to send Viju to Udipi as a 'promotion' to be in charge of the shock troops and their training, far away from Bombay and any potential trouble. Prakash was sent away to Australia as a 'punishment', but everyone knew it was just a smokescreen. Prakash Shetty lived in Melbourne for two years in a fancy penthouse, drove a Maserati and a Range Rover Sport, and partied with the elite society of Melbourne before returning and resuming the post of an heir apparent. Viju took Sonali and left Bombay; he kept his hatred in check, and pretty soon, it was in everyone's forgotten past. But Viju never forgot and never forgave. He trained with the troops, building a name for himself, and quietly waited for the day when all scores would be settled."

"And in stepped Arjun. Pretty smart. But what I'm not getting at is how Arjun would know about this family feud and how did he get access to Viju?" asked Shalini.

Shinde took a sip of his beer and said, "Arjun knew that eventually, the truth about the shoot-out would emerge. Somebody always talks. And he knew that eventually, there would be war again. So he sent special emissaries south to meet with Viju secretly. It was all about applying the right pressure and providing the right incentive. Viju had never given up on the idea of settling the score with the old don. Still, it seemed that he was doomed never to be able to exact revenge on the father or the son. Hence, the bold proposal put forward by the emissaries of Arjun tipped him over the edge, as it opened the door to a plethora of new possibilities. You see, Ms Shalini as

I said earlier, the most powerful motivator of all is power. And this is what Arjun offered his old friend Viju."

"What do you mean, old friend? You mean they knew each other?" Shinde nodded as he emptied his glass and said, "On the face of it, they came from two different worlds, one never destined to meet the other, but the reality was something entirely different. Arjun had a group of friends in college: two brothers called Brian and Stuart, Venkat and Timpy. They all played in a famous local band and were well-known on the college circuit for playing a number of concerts. They had even played at the famous Aid Bhopal Concert raising money for the victims of the Bhopal Gas Tragedy. Viju was already a famous street fighter, feared by all. Now, as I said, these two worlds should have never collided, but love has a way of doing the impossible."

Shalini lit a Gold Flake and said, "Just like politics, it makes for the strangest of bedfellows. What's the connection here?"

Shinde took a big gulp of his beer and continued, "Sonali was a good friend of Stuart and the band and was always at all the rehearsals and concerts. It was at Malhar, the annual college festival of Xavier's College, that Viju saw Sonali, and it was love at first sight. But Viju wasn't a fool, and he knew his chances were minimal at best with a direct approach."

"I get it," said Shalini, "He needed a way in, and that was through Arjun and his friends. The lateral approach possibly had a better chance of working because it would give him time to get to know her and for her to get to know the real Viju. I can appreciate that type of commitment."

"Exactly," said Shinde, "He became a regular fixture, hanging out with Arjun and the band at Elphinstone College, and he used to be the muscle that dissuaded any potential hecklers at the concerts. The band got free protection, and Viju got a chance to be close to Sonali. It was a win-win situation for everyone. But Arjun, being extremely perceptive, realised that Viju wasn't hanging out with them for the music and understood his amorous intentions. Surprisingly, he saw that Sonali was not too averse to Viju's attention but had her reservations, given the Shetty boy's reputation. Arjun also realised that Sonali just needed a mild push in the required direction and played matchmaker and messenger during the initial days of the courtship. Viju was strong-minded and loyal, and Sonali was swept off her feet by the intensity of his emotions; it turned out to be a match made in heaven. Without Arjun, Viju would have never found love and never forgot who had made that possible."

"This bartender really had a lot of luck, didn't he? Right place at the right time. Chaos theory at its best definition," said Shalini.

"It is called situational awareness, and Arjun was very aware, to say the least."

"And power? What did he offer?" asked Shalini, "He offered Viju the Shetty leadership on a platter. Once Homi had been spotted by Billimoria going to Sammy's joint, and once Arjun got the full report from the very same plain-clothed *hawaldar* who Billimoria had tasked to follow Homi, he knew it was only a matter of time before the Shettys would come calling. He had immediately sent Sonam, the long-haired fighter from

Darjeeling, and Vasu to meet Viju and had his informants in Colaba Police Station keep him updated with Billimoria's movements. Arjun knew that Billimoria would not reveal such explosive information on the phone. So, Arjun made sure his movements were closely monitored and his phone lines tapped.

"Arjun also knew that Sharad Shetty would never move against Strand with only Irfan Pathan and his depleted army. He knew the Shetty don would send for his shock troops and Viju Shetty. The rest just fell into place. Viju sat at the war table and was privy to all the plans, which he then passed on to Arjun. They waited for Yeda and Kalia to arrive at the bar, and then Arjun made his move that would alter the balance of power in the Bombay underworld. All Viju had to do was cut the power at Lhotse for thirty seconds, giving Arjun and his men the time to breach the walls. Viju, however, took it upon himself to slaughter the soldiers at the control centre and in the general surrounding area and take Irfan Pathan's head.

These were men who had been loyal to Prakash Shetty and had laughed while Sonali was being slapped around all those years ago.

* * *

"To the rest of the world, it was a coup d'état, with some welcoming it while others graciously accepted the new order in the Shetty house and prepared for the negotiations that would surely follow. The underworld is, in the end, a slave to economics; business had to proceed as usual because the one true God of the underworld was money. No one ever knew of Arjun's involvement. Viju took control of the Shetty empire,

Arjun had the crosshairs off his back, and a covert alliance was formed between Colaba and the Shettys. Then, around the same time, Wastra rose to prominence, took over, and controlled South Bombay with an iron hand. It was then that an era of criminal peace commenced."

Shinde finished off his beer and looked at Shalini, who said, "The king is dead; long live the king."

Shinde nodded, "That is, until the day, Wastra learned about Lesley's death?" asked Shalini.

"So you haven't lost track," Shinde replenished his glass and looked inquiringly at Shalini's glass. She shook her head.

"I need a break. My liver can't take much more of this damage."

"Actually, this beer is freshly brewed and is quite healthy. I'll order you some more *jhingha masala* and *roti,* though. It goes very well with the beer, don't you think?"

Shalini nodded gratefully, and Shinde continued, his thirst unquenched. "So, like I was saying, later that same evening, following the gang meeting, Arjun was at the Everest Bar surrounded by his guard dogs—"

"The youth brigade?" interrupted Shalini.

"Yes, and as I happened to mention earlier, they were always around Arjun. You couldn't get within five yards of him without one of them either blocking your path, asking your business, or if it was someone known, then at least one of them would be hovering around, just out of earshot, but always within striking distance if the need presented itself. They always formed a protective net around him. There was a bond between them that no one could understand. They were fanatically loyal to him.

They showed respect to Richard, Vasu and the senior warlords, but it was evident to everyone around that they took orders only from Arjun."

"The photograph!" Shalini exclaimed.

Shinde smiled, "Ah, the penny drops! Very astute, Ms Shalini. What are your conclusions?"

"I have been searching for the guys in the photograph. When you first saw the photograph, you talked about the mysterious Wastra. The shoot-out at Gateway, the attack on Lhotse, and the rise of Wastra are all connected. Arjun and The Canon Bar weren't just other establishments filling the Wastra pot. Arjun didn't pay homage to Wastra. That was the elaborate subterfuge. That was the tree hiding in the forest. Arjun was Wastra!" Shalini lit a Gold Flake, took a deep drag and let the smoke roll out slowly as she contemplated what she had uncovered.

"Wow," was all she could say.

Shinde smiled as he refilled his glass and lit a Gold Flake, "Yes, you are absolutely correct in your assumption. This was a masterpiece of deception. With the exception of the inner circle warlords, who had been hand-picked from the outset, no one knew about the subterfuge. If manipulated correctly, the human mind is such that it will accept any reality. And that's what Arjun did. He knew that eventually, Colaba would fall unless an illusion of a superpower was created. Anyone with the right motivation will kill a King, but no one would ever think of killing a God. The common man will believe and worship anything if pointed in the right direction. He will maim, kill, and commit atrocities in the name of his God. The trick is to manipulate him into believing in the right God. Of course, the level of education is inversely proportional to belief. The less educated the man, the greater his belief in an omnipotent force he can't see.

Arjun just took a page out of the book of indoctrination and created the omnipotent Wastra. Plying the uneducated and impoverished locals with food and money, the warlords spoke of the great Wastra, the protector of the poor, the one who would lead Colaba into the light. After several such drunken sessions in different parts of South Bombay, the story got a life of its own through the drunken re-telling at the various bars and street corners, in the market-places and restaurants, and became a legend that grew to monstrous proportions. After a while, no one even thought to question the existence of Wastra. They just accepted and propagated the new reality. It's like God, my dear. With a couple of holy books and a couple of vociferous acolytes, or in this case, bottles of Old Monk rum and Gilbey's Green Label whiskey, the inner circle warlords and the human mind, without further question, willingly accept the existence of an all-encompassing supernatural power that single-handedly controls every single aspect of every single organism on the planet. But it took significantly less time to create the reality of Wastra."

"Incredible," whispered Shalini into her beer, "And no one thought to question the reality?"

"There were a few. Not everyone believes in God in the same way. Billimoria, for example, decided to grow a pair finally and began to question these stories. He had his suspicions but couldn't prove anything. Even the coup in the Shetty clan didn't stop him from investigating on his own until the day the gas mains in his secret Cuffe Parade flat exploded and killed his mistress.

"He was lucky, and he knew it. He was coming up in the elevator when it happened. A few minutes later, he would have joined his mistress in the ever-after. He knew he was now a target, and his enthusiasm evaporated like water on a hot day, so he applied for and was immediately granted a transfer to Navi Mumbai, which was still in its fledgling state of development. He would not be heard from for a long time. That also put an end to the disbelievers and potential rebels.

"Billimoria was feared by the underworld, and if he had run off to the outskirts of Bombay, tail between his legs, no one in his right mind would question the existence of Wastra. Long life is a deep thirst for the underworld. Doesn't always happen, tough. They say there are old dons or bold dons, but no old and bold dons," Shinde chuckled at his own humour.

Shalini took a sip of her beer, "I have a few questions. You talked about guys with Kalashnikovs backing Arjun in Lhotse. These were not the regular fighters, were they? They sound differently trained and very military to my ear. Who were they?"

Shinde smiled, "Very good, Miss. You didn't get lost in the beer and cigarettes. You're asking the right questions."

SIXTEEN

FILLING THE BLANKS

The waiter got some *jhingha masala* in a medium-sized metal *thali,* along with five *chapattis.* Shalini broke off a piece of the warm bread, rolled a prawn into it, and stuffed it into her mouth. There was an explosion of flavour, and her taste buds were overwhelmed by the delicious mix of prawn, tamarind, chilli, and turmeric that had been blended with some other stuff she could not identify.

Surmai Fry, the local fish delicacy, cooked to its spiciest Malvani best, arrived shortly thereafter, and for a while, they sat in companionable silence as Shalini ravenously went through the food like a marauding invader, and Shinde destroyed three large mugs of beer, all the while looking admiringly at Shalini's ability to demolish the enormous quantities of food before her.

After Shalini finished her meal, she leaned back, took a sip of her beer and said, "It's an amazing tale you weave, but I have questions that I hope you'll be able to answer in order for me to get a perspective on things because right now there are some huge blanks that need filling."

"If you didn't have any questions, I would be most disappointed, Ms Shalini. It would mean you weren't really listening. Let me see if I can help wave the clouds away."

Shalini took a deep breath as she collected her thoughts. "Let's start at the beginning. Why did Richard agree to help Arjun in the first place? They were not friends or related by blood. Arjun didn't pay Richard for his services, and at least from what I know, these underworld types are not charitable unless it's to themselves. Plus, the cost of taking on the Shettys would have been prohibitive, to say the least. So why agree to help almost a total stranger, especially since it meant almost a certain war? I don't understand that. Why risk an all-out confrontation with a much more powerful force for nothing?"

Shinde nodded approvingly, "Very good questions, Miss. On the streets, do you know what is the most valuable commodity is and what every gang lord's ultimate goal? The one thing that will make a man in this line of trade sell his mother willingly?"

"Money, sex? Oh wait, I remember. It's power, isn't it?" said Shalini.

Shinde nodded his head, a trifle pompously from Shalini's point of view, and said, "You have a very retentive brain, Ms Shalini, and you are absolutely correct. The most valuable commodity is information, and the ultimate goal is power. Money and sex are just add-ons. For the smart man, the biggest motivation by far is the ultimate goal of power because once you have power, everything else will be attainable with minimum effort, and that is what Arjun offered Richard. The power that would make him a man of reckoning in Bombay. A chance to be free of the Subash Raut umbrella that Strand Company was a part of."

"The Kalashnikov-wielding men at the Shetty stronghold," things started making sense to Shalini, "This wasn't a 'charity case' act by Richard. Having those guys taking care of business for you would make you a big boy in the pond, wouldn't it? But who were they?" She snapped her fingers as a piece of the puzzle fell into place.

"They were the offering from Arjun, the quid pro quo, if you will. But that would mean..." Shalini let the words trail away as another scenario began to slowly come into focus.

Shinde took a large swig of his beer, lit a Gold Flake, and smiled, "You're getting there, Ms Shalini, much faster than I expected. Arjun could have gone to war with the Shettys all on his own. But had he done that, he would have exposed a closely-guarded secret that would have had far-reaching political consequences, which could not be afforded at the time."

Shinde took another swig of his beer, refilled his mug, looked at the waiter, lit a Gold Flake and continued.

"A good general chooses his battles. Prakash Shetty was dead, along with his father and his father's legacy, the moment he laid hands on the elderly couple. He just didn't know it at the time. While he was sitting in Lhotse, along with Kumar Vaswani and the rest of the assailants of Arjun's parents, he had been receiving real-time reports of what he considered their feeble efforts to have a case registered against them. Although there had been a number of witnesses to the beating, none had come forward to testify. Such was the fear the Shettys and Billimoria generated amongst the common man. And let me tell you, Ms Shalini, it's not that Richard and Strand Company were not aware that the assault on Arjun's parents was yet another infraction in their territory," said Shinde.

"I was thinking about that," said Shalini. "This happened in an area under Strand Company's control, and these gang bangers are territorial beasts. This Richard must have been rather annoyed, euphemistically speaking."

Shinde nodded, "Richard had been enraged and had gone to Subhash Raut, demanding retribution against Prakash Shetty and his cohorts, but Raut was not willing to lose money in some war over some inconsequential civilians, and Richard had been asked, none too respectfully, to keep his ego in check, be a team player, and had been categorically told to take one for the team."

"One more, you mean. So Richard was already primed for rebellion when Arjun approached him for help. But that couldn't have been enough, could it?" asked Shalini. "It had to have been something big enough for him to buck his master and go against the specific orders not to retaliate?"

Shinde took a large swig of his beer, lit a Gold Flake, and said, "Have you heard of the LTTE?"

Shalini was amazed yet again at his ability to seemingly go off point and be able to knit what would seem to be fractured pieces of information together and make a coherent story.

"Arguably, the greatest rebel force to have ever existed on planet Earth? Who hasn't heard of them? The stories about them are the stuff of legends, but I'm not too clear on the connection here. They were operating in Sri Lanka, weren't they? What's their connection to this story?"

"The origins of the relationship between Arjun and the LTTE are shrouded in fog. No one really knows how it all began, but there are stories of a girl, a foreigner, Belgian maybe. I have heard the name Muriel Steyns mentioned, but I can't be sure. What I am fairly certain about is that it all began with an incident one night on the Bangalore-Chennai highway. Back then, it was known as Madras."

"I swear to God, Shinde," said Shalini, shaking her head, "You're making my head spin. Another name in the mix. We have been moving in very different circles. Where do you get your information from?"

"These are not things you read in a newspaper, hear about on the radio, or watch on television on your favourite news channel. I have an ear to the ground, Miss. Travellers pass through the various bars that I have frequented over the years. These are not the high-profile establishments that members of the so-called upper echelons of society like you go to imbibe and fraternize. The people going there are extremely superficial, and apart from the quick fix of a temporary good time, you cannot expect anything more from them. Having said that, Ms Shalini, I must admit that you definitely don't fit the mould."

Shalini smiled and doffed an imaginary cap.

Shinde continued, "Down here in the Styx, it's real; there's quality, both of matter and mind. Travellers looking to stay off the beaten path are more receptive to sharing their experiences with a fellow transient. Sometimes, like today, I can share some of the stories I hear with a willing audience like you."

Shalini took a sip of her beer and said, "So you're the bar-room shrink, is it? And is that how you see yourself, as a transient? Somehow, I don't think you got all this from some random passer-by," Shalini understood the concept of protecting the source and decided not to push any further.

***

Shinde drained his glass, rolled with the punches and continued, "So, as I said, no one was sure of what happened on that fateful night so many years ago, but it was traumatic and had a devastating effect on Arjun's mind. He was young then, just sixteen, when the incident occurred. He came back to Bombay completely changed. He was no longer the happy, carefree kid who had gone to play a tennis tournament in Bangalore. You couldn't quite put the finger on it because, on the surface, he was still the same— a little chatty, a little brazen, as only the young can be—but there was an underlying hardness to him that only extreme circumstances can bring about."

Shinde lit a Gold Flake and continued, "The first casualty, along with the loss of innocence, is the eyes. The wide-eyed openness is lost forever, replaced by what is commonly referred to as maturity. A lot of people put it down to the developing match toughness of the young tennis player. The more knowledgeable said it was due to the constant travel and pressure to win tournaments and blamed the parents who put unnecessary pressure on their kids. But the ones closest to him knew it was something else, more profound, more shattering. He would never sit on Marine Drive again with Amili Setelvad under the scorching heat, their sweaty palms clasped together, burning up, but happy as only the innocent can be. In an instant, it was all gone. Something irreversible happened on that fateful trip to Bangalore. The kid had disappeared, and a tough stranger had taken his place. Amili was heartbroken, and he didn't care."

"Who's Amili Setelvad?" asked Shalini, her feminine senses coming alive.

Shinde just shrugged the question away, "She was a fleeting moment, lost too soon in the sands of time."

Shalini grinned, "Ah, women! I was beginning to think this guy was all guns and no roses."

"You couldn't be more wrong. But with Amili, it was different. They were kids, she was his first crush, and he was hers. This was much before the traitorous bitch called love kicked him right between the eyes. With Amili, it was beautiful in an innocent, cheesy way."

Shalini sighed, "I hear you loud and clear, Shinde, more than you can ever imagine, and to be honest, I could do with some cheesy innocence in my life."

Shinde nodded profusely in agreement, "It's a cynical world we live in. Everyone is judged by his bank balance, while honour, dignity and respectability are available for a price. In a couple of months, Arjun was gone again. Everyone just assumed it was for another tennis tournament. This was before the world shrank to a SIM card, and the iPhone was able to track you through space and time. Back then, it was snail mail and long-distance calls that set you back an arm and a leg. No one, especially his self-absorbed parents, thought to question his disappearance. Everyone just assumed a convenient truth."

Shinde continued, "At that time, the invasion of Afghanistan by Russia was underway, and, as a result, the shady sea-front motels and hotels of Colaba were full of Afghans. Some were there fleeing the war, but a large number of the Afghans in Colaba at that time were hard-core fighters who had been tasked with the job of protecting the drug lords selected by the Afghan high command, which was in charge of financing the defence of their country by setting up distribution lines for their heroin. The Afghans, fighting an effective guerrilla war, were self-sufficient in terms of fighters, and the high volumes of income generated by their drug trade were being used to buy weapons, which were then sent to the Mujahideen, who were giving the Russians a taste of Afghani cuisine, which just didn't suit their palate."

Shinde laughed and then, in a more sombre tone, continued, "But Arjun was interested in a war to further to the west, where there was an army desperate for human resources. What that war had to do with the incident on the Bangalore-Chennai highway is rather complicated, and it's probably best to talk about it another day. The fact is that Arjun was searching for answers, and so, with the help of the Afghan warlords, he found his way to Iran, which was involved in a do-or-die struggle against its Saudi and American-funded neighbour, Iraq. "Outmatched in terms of technology and weapons, the Iranians were dependant on their superior manpower and a generous dose of mercenaries and had been able to hold their own in a series of ground battles, nullifying the technological superiority of the enemy by sheer volume, and it stood to reason that there was a perennial demand for willing fools, ready to lay down their lives for a salary. Arjun was a part of one of the many cannon fodder regiments that were thrown into the front lines to blunt the tanks and heavy artillery of the Iraqis. No one expected him to last more than a fortnight because that was more or less the shelf life of a front-line grunt matching up against the Iraqi war machine.

"But, as he was to do several times later in life, he proved everyone wrong. Right from the outset, he displayed an animal-like ferocity and an ability to inspire. At the peak of one of the battles, it came down to hand-to-hand combat, and eyewitness accounts credited him with over one hundred kills in a single night. The same eyewitnesses also reported that he used his teeth and hands once he ran out of ammunition. This caught the attention of some of the senior commanders, and he was sent to train with the elite Revolutionary Guard. He was made a full-fledged captain, something unheard of, especially since he was so young and a foreigner and they say he was at the battle of Ramsar and led the final assault that broke the Iraqi defence."

"From tennis player to a gun for hire! That's a serious career change. And according to you, it was the direct result of some episode on some highway. It must have been a rather serious episode, don't you think? And what you're saying is that he went to an active battlefront of his own volition? Don't you think it's rather odd, to put it mildly? Either you're being selective with the truth, which makes me wonder why, or maybe you don't have all the facts. But I cannot believe that it was all because of some girl. There had to have been something else and something earth-shattering. The bottom line is that it's quite obvious that he had a proclivity for killing. The desire to kill was deeply instilled in his veins. Maybe he was born with this talent, like Roger Federer, but only in a different line of work. Maybe this Belgian girl was just a trigger for something that was already there, lying dormant and waiting. You know there's a clinical term for someone like this. It's called being a psychopath."

Shalini paused as she took in a deep breath. What Shinde was saying didn't make any sense. There had to be something else that had happened that night on the highway that had triggered such an extreme response in that young kid, and she wanted to know what that was. Then again, maybe he was just bad from birth. Somewhere along the way, she had lost her objectivity, and she knew it would be a struggle to regain her neutrality, such as the craziness and improbability of the story.

Shinde squinted at Shalini. This girl was bright.

"Be that as it may, the bottom line is that this young man found himself neck-deep in the Iran-Iraq war. The Iranians were recruiting mercenaries in droves to bolster their frontline troops, and they were not being picky about who signed up. There were more than fifty nationalities fighting as mercenaries in the Iranian army. If you had the heart, stomach, and balls, excuse my language, the Iranian army would give you some weapons and basic hand-to-hand combat training at no extra cost and then let you find your battle legs by sending you to meet the Iraqi army and Air Force for some personal time at the battle-front. Arjun had the desire, and he soon found out that he had the balls as well. When he first joined the 57th Brigade four hundred miles west of Tehran, the battle-hardened soldiers couldn't control their mirth, and many ribald comments were passed about lonely nights on the battlefront and how some sweet fruit could help ease the pain.

"Then one night, the Iraqi fighter jets launched a bombing raid on the encampments of the 57th, followed by a tank attack. Finally, the Iraqi infantry, confident of an easy victory, advanced on the enemy positions. Many of the veteran mercenaries of the 57th Brigade were of the mind to retreat.

"There seemed to be only one possible outcome, and the general mood, as the air rained bullets and mortar fire, was to live to fight another day. Then, Arjun showed these men of violence what violence was really all about. Telling the Captain of the 57th to wait for his signal, he rallied a small section of the demoralised mercenary troops and slipped past the Iraqis through their left flank, which, by his calculations, was the weak link. With four hand-picked soldiers, they got under the line of fire of the tanks. Arjun blew the tracks of one vehicle with well-placed grenades, then popped a couple of flashbangs down the hatch of the immobilised vehicle, and when the disoriented and confused gun crew came up for air, killed them all and then turned the tank on the attacking Iraqi infantry. The temperature had dropped, and the moisture-laden air coming in from the west condensed to a light fog, limiting visibility, making the Iraqi tank units unaware of the surreptitious takeover of one of their vehicles, and so they were entirely unprepared for the 'friendly fire', and several Iraqi tanks were destroyed in a matter of minutes.

"The remainder of the fighters held in reserve attacked the confused Iraqis from behind, from where they were expecting nothing but support, and the bulk of the 57th infantry, recognising the chaos as the signal they were waiting for, charged forward across the unofficial no man's land, catching the Iraqis in a vice. Once Arjun and his men ran out of tank shells, they joined their comrades on the ground. At close quarters, it degenerated to hand-to-hand combat."

Against her will, Shalini was mesmerised by the impossible tale. "That's where he showcased his canine skills. I get it. The highlight of his teenage life. It's quite horrific."

Shinde had a grim look about him, "As I said, following the battle of Rayat, he was sent for special training and was promoted to captain. A lot of his missions after that have been classified and are probably in some defence archive in Tehran, but they mostly involved behind-enemy-lines action. His ability to launch crippling attacks from behind the enemy lines while being invisible earned him the nickname *rooh,* or ghost, and made him feared and respected by friends and foes alike. His identity was kept a closely-guarded secret, and he was given special privileges; he didn't have to serve full time and travelled back and forth between India and Iran, always taking the less beaten path to avoid passport control."

Shinde emptied his glass and lit another Gold Flake, "He was no longer a part of the regular army and was tasked only with covert military operations. He would fly to Sharjah, where he would be met by an agent of the Iranian government and would be given false papers for his flight to Tehran. Of course, today, you wouldn't be able to get away with stuff like that, but back then, customs and immigration in the UAE were rather lax."

"But didn't anyone ever question his whereabouts? Friends, teachers, his parents? It's pretty sad that no one would miss you if you were gone, don't you think? Especially when you're so young. The teenage years are so difficult, the internal rewiring, hormonal imbalances, and the resulting insecurities. I hardly think that being an assassin at the age of sixteen makes for anything positive as far as character-building goes."

"You are so correct, Ms Shalini. I believe that what a teenager needs most of all is a home he can come back to, where he can find peace. But if you have a drunk and abusive father, a mother who was most likely cheating on her spouse, and no sibling that you can reach out to, then peace is a luxury that you cannot enjoy."

"I hardly think that some blood-stained battlefield is the answer. So that carefree teenager who went to Bangalore for that tennis tournament wasn't really a happy bunny, was he? I'm no shrink, but I think the Bangalore incident was just waiting to happen. Maybe he went looking for trouble, and it found him. I think it's terrible and tragic that he lost his youth and innocence so needlessly. Your school and college years are supposed to be fun. He was killing at sixteen in a foreign land. That's not what you put on your resume when you apply to Harvard, don't you think?" asked Shalini, her tone combative.

"Not really," said Shinde wryly, "but unfolding events might have never occurred, and you wouldn't be sitting here on the cusp of the greatest story of your career."

"Well, there is that. Do go on," said Shalini.

* * *

"It was at the Battle of Mehran that Arjun met Ramalingam. He was Tamil, but he was not from India. He ran a specialised team that provided weapons and ammunition to the Iranian army at exorbitant prices. But he was reliable, his products were top-notch, and the Iranian high command was more than happy to pay. From Ramalingam, he heard about the great leader who had emerged for the Tamil people of Sri Lanka. Velupillai Prabhakaran had galvanized the resistance movement of the Sri Lankan Tamils into an all-out war with the Sri Lankan army. The fighting force of the Tamils was known as the Tamil Tigers. Trained by the Mossad were fearsome guerrilla fighters and had won a series of battles against the Lankan army. Stories of their exploits and victories against a numerically superior force and of their charismatic leader stirred the Tamil blood in Arjun, and he left Iran along with Ramalingam for Sri Lanka. As I said, the origins of the relationship between Arjun and the LTTE are not entirely clear, but from so many stories, this could be the most plausible one."

"True or not, the story is pretty incredible. Please go on," said Shalini, totally in a groove, supported ably by cigarettes and beer.

Shinde smoked and smiled and continued.

"For the next two years, Arjun ran guns, ammunition, and food supplies for the LTTE and also trained under the Mossad, further developing his uncanny knack for guerrilla warfare and covert operations."

"That's how he was able to plan the Gateway shoot-out so meticulously. Those mafia boys had no idea what they had awoken," said Shalini.

"Very good, Miss," said Shinde appreciatively. He learned to kill in Iran, but in Lanka, he learned the art of war. Many southern political parties had sworn their allegiance to the LTTE, some covertly, and some pretty much put it all out there, unfettered by political correctness. So, with an armada of fishing boats, under the collective political blessings of the ruling and opposition parties of Tamil Nadu, protected by the Indian coast guard and under the command of Lt CDR Moses, Arjun launched off from Rameshwaram and maintained a continuous supply line of food, ammunition, and weapons for the rebel fighters. The Sri Lankans, not very well known for their courage under fire, were not inclined to challenge Moses and his flotilla of well-armed coast guard cutters. Complaints by the Sri Lankan government fell on deaf ears. No one wanted to harm the 'poor fishermen' who were just trying to earn a living."

"Moses?" asked Shalini, "Another name in the mix!"

"Moses was the Indian Armed Force's tennis champion and Arjun's doubles partner. They had won a series of tournaments and even taken the famous Batra brothers to five sets in the national men's finals. Theirs was a bond forged by blood spilt on the tennis court, and Moses, being a rebel himself, found the supply line operation to be his calling in life. It didn't end well for Moses, but that was much later and is another story, not for now."

"I have to admit that this Arjun was an interesting guy. I think women would go for him because he had all the qualities they would never want in their boyfriends or husbands," said Shalini speculatively.

"The one thing that I have learnt in life is that the darker the character of a man, the stronger is the emotional response from a particular type of woman," said Shinde, as his eyes twinkled. "I've also observed that this type of woman is normally very attractive. Shall I continue?"

"Yes, yes, of course," said Shalini, snapping out of her reverie.

"Then, there was a change in Arjun's life. In the late '80s, he went off on a tangent. Deciding to be a pilot, he went to Texas, where a lot of Indian youngsters were going to get their pilot licences because you could finish your entire training in six to eight months. In those days, you didn't need to go through a lot of red tapes at the various American embassies in India to get a student visa, as was required if you wanted to join a flying school there. You just applied for a tourist visa, and off you went to become a commercial pilot. The flying schools in America were just interested. If you could pay, that's it. He left Kalia Anton from Antop Hill in charge of the supply line operations, and Anton proved more than able for the task. Again, there is some story of a girl who gave him a sense of purpose, a direction away from violence and death. She gave him stability and love, which he had never got at home or from anyone."

"A girl was able to do that? Who was she? She must have been something special." Shalini was curious about the girl who had latched her fortunes to a killer.

"I am given to understand that she was. She was older than him by a few years and lived in a different world than him. Normally, their paths would have never crossed, but as you've probably worked out by now, there is nothing normal about this story. Against all odds, he was able to make her love him, and the truth is told, he loved her back, if only for a short while. He was too damaged for any permanent emotional contact with a woman. He had tasted blood and could never drink milk again. The lion and the tiger may be stronger, but the wolf does not perform in the circus, and that's what he was: a wolf, a hunter, a killer; intelligent, vicious, and absolutely without remorse, capable of blending into his surroundings with effortless ease and impossible to be completely domesticated.

"After returning from America as a fully qualified commercial pilot, he had, unbeknownst to her, reacquainted himself with Kalia Anton, who had left the supply line operations out of Rameshwaram and had been reassigned to Bombay and was in the process of setting up the most incredible and audacious programme in Antop Hill. Her biological clock said family, and his said action, and he wanted back in the game. While he had been in America doing his flying training, an idea had taken birth that would have far-reaching consequences much later on."

Shalini said, "So she was vegan, and he was anything but. She must have known that her boyfriend was a little next to the tracks, euphemistically speaking…"

Shinde lit a Gold Flake and filled his empty glass to the brim, "Anyway, Ms Shalini, the 'twain' just didn't meet. It wasn't that he didn't want to, but his orders were clear and unambiguous. There could be no complications to the greater plan. He was merely transiting through Bombay, and there was no room for excess baggage. He felt a certain amount of relief because the claustrophobia of a monogamous relationship was closing in on him like huge implacable steel walls, sucking the life out of him."

Shinde lit a Gold Flake, took a swig of his beer, and continued, "But the girlfriend was no fool and was already making her own plans. In the summer of 1991, she disappeared with her colleague, migrating to a foreign land. He was surprised by the effect her departure had on him. He had hoped that she would leave, knowing he would feel some sort of regret when she left, but it was sudden and without warning. She disappeared one morning without so much as a goodbye, and he felt that someone had taken a sledgehammer to his heart."

Shalini felt a wave of sadness engulf her. It wasn't only for this kid but also for the unknown girl and the demise of love. She had to have known how absolutely far from normal her man was. Still, she had stuck with him. That, in Shalini's book, denoted character. She must have loved this crazy killer and must have seen some good in him. It was a betrayal of trust that would have led her to the arms of another man. Then again, maybe it was too much too soon. Maybe Arjun had been too young to get tied down? Maybe he wanted to live a little before getting married? Then she remembered that there was nothing normal about this young man. It was a bit like calling a tiger a cat. He was a killer, following orders from a higher power, and she realised it was a simple case of indoctrination versus the heart, and it was pretty clear who the victor had been.

* * *

Shinde finished off his glass, refilled it and continued, "He struggled to maintain his sanity. He frequently visited the many bars that were springing up all over Bombay, partied hard with the pretty young things of the night, and numbed the pain with copious amounts of alcohol, the beast in him coming back to life as he teamed up with Kalia Anton and the LTTE, setting up the Antop Hill operation. He trained mercilessly with the LTTE instructors, honing his close combat and shooting skills. With Atul and Lhoncha, he perfected his weapons training. A sort of coldness began to wash over his soul as the wolf came back to life, and then his parents got beaten up, and an opportunity presented itself."

Shalini let a long-drawn-out breath from pursed lips, "And here we are. I guess his destiny revealed itself, huh?"

Shinde nodded, and Shalini continued, "Yes, it did, and here we are. Do you know what I find troubling? When subjected to the trauma of war, grown men return home devastated in their minds. It's called post-traumatic stress disorder."

Again Shinde nodded, "I am aware of the condition called PTSD. It was first officially recognised in soldiers returning from the Vietnam war."

Shalini nodded and said, "Soldiers suffering from PTSD normally need a lot of therapy, and even then, most never return to a state of normal equilibrium. But this kid, he killed with his bare hands and teeth, lived and breathed death and destruction at a very young age, and then what you are trying to say is that he returned to his teenage life in Bombay with absolutely no signs of degradation of his mind? And what's more, he kept doing this for a while?"

Shinde nodded, and Shalini continued her line of questioning unabated, "So, he was flitting between extreme violence and playing music with a college band, with no visible ill effects to his mind and body? Then he gets some sort of grounding through this girl he meets. He gets a legitimate profession, finds love, but then gives it all up because he believes in a higher cause. I know you think you are talking about some sort of legend, but the truth is that he must have been tortured by guilt and regret and anger, like any normal human being. I'm not a shrink, but this is a psychopath in the making, maybe even a serial killer. His parents should have been put in jail. It's absolute negligence at the very least on their part, bordering on child abuse at the other end of the spectrum... Would it be alright to use the facilities at your friend's apartment? I really need to get some air."

She smiled a small smile at Shinde, and he understood that she was apologizing for her outburst, but at the same time, hoping that he understood her confusion and mixed emotions. He nodded, and her smile widened as she understood there was no animus, only understanding in Shinde's eyes.

As she got up to leave, Shalini had to admit that this was sounding less and less like a fairy- tale and more like a biography. Not for the first time, she wondered about the relationship between this alcoholic and the mysterious figure he was painting. And she wondered about the girl.

SEVENTEEN

MASTER OF MASTERS

Shalini called Shantanu on her way down from Karate Vilas' house. She was still upset—not at Shinde, but at herself. It had been hammered into her very being that a good reporter did not get personally involved with the story because it compromised objectivity. But the tale was so gripping, and Shinde's ability to bring the tragedy of this young man to vivid reality made it difficult to be neutral. As she called Shantanu, she hoped her emotional outburst hadn't ruined everything. He answered as she carefully navigated the rickety wooden steps.

"What's up? I hope you're calling with some news," Shantanu was never the one for unnecessary pleasantries.

"Just checking in, boss. Thought you might be concerned for my safety. Didn't want you to get worried or anything. I'm fine."

"Waxing sarcastic, are we? You're an investigative reporter. If you wanted to be safe, you should have gone to fashion school or something like that. This is the school of hard knocks, and you either get up to speed or get out of the way."

Shantanu's tone softened, "Sorry, I've been having a tough day. The Home Minister is playing coy about giving me an interview. I wanted to ask him about his dead security chief, but he's dodging me. I keep getting his stupid secretary Naveen Singhal, that short, fat, corrupt piece of shit who keeps telling me that the minister is in a fucking meeting! And I've heard Billimoria has beefed up security around the hospital. He's brought in more of his goon squad, George's Hospital has become a no-fly zone for reporters, and he's trying his best to get the Dean suspended for interfering in an official investigation. Once he gets all the doctors out of the way, he'll make his move, and I think the junkie will mysteriously commit suicide or will be shot dead in self-defence.

"Someone up on high has put a kill order on the junkie, and the Faruzi attack dog is in the hospital to do his master's bidding. And he doesn't want any witnesses. What I'm not able to understand is why they haven't been able to remove the Dean. He's the only thing standing between our resident in-house druggie and an encounter. You need to push that alcoholic. Somewhere in his story is the answer to our junkie question."

"Shinde is a mean storyteller boss, there is no doubt about that, but so much of it seems to have a personal feeling about it. It doesn't sound like hearsay or bar room chit-chat to me.

Sometimes when he's talking, I feel as though he was actually there, and I know that's not possible, but then again, that could be the effect of the beer, and I have to tell you, boss, there's been quite a bit of that going down."

"You'll have to play his game, you're on his turf, and it's his rules. He'll tell you what you want to know, eventually, but you'll have to suck it up, knock it back, and enjoy the ride. Just remember that there's a hangover that follows," said Shantanu as he hung up.

When she came back into the bar, Shinde was lighting up a Gold Flake while one of the waiters filled his glass. He looked up at Shalini and intuitively said, "Reporting to the boss?"

She thought about Billimoria and his gang of criminal cops setting the stage to do their dirty work at the behest of an invisible master or masters, and she thought about Babu lying unconscious and helpless at their mercy and said, "I'm sorry, I lost it a bit earlier, but my frustration was not directed at you."

Shinde smiled, "It's not easy to be unaffected by the story, Ms Shalini, but you have to try. The road to immortality is paved with heartbreak and broken souls, extreme circumstances being the roadmap to greatness. If you don't know true suffering, you can never be really great."

"Losing one's soul in the pursuit of greatness is a high price to pay," said Shalini. "But let us agree to revisit this at a later time. I'd like to talk about LTTE. What were they doing so far from home? And what is this Antop Hill operation that you are talking about?"

"Do you know where Antop Hill is? I mean, you are from a more ritzy part of town. There wouldn't be anything of interest for you there," said Shinde, taking a deep swig of his beer.

Shalini replied a trifle aggressively, "I'm a reporter, and I go wherever the story takes me. Believe me. I'm tougher than I look. I'm here, aren't I?"

Shinde nodded his agreement, a small smile playing around his lips and carried on. "Antop Hill is the Tamil heartland, right here in Bombay, and all its inhabitants, right down to the lowest *chaiwala,* have always been fervent supporters of the Tamil cause in Lanka even today, although that island faces no more war. That doesn't mean that the dream of an independent Tamil nation has died. I have no doubt that we will hear the roar of the tiger again. But I digress. During the freedom war, Antop Hill contributed a lot to the cause by means of food, money, and even volunteers."

Shinde lit a Gold Flake, refreshed his glass, and continued, "Far away from the prying eyes of the Sri Lankan secret service and other similar agencies, Antop Hill was converted into a training ground for the LTTE, with firing ranges and obstacle courses designed to resemble the jungles of Sri Lanka, but built completely underground. Volunteers, drawn by the magnetism of Velupillai Prabhakaran and his promise of an independent Tamil homeland, came in droves from all over the world to fight in the LTTE's war for independence.

Instructors from the front lines of the war came in turn to train the recruits in guerrilla warfare.

"They came by the fishing boats to Rameshwaram, then by road to Chennai, and then, by one of the many Indian Airlines flights, to Bombay. They provided extensive training in the use of small arms, camouflage, and the art of the silent killer, which was the signature tactic of the Tamil guerrilla fighters, and which struck fear deep in the heart of Colombo. Once the volunteers were battle-ready, they took land routes by bus and truck to Rameshwaram."

"And then Moses would escort all of them to the Lankan shores," Shalini whistled silently.

"That must have been one heck of an operation."

Shinde smiled, "It wasn't just the operation that was amazing, but the fact that it was conducted in a metropolis, right under the noses of multiple law enforcement agencies completely undetected, that made it a thing of beauty."

Shinde took a deep swig of his beer, checked his mobile phone for messages, saw that there were none, and continued.

"Then the attack on his parents happened, and Arjun put his proposal forward to Kalia Anton. He had earned the trust and respect of the LTTE high command more than enough, all the way back to the supply line operations, which were still running successfully and unabated, now under the command of his friend Karthikeyan. It didn't take long, and one evening, a week later, as he supervised the demolition training at Antop Hill, Arjun got the news that his plan had been green-lit by the great man himself. "How much more audacious could a plan be than the plan to operate a training ground for an external rebel force, which is fighting a war in another country?"

Shinde took a large swig of his beer, "Remember when I said Arjun was always circumstantially aware?"

Shalini nodded. "I remember."

Shinde lit a cigarette, "The assault on his parents presented Arjun with a unique opportunity. With a cold, detached mind, he saw a way to kill several birds with one stone. Wastra would be able to provide enhanced logistical and financial support for the Antop Hill operation. The LTTE would provide armed support for Wastra's organisation when things got tough.

Nothing like having a bunch of guerrilla fighters back you up in street battles. His brief encounters with Richard over the years had impressed him. Unlike others of his ilk, Richard had an honour code, which he followed and enforced amongst his men. He was well respected on the streets and wasn't too greedy.

"At a secret meeting in Richard's Mohini Mansion flat, Arjun made his play, where he proposed giving Richard the support of the LTTE fighters based in Antop Hill whenever he needed them. This would make Richard stand alone, make him the king of Strand, and would remove him from serfdom forever.

"Arjun knew that Richard craved his own place under the sun. This would guarantee that. In exchange, Richard had to present himself and his fighters in the field of battle against the Shettys."

Shinde laughed, "It was much later that Richard realised the extent of Arjun's vision and his ambitious plan of an empire. On Arjun's part, his assessment of Richard had been spot on. Richard came from the Sundernagari fishing village, where his parents had made their money bootlegging alcohol and had been able to buy a small flat in Mohini Mansion, right opposite Strand Cinema. Although Richard had a very basic education, he was a skilled orator and had a surprisingly good grasp of the English language. He was capable of extreme violence and extreme empathy, with a good level of intelligence thrown into the mix. He had been able to mobilize an effective fighting unit known as Strand Company, and they ran a localised protection racket in Colaba, bootlegged alcohol, and had a pretty lucrative money lending operation going."

Shalini shook her head, "The poorer the Indian, the greater the need to show off."

Shinde nodded, "There always was a festival or a wedding that was entirely beyond the financial capability of the average citizen of Colaba. But the need to prove their financial prowess to their neighbours would eventually lead them to the doors of Strand Company, which were always open. God forbid, however, if you did not pay the interest rates on time. To keep the police and other predators at bay, Richard had allied himself with Subash Raut, which meant he was part of an umbrella that had weak political backing. It galled him to have to pay the weekly tribute to Raut, but his hands were tied. He also had to endure the term '*chotey*' as a constant reminder of his position in the food chain, and it wasn't like the police had stopped their harassment. In the end, Richard had to view everything in terms of degrees. Either he paid up to Raut, and the degree of harassment would be palatable, or he stopped paying, and the degree of harassment would increase exponentially, and nothing was off the table."

"So, Arjun's proposal was a godsend for Richard. Even so, this was quite a risky move on Arjun's part, wasn't it?" asked Shalini, pouring herself a stingy amount of beer. "There was quite a strong possibility that Richard could have refused outright or even agreed and then sold him out to the Shettys. That would have earned him valuable currency, wouldn't it have?"

"There was always a chance that something like that could happen. Arjun had stationed twenty LTTE fighters in five fast and souped-up Maruti Suzukis just out of sight, near the Hanuman Mandir. If they didn't get an all-clear in thirty minutes from Arjun himself, they had instructions to go in and kill everyone in Richard's flat. After that, they had his phone line tapped for a few days, just in case he had a change of heart. Nothing was left to chance."

Shinde stifled a belch as he reached for the pitcher and poured himself a healthy serving of beer. "As it turned out, the precautions proved unnecessary. Richard was more than amenable right from the start. He couldn't wait to stick it to the Raut conglomerate, and he was still upset at the killing of the flower seller. Then Arjun got the green light and took Richard to Antop Hill. After Richard witnessed the Antop Hill operation in full swing, he realised he was out of his league and thanked God for making the right choice. He wondered about many things, the least being how long had all of this been going on and how he could not have figured out the deeper truth about Arjun. He realised that there was a bigger plan afoot, but as long as that plan included the end of his dependency on the Raut conglomerate and his confirmation as King of Strand, he was in for a penny and the damn pound."

Shinde took a large swig of his beer, "Between the time that Richard agreed to help Arjun and the actual shoot-out, Arjun sent a mix of Strand warriors and fisherfolk from Sundernagari to train with Anton and elite LTTE instructors at Antop Hill, in addition to the street combat techniques dished out by 'China Ryan'. By the time of the shoot-out a month later, all forty of them had been trained into a cohesive killing unit. Arjun reserved fifteen LTTE fighters in three jeeps at Regal. They were to stay out of sight, controlling the entrance from the north, with orders to enter the battle if and only if Arjun sent a runner with a pre-arranged code," Shinde laughed.

"It turned out that the LTTE instructors exceeded their targets, and the fight simulations created by Arjun were tactical marvels. The destruction wreaked by their trainees at Gateway was devastating. The kill -ratio was a hundred per cent, with no losses suffered. To call it an unqualified success was an understatement. During the attack on Lhotse, Arjun displayed his remarkable military acumen, splitting up his forces, using only LTTE fighters from Antop Hill, while the Strand warriors and the fisherfolk took care of Yeda Hussein and Kalia Sunil at his Bar, and then buttoned-down Colaba in case of any further Shetty strikes. This was cool-headed planning beyond anything Richard or any of the warlords had ever experienced. They realised that they were in the presence of greatness, and they submitted willingly to a higher power."

Shalini shook her head in amazement, "And all this eventually was the foundation for the birth of Wastra."

Shinde nodded. "The shoot-out made Arjun famous, and the destruction of Sharad Shetty with such apparent ease made him the undisputed king. But Arjun knew that the key to longevity was anonymity while maintaining friendships and alliances. He knew it was important to create a persona of mystery that even he ostensibly answered to.

"People are more scared of the unknown, even if it is the figment of imagination and creativity. Only ten of the forty who went to train at Antop Hill knew who had organized it. They became the inner circle of warlords, and the loose string that connected them became tight as they realised the significant advantages of keeping the faith, as opposed to the wrath of God that would befall the treacherous.

"The rest of them were told of the great warrior who had made a decision to make Strand his home and of his close bond with Arjun. It was automatically assumed that it was this unknown fighter's ties with the army, which was training at Antop Hill, that had facilitated their entry into the underground facilities. Once the intense training began, any further unanswered questions were forgotten. After Lhotse, there was a delegation of power, and all the ten were rewarded with their own areas of power, with Lhoncha receiving the lucrative RC Church area as his protectorate. Richard was made ruler of Strand, which made him king of Colaba. Arjun took over the Canon Bar along with Vasu and, true to his nature, stayed under the radar and, for all practical purposes, owed, like all business establishments in the area, fealty to Richard and Wastra."

Shalini spoke with untainted respect, "In this particular case, the throne itself was an illusion. What better way to preserve power than to keep the identity of the king a secret while allowing his powers to flow through his chosen ones? The warlords became powerful, and they pledged their allegiance to Wastra, all of them knowing that they ruled at the pleasure of the bar owner, with the only condition that the identity of Wastra is kept a secret. They also knew that any road to betrayal would lead back to them, and none of the warlords lived in an illusion that they could defeat the bar owner and his terrifying invisible army. On the other hand, they were getting impossibly rich, powerful, and respected, so only a fool would mess with this apple cart. That fosters omnipotence, and that is how legends are born. Am I correct?"

Shinde smiled as he paused to take a swig of his beer and light a Gold Flake before continuing, "You have understood the grand plan with remarkable clarity, Ms Shalini. Of course, the strategic takeover of all the areas of South Bombay caught the attention of several key players, including the police. However, with the brutal elimination of some dissident warlords and pay-offs to key police officers right at the top of the food chain, the threats were slowly but surely neutralized."

Shinde lit a Gold Flake, "Then there was the final severing of ties between Richard and the Subash Raut conglomerate."

"I was going to ask you about that," said Shalini. "That must have been a painful experience for everyone concerned."

Shinde laughed and said, "Parting is such a sweet sorrow. The first sign of trouble popped up when the monthly tithe did not arrive at the Cuffe Parade penthouse in Jolly Maker 'B' block. Raut sent Dushyanth Joshi, a tall, burly, ugly man, famous for his bad breath and bad teeth, to collect the money and give Richard the required tongue lashing."

Shalini wrinkled her nose, "Two things I can't stand both in men and women are bad breath and stupidity, not necessarily in that order."

Shinde smothered a laugh in a huge swig of his beer and continued, "Suffice it to say that there was confusion and anger in equal amounts at the Raut residence when Dushyanth did not return. Several attempts by Raut's henchmen failed to turn up any clues as to his whereabouts.

"He seemed to have vanished into thin air. After a few days of futile waiting, Raut finally called Richard's house himself and was surprised when Richard answered the phone. He had expected Richard to dodge his phone call and was preparing a slew of choice verbal abuse at whoever answered. He was even more taken aback at the nonchalant tone. Richard could have been talking to the mailman, for all it was worth.

"Subash Raut's fair skin mottled with rage, and he screamed at Richard to present himself along with the required amount of cash immediately at his penthouse. Richard promised he would be along shortly."

Shinde looked at the waiter and made a sign with his right thumb and forefinger like an inverted 'C' signifying a box. Another packet of Gold Flakes arrived. Shalini wasn't sure if she was paying for the booze or both but decided not to raise the issue.

Shinde lit a Gold Flake and continued, "It was another five days later, when a junior minister was at Subash Raut's residence, that the security announced that Richard was at the entrance, awaiting an audience."

Subash Raut was overcome with unbridled rage at the audacity of this lackey arriving unannounced, especially when he was hosting a political ally. Through gritted teeth, he told his security to allow Richard into the penthouse. 'Just see what I do to him,' he promised the minister. "Strand might be short of a chief tonight." The elevator brought visitors directly to the penthouse and opened into the plush living room. Normally, Raut was used to murmurs of awe when visitors first arrived at the penthouse. As usual, he presented his back to the elevator for further effect, looking out through the massive glass windows at the Arabian Sea, and pretended to be engrossed in conversation with the minister.

"Subash expected some sort of sign, maybe the shuffling of feet or a discreet cough from Richard, and was preparing to make him wait for a while. But there was silence. The elevator doors had closed, and the elevator was whirring its way back to the ground floor. Enraged, Raut turned to see what was going on behind his back, and the vitriol that was about to emerge from his paan-stained lips died away, unspoken.

"Richard stood before him with a cardboard carton in his hands. There were four dark men standing behind him. It wasn't that they were not scary—they most definitely were—but Subash Raut was pretty certain those were Kalashnikovs they were carrying, and he made sure that he didn't make any sudden movements."

Shinde took a large sip of his beer, made sure Shalini was still mentally there, and continued, "Richard stepped forward and placed the carton on the designer coffee table that must have cost a fortune, and making a namaste sign said, 'Subash Bhai, this is for you.' Subash Raut and the minister visibly relaxed. Obviously, there had been some misunderstanding. Richard was still the chotey they knew. As he opened the carton, Subash Raut made a mental note to himself to make enquiries about the machine-gun-toting men with Richard. He needed a few of them around to boost his image. Both the minister and

Subash Raut gagged at the obnoxious stench that emanated from the carton.

"Subash looked inside and almost threw up, but the minister showed no such control and emptied the contents of his stomach on the expensive Persian carpet that draped the floor.

Richard took on a hard tone, "Take it out, Bhai." It was not a suggestion. Subash Raut took out the contents of the carton, and the minister vomited again.

Dushyanth Joshi's head had been severed at the neck with some sort of hacksaw. He'd been dead for a few days and looked even uglier in death than he had in life.

Richard spoke quietly, "There is no more Subash Raut conglomerate. All your members have joined the new order. There is only one king, and his name is Wastra. You have twenty minutes to leave this apartment, or else I will have you thrown out by your own bodyguards." On cue, the four bodyguards with Subash left his side and took up positions behind Richard.

Richard continued, "You have not been unnecessarily cruel or greedy, unlike this dog on your table, so your life will be spared. But you will leave Bombay tonight, never to be seen here again. Do not think of taking up arms against Strand. We will know, and there will not be any mercy."

"Then Richard looked at the shivering minister but didn't have to say anything. The minister was now Wastra's dog."

Shinde said, "Wastra became the way, the truth, and the life that everyone began to believe in, and no one dared to dispute."

"But what happened? How did everything come to an end?"

"It was perfect governance. The poor were content, the rich were not taxed extensively, and the greed of the police was kept in check. Only an act of God could have brought the house down, and that's what happened."

Shalini looked at some of her handwritten notes, which she had been keeping for ready reference in conjunction with the recorder. "The death of Lesley? Is that it? Are you telling me that the death of one girl brought about the downfall of a carefully constructed kingdom?" Shalini shrugged, "Well, Helen did launch a thousand ships."

Shinde looked at Shalini as though undecided about his next step, "Yes, but nothing is what it seems. Lesley's death was the trigger that set in motion a chain of events with cascading consequences. As I've said before, this is a dark road, and I don't know whether you want to follow it. You might not like what you see if you look into the abyss."

Shalini leaned back in her chair, looked at Shinde through hooded eyes, and said, "I think we are already halfway down that dark road. There is no doubt in my mind that this Wastra was a psychopath. Don't get me wrong, Shinde, I'm not saying he was crazy; in fact, far from it. But the clinical psychopath or serial killer follows a different set of rules. He is highly intelligent and methodical, and patience is his forte when he is stalking his prey, not unlike a CEO of a company. The dark road you talk about has one end at George's Hospital. I want to go all the way. Let's go the distance, shall we? Hopefully, I'll find my pot of gold or something else at the end of this rainbow."

Shinde nodded. For the first time that day, he chewed on a piece of fish and said, "Do not judge in haste, my dear. The story still has a way to go."

EIGHTEEN

THE KEY TO LOYALTY

Shinde finished off his fish, leaving a tiny heap of bones in the metal *thali*, and contemplated over his beer while Shalini stuffed another prawn into her mouth and waited expectantly.

There were a lot of customers coming into the bar, and Shalini realised that it was growing dark outside. The pink glow that streaked the evening sky seemed to caress the deepest recesses of the drinking establishment she had currently taken residence in. She checked her watch and saw that it was a quarter past six in the evening. Almost six hours had passed since she had entered the hallowed halls of Sujatha Bar. As she turned around in her seat to take in the beauty of the twilight, the streetlights of Colaba Market came on. The night seemed to come swiftly to Strand, enveloping the area in a lover's embrace.

The dark, dingy interior, the intriguing alcoholic, and the fascinating tale he was weaving, along with the copious amounts of alcohol and food that were being consumed, had made her forget about the time. She was aware of Shantanu's instructions about the lack of luxury thereof, but she also realised that Shinde was too smart to be pushed around, and he would finish his story at his own pace.

The customers were mostly locals. They were employees from the many shops of Colaba Market and the surrounding area, stopping by for a quick nip and some gossip before heading back home. But there were also a few tough boys who had dropped in for a few early rounds of the local country liquor and were creating a bit of a ruckus like all young bucks tend to do, but they left Shalini and Shinde alone in their corner. Obviously, Ganpat, the manager, had told them to stay away. There was certain respect, for want of a better word, given to Shinde, and Shalini, for some incomprehensible reason, knew that she was absolutely safe in what she realised could suddenly become a very dangerous part of Bombay.

"Indoctrination is the key to loyalty," said Shinde, breaking into her thoughts and off on another tangent. "If you catch the right people at the right time and give them the right training, you will have an army that will follow you unquestioningly to hell and back. The trick is to mould their minds until their truth is what you want them to believe it is."

"Agreed," said Shalini, in between mouthfuls. "But isn't that the basic philosophy of all the terror groups that seemed to have sprung up around the world?"

Shinde nodded as he lit a Gold Flake and continued, "And it works with spectacular success for them. They have all the fodder they need to slake their unquenchable thirst for blood due to the intense indoctrination programmes they dispense to their uneducated and disgruntled acolytes. Most of their suicide-bombers go willingly to their deaths after six or so months of brainwashing. And as a pragmatic man, the factor that I feel will contribute most to their eventual success is time. They have time on their side. They can fail a thousand times, but they need only one successful mission. It's Murphy's Law that they will succeed eventually if they put enough missions into play. They just need one successful attempt, and all the failures would have been worthwhile. But for the governments and their agencies fighting to prevent exactly such a disaster, they are battling the clock and have to succeed each and every time. Eventually, the governments of the world that are cooperating with the so-called 'war on terror' will be forced to the negotiating table. There can be no other way.

These men, these terrorists, do not fight for money, country, or even family honour. They fight for their God, and you cannot compete with that type of commitment. But I want to be absolutely clear, Ms Shalini. I do not condone any of their actions. They are a bunch of cowards, in my opinion, who wage war on innocent civilians."

Shinde took a deep swig of his beer, "The LTTE has been labelled a terrorist organisation, but I must remind you that it was first a legitimate organization, battling an oppressive Sinhalese government, and its armed struggle was recognised and even applauded by most members of the United Nations for years until the very governments that had given it international legitimacy a volte-face and literally overnight labelled it a terrorist organisation. It had its headquarters in the UK and even had its own radio station.

"Everything changed after that. They were forced to shut down their operations, and the leaders went underground, but that's yet another story for another time."

"I think it might have had to do with the assassination of Rajiv Gandhi if I remember correctly. They crossed the line that day, and there was no coming back after that catastrophe. I have often wondered why they did something like that," said Shalini.

Shinde bristled, "What would you do if someone sent highly-trained armed forces into your backyard, ostensibly to 'keep the peace,' but with the actual objective of destroying you? On the other hand, they sold weapons to you through independent contractors to combat the very same peacekeepers that were now in your backyard? It's one thing to be capitalistic, another thing to be so greedy that you don't care how your coffers are filled. It was a disgraceful ploy by the political son of a dynastic family. The LTTE had no choice but to retaliate in the way they did once they understood the devious game."

"My knowledge of the LTTE is rather rusty," said Shalini hastily. She wondered why this alcoholic was so defensive about a war that was long over. Maybe it wasn't the best course of action to fact-check the storyteller while he was telling the story.

"I'm sure you'll have a fair working knowledge before the night is over," laughed Shinde good-naturedly. "To be perfectly honest, the decision to assassinate the ex-Prime Minister of a neighbouring country, who seemed on the road to another term in office, did not sit well with most of the LTTE high command.

Velupillai Prabhakaran's word was law, and what followed was the tragedy in Sri Peremur."

Shalini nodded sombrely, remembering the assassination when he was presented with a bomb-laden garland that had exploded, killing the ex-Prime Minister and scores of onlookers who had come to watch his speech. She remembered reading an article about the slain ex- Prime Minister's wife, about how she came from a land where scores of villages had lost all their menfolk to vendetta. She remembered the article talking about how families waited for centuries to take revenge. Maybe the LTTE should have remembered the old adage of removing anyone from the equation which was capable of settling the score in the future. She hastily thrust the troubling thoughts aside. Objectivity, Shalini, objectivity!

* * *

Shinde lit a Gold Flake, took a swig of his beer, and continued, "Arjun knew that eventually every leader gets betrayed. The reasons ranged from economic to personal. But they didn't matter; the fact that it had happened time and time again over the millennia to almost all leaders was all that mattered. In order to try and prevent a future assassination or coup, it wasn't enough to just have loyal fighters around him. He needed fanaticism. He needed a group that would protect him and dies for him if required, irrespective of whether he was right or wrong."

"He needed men who would die for their God. Enter the entourage," said Shalini softly.

"Most excellent, Miss. That's correct. The entourage wasn't some random friends he had picked up along the way. Trust is good, but control is better. They had been carefully chosen from scores of street fighters and other denizen of the streets. They were young, tough, came from broken families, and were ripe for the plucking. Arjun had tested them in street fights, attempted to corrupt them through unconnected sources by threats and bribes, and had found them absolutely lacking in fear and loyal to a fault."

"They had the right mindset. So, he was creating his own invisible armour. That's pretty impressive!" said Shalini.

"They needed a lot of discipline and training before they could become all they could be. So Arjun sent them south, to Lanka, to train with the feared Black Lions of the LTTE. There in the Tamil heartland, they trained their bodies and minds. Mossad agents trained them in the art of killing, and they learned the lessons of loyalty and sacrifice at the feet of the great Prabhakaran himself."

"So while everyone thought they were getting drunk and high in Goa, these kids were being moulded into Arjun's special bodyguard unit."

"Yes," said Shinde, lighting a Gold Flake. "But apart from combat, they also learned the arts of deception and subterfuge, the art of how to hide in plain sight. When they came back, to the casual observer, it seemed nothing had changed and that they were still crazy drinking buddies of Arjun.

The reality was completely different. They had left Bombay as boys and returned as highly-trained killers. They blended into the fabric of the streets like the chameleons they had been trained to be. They looked for spies, police informants, disgruntled partners, or employees and quietly eliminated potential threats to the throne. No one suspected them at all. They frequented all the bars and other dens of iniquity, developing their own social circles, building friendships, and developing loyalties, but always keeping their ears to the ground. Everyone saw them as freelancers for Strand Company, independent and available for hire, with a weird, inexplicable affinity to Arjun. And after a while, as is such in the telling of such tales, it became common knowledge that they were loyal only to themselves if push came to shove. The reality was that they were his invisible and final line of defence. They were his wolf pack, and he was their alpha," Shinde paused to refill his mug, took a large swig, and continued, "Arjun summoned the entourage for a meeting far away from the Strand. They met at Topaz, which was a famous dance bar. There, amidst the pulsating Bollywood music to which scantily-dressed dancers gyrated and frenzied customers threw away their hard-earned money on the dancefloor, Arjun laid out his plan that would eventually and unwittingly plunge Strand and Bombay into a war of monstrous proportions."

Shalini was fascinated, and it showed on her face, "What I don't understand, though, is how come this junkie, Manzar Alam or Babu, ended up becoming one. He was obviously highly trained and disciplined. Even in his weakened state, he decimated so many of his attackers that I wonder about the outcome had he been at full strength. There are so many crucial parts to the story that are missing." Shalini took a large sip of beer and lit herself a Gold Flake. She knew Shinde would help her piece the jigsaw together as he moved the story along, chugging down enough beer to sink the Titanic in the process. She mentally settled down for the continuation of the long ride.

Shinde took a swig of his beer and said, "Nothing is ever what it seems on the streets of Bombay. You may think you have the answer, and then you realize that you didn't even know the question. I can tell you one thing for sure, Ms Shalini, that everyone has a price. Even the most carefully inculcated warrior can be bought, and there is no sure bet when you live in the darkness."

"Is that what happened? Did Babu betray his master? Why was he allowed to live? And how did he end up a slave to the needle?" Shalini snapped the questions off in rapid succession, although she knew it was futile to expect rapid answers.

Shinde smiled as he lit a Gold Flake and, as though reading her mind, said, "I promise you answers to all your questions, and at the cost of repeating myself, the fruit of patience tastes sweeter, Miss Shalini. If I jump ahead, the true significance of this story will be lost. Let's get back to the day Arjun learned about Lesley's death. For Rasul, and the rest of the inner circle warlords, the conversation was forgotten minutes after the meeting concluded.

"Although he had not made it visible, the news of Lesley's death had shocked Arjun to his core. He knew there was nothing that he could do now that she was gone, and he did not blame Rasul for his callous reaction to her death. The streets were mean and unforgiving and swallowed the unwary, whole soul. But he was determined that her death would not go unpunished. At the same table where he heard the news of Lesley's death and where he supervised the celebration plans for the petroleum minister, Arjun silently swore an oath to avenge her unnecessary death. He made a decision that would affect everything.

"He decided to kill Santosh Saukar."

The confusion showed on Shalini's face as Shinde casually dropped the bombshell, and he nodded in agreement.

"Arjun was such a consummate professional. It seemed unthinkable and entirely out of character for him to take such a drastic decision. He knew that even his closest friends, his inner circle warlords, would oppose this. Vasu and Santosh Saukar were chillum buddies and had been at Bhavan's College together. Then there was Richard, who had known him all his life and had been his neighbour in Sudam Jhopadi. Not to forget that Madhya, the head of Paanch Pairi, another inner circle warlord, was related to Santosh by marriage."

"There are many ways to skin a cat. So rather than risk a rebellion, he used his wolf pack. It's very important to have unquestioning loyalty when you are about to do something that would be viewed as rather unpopular by the masses," said Shalini, understanding the plan but not sure of the reason behind it.

Shinde emptied his glass, "When he told them of his decision to eliminate Santosh Saukar, the four did not even blink an eye. They ordered several rounds of whiskies and just set themselves to the task of whacking the drug king."

* * *

Shalini realised that she was still hungry and would have welcomed some *surmai masala* with some rice, *papad* and prawn pickle, but she knew it was criminal to subject her body to unbridled eating while engaging in such relentless alcoholism. It was an old wife's tale that you were protecting your liver if you ate while you drank. All you ended up doing was piling on the pounds because the liver would prioritise the alcohol for metabolism and ignore the food, which would get stored as fat. Now, this was no excuse to indulge in crazy alcoholism, but difficult situations called for hard choices. *And sometimes you had to take one for the team,* and she thought piously to herself as she poured herself yet another glass of beer.

"I know I should expect the unexpected, but I don't understand why he would take such a rash decision?" asked Shalini and continued, "From what you have told me so far, Arjun was a clear-headed thinker. You can't expect to have a happy home when you start eliminating family members."

Shinde bobbed his head in agreement, "The relationship between Lesley and Arjun was one of coincidence, although the truth is told, I'm not sure I believe in coincidences. I believe everything is fore-written and is meant to be."

"So what you're trying to say is that everything happens for a reason. Look at the war in Syria or Yemen. How can you say that was meant to be? They say that the situation in Yemen is the worst humanitarian crisis ever. How could that be fore-written, and what possible purpose could that serve?"

"I don't mean to sound cynical, Ms Shalini, but I believe that it is Mother Nature's way of balancing the equation of uncontrolled overpopulation and consequent depletion of her resources. I know it's a callous way of looking at things, and I am not a callous man, but the facts speak for themselves.

You find disease and war occurring in the most overpopulated parts of the world; you will also find that these places are often systematically stripped down to the bone for their natural resources. I feel that humans are the ultimate supervirus in many ways. Mother Nature just needs to step in from time to time, using war and disease as effective tools to combat the scourge," Shalini shook her head, amazed at the complexity of this alcoholic's thinking but not totally convinced by his cynical arguments. Shinde continued, returning to the original topic.

"It was almost impossible to believe that there was any connection between Arjun and Lesley. She was older and moved in different circles; their paths should never have crossed, and as far as everyone knew, they never had. But the fact of the matter was that once, a long time ago, she had saved his life, in a matter of speaking."

"Whatever do you mean, Shinde? Are you trying to tell me that this girl who was a junkie saved Arjun's life?" Shalini was askance, to say the least. She couldn't make any connection between the two. She took a sip of her beer and said, "Let me guess. She saved him from the police a long time ago. A little Bollywood, no?"

Shined smiled and said, "There are many ways to save a person's life. For the ten-year-old Arjun, she had been a lifesaver, giving him food and shelter when he had none."

Shalini was silent, smoking a Gold Flake as she waited for Shinde to continue.

"She had found Arjun wandering around the streets of Colaba with his tennis racket in hand. He was obviously not one of the regular urchins, and she was initially curious. But that turned to shock when she found out that he had been thrown out of his house by his mother, who was entertaining some 'uncle.' Upon further questioning, she found out that his father was out of town, and this was a common practice followed by his mother during such occasions. The young Arjun had no idea when his father would be back. Lesley knew that this innocent child was easy meat for the sexual predators on the mean streets of Colaba and took him back to her place. This was the first time Arjun met her brother, Mario, and her boyfriend, Greg. They got him into a shower, gave him some oversized pyjamas to wear, and stuffed him with some delicious *chicken vindaloo and pav*. He ate ravenously before collapsing into a deep slumber and didn't wake up for twelve hours."

"What an absolutely spectacular mother!" said Shalini. "If this happened today, she would be in jail for child abuse." Shalini was appalled and silently thanked her stars that while she considered her family mildly dysfunctional, they were paragons of virtue compared to the family being described by Shinde. The father must have known; there was no way her cheating could have gone unnoticed. Maybe that explained the alcohol abuse.

Poor man, thought Shalini. *Why hadn't he just divorced her? Maybe he had just been a very weak personality.* The seeds for the creation of the killer had been sown at a very young age. She felt anger, frustration, and sadness in equal parts.

Shinde agreed, "Those were different times. Divorce was not the norm, and child abuse didn't exist. It was never the fault of the parents. They were only disciplining their children. When Arjun woke up, he didn't show any desire to leave, and Lesley, with her maternal instincts all aflame, was more than happy to have him stay. And stay he did, for almost three weeks. It had been the best time of his young life. Eventually, he did return home when, after several conversations, Lesley learned of his famous grandfather in Chennai. She had called the 'iron man,' as he was known, who flew down and retrieved his grandson personally."

"He should have taken his grandson back with him. What made him leave that poor child with those unfit parents? At least that poor boy would have had a peaceful childhood," Shalini was upset, and her face showed it.

"He did take Arjun back to Chennai, and had Arjun stayed there, he might have lived a quiet, peaceful, and unremarkable life, but it was not to be. Perhaps it was because Arjun's father begged and pleaded, and finally, against better judgement, Arjun went back to live with his parents in Colaba, eventually resulting in your presence in this bar. But I feel that the old man wasn't prepared for fatherhood all over again, and the reason for allowing Arjun to go back was most probably selfish. Like I said, Ms Shalini, everything happens for a reason. All the terrible things that occurred in Arjun's life moulded him into the person he became, which culminated with you being here in this bar with me, listening to a great story."

The father had most definitely been a relatively good man, trying to live with a cheating wife.

Why hadn't he just divorced the bitch, thought Shalini again, as she clicked her tongue irritably. "There's always another story, Shinde, believe me. It's like a bus or a taxi. Never run after any of them because there's always another one coming along in a few moments."

Shinde smiled as he took a long drag and topped up his glass, "Not like this one, Ms Shalini. Not too many like this one, believe me. Anyway, as usual, I digress. Arjun was a constant fixture in Lesley's house for the next couple of years or so. He enjoyed being with Lesley, Mario, and Greg, and they, in turn, adored the young tennis player and treated him like their baby brother. Then the visits to Lesley and Mario became less and less as he started to grow older. Acclimatizing himself to the abuse and trauma, he got hard in heart and mind. As he got on with his life and they got on with theirs, the visits became a trickle, and then after the incident on the Bangalore-Chennai highway, they ceased altogether."

"I guess operating behind enemy lines in a faraway war, running supply line operations for a rebel outfit, falling in love, and trying to get a career going might do that."

Shinde nodded. "He hadn't really thought about them for a long time until that fateful day when he heard how Lesley, Mario, and Greg had died one by one, like street dogs—with no honour, struck down in the prime of their lives by the dreaded needle."

"Shinde, I don't want to press home too fine a point, but these drugs were being sold in Wastra territory by drug peddlers who were protected by Wastra. How many lives have been destroyed by the white powder or the brown? He was just as much to blame as the guy who sold Lesley the drugs."

Shinde nodded his agreement, "Lesley's death shook Wastra to the core. He knew he was just as culpable as Santosh Saukar in Lesley's death. But he knew that he could not bring back Lesley, her brother, or her lover. He could, however, try to make things right. He also knew that an order to stop drug dealing in South Bombay would lead to open revolt and bloody war with close friends, which he wanted to avoid." Shinde lit a Gold Flake, took a large swig of his beer, and continued.

"So he decided to approach the problem laterally and start a drug war between the drug dealers. Let the dogs kill themselves. And that's when another organisation was born. It didn't have a name per se, but in certain extremely restricted circles, they called members of this organisation 'the white knights.' A rather dramatic name, I must admit, but those were dramatic times.

Shinde continued, "but the story of the white knights, like many of my other stories, is for another day. Could I interest you in some more food?"

Shalini nodded animatedly as she poured herself a glass of beer and checked the battery level on her recorder.

NINETEEN

SANTOSH SAUKAR

"Santosh Saukar made his first kill at the age of twelve. Another boy, roughly of the same age, also an orphan who survived the deadly streets every day by his wits, just like Santosh, had procured a packet of Marie biscuits from a hippie couple at Gateway. Like most street kids, he did not have any desire to share his loot. The gutters of Colaba had vomited Santosh Saukar into this world. He was found in a rubbish dump, near Fariyas Hotel, by a municipality chawl worker who was combing the trash cans at night, hoping for some discarded drugs or food. This was not some kind of old person who then adopted the newborn; he was a nasty, old alcoholic who put the infant in a dirty plastic bag and deposited the screaming baby at Colaba Police Station. The constables on duty, an equally callous bunch, had taken young Santosh to the Charni Road orphanage and handed him over to the caretaker after six hours. There was no postnatal care for Santosh, just the cold hard floor of Colaba Police Station. He had screamed till he was exhausted before lapsing into unconsciousness, and it was a miracle that he survived the night. He was a beautiful baby. The most probable explanation for his abandonment was that his mother was one of the many whores that wandered up and down Colaba Causeway and the various side lanes. The red streaks in his black hair and coloured eyes spoke of a Caucasian father, and he was easy prey in the orphanage. He had been raped repeatedly by older inmates and the warden, who enjoyed a fresh piece of steak from time to time.

"When he was nine years old, Santosh had been on his knees at the warden's office, pleasuring the paedophile with his mouth. At the point of orgasm, he had taken out the knife that he had hidden in his trousers and had sliced off the warden's penis and his testicles. He had left him screaming and bleeding on the floor after he had taken the keys from the thrashing body. He slipped past the sleeping guards and let himself out into the polluted air of Bombay. Now, three years later, he was well-versed in the art of survival as he stalked the kid with the biscuits, waiting for the right time to strike. He trailed his prey at a discreet distance, and once the kid felt certain that no one was following him, he ducked under a fence and went into Sunderbhai Chawl, an abandoned decaying structure that was soon going to be bulldozed, and it was rumoured that twelve storeys of luxury flats were going up in its place.

"Santosh picked up a rock and silently climbed up the stairs to the first floor, where the other kid was sitting in the dirt with his back to Santosh, a beedi in hand, puffing away contentedly.

The packet of Marie biscuits lay opened on the floor in front of him. Like a panther, Santosh crept up on the unsuspecting boy, and in a blinding flash, he attacked. He struck several times, just to be sure, although the first blow had been enough, cracking the skull open cleanly like an egg as he toppled sideways. The subsequent blows crushed the skull, and brain matter splattered all over the ground like some spongy, grey, bloody mushrooms. Santosh Saukar tore a piece of cloth from the shirt of the dead body and wiped the sticky mucus from his face and skinny arms. He picked up the Marie biscuits, inspected them closely to make sure there wasn't any brain matter with the biscuits, and ghosted away into the Cuffe Parade skyline.

"Iqbal 'Bangdi' ran, a street gang in Fort. He was older and extremely vicious, and he became Santosh's idol. Very soon, Santosh was selling *ganja* and *charas* for Bangdi all over Colaba, Flora Fountain, and the Fort areas. His customers were the hippies who thronged the many by-lanes of Colaba and Fort and local teenagers looking for a quick fix and a cheap high. Nobody suspected the young Santosh because of his innocent, childish looks, and in a relatively short period of time, he was the prime distributor for the Bangdi Gang, as they were known. Santosh grew to slightly above six feet in height by the time he was sixteen. He was naturally brawny, had long, wavy black hair with the signature red streaks, intelligent hazel eyes, and high cheekbones, betraying his foreign genes."

Shinde signalled to the hovering waiter as he lit a Gold Flake, and another pitcher appeared, "The good looks were where it all ended. Santosh was dead inside. All vestiges of decency had been wiped out a long time ago in the orphanage and then while growing up on the streets. But he had a magnetic personality and was a courageous and skilful street fighter.

The young bucks of the streets naturally gravitated towards him, and very soon, he was the leader of his own tough street gang. There was the eventual clash, the old lion versus the challenger to the pride, but Iqbal Bangdi was betrayed by his own men. They had been promised much bigger shares in the company business, and he was gunned down by his own bodyguards at the Worli Naka gas station. Shortly thereafter, every man who had betrayed Bangdi started turning up dead as Santosh sanitized the gang of all the traitors. He had readily joined the Wastra umbrella after listening to Vasu, Richard, and Madhya talk about the new king. He was irritated that none of them, no matter how high he got them, would ever reveal the identity of Wastra. He had even considered kidnapping Vasu and taking him to Elephanta Caves to interrogate him there at his leisure, but he knew he would have to kill Vasu after that.

The fear that Wastra generated far outweighed the need to find out his identity, and Santosh waited for his time to be propitious and let sleeping dogs lie. He made his payments on time, and his business flourished as the police and other predators faded away under the orders of the new king, and after a while, he decided that it was best not to change a winning formula."

Shinde lit a Gold Flake, took a large swig of his beer, and continued, "But as far as business was concerned, Santosh was ruthless and trusted very few people. There was always another Santosh waiting to take his place, and he had no intention of ending up like Iqbal Bangdi. So, his security was tight, and, more importantly, his bodyguards were loyal and had been with him for years. Wastra realised that taking out Santosh Saukar was not going to be easy and required meticulous planning. The entourage was assigned to only one task, and that was understanding Santosh's timetable and thereby figuring out his Achilles heel. Amjad, or 'pretty boy' as he was known in the gangland circles, found the chink in Santosh Saukar's armour."

Sujatha Bar was quite full. Surprisingly, the ilk of the customers had changed, and a lot of them were well-to-do youngsters. Apparently, the bar brewed its own beer, which was a hit with the well-heeled 20-somethings. The recipe for the fish and prawn fry was also a well- kept secret and had caught the imagination of the night birds. Most importantly, the fact that the bar was open till the wee hours of the morning with little or no police interference was the main attraction.

"Hang on just a minute! Did you say that Wastra decided to start a drug war?" But she was talking to his back because without warning, and for the first time since Shalini had entered Sujatha Bar, Shinde had actually gotten up and left to use the restroom for gents located at the back of the bar. Shalini had got a good look at him and was rather surprised. He was tall, maybe six feet or just about there. He was lean, tough-looking, and didn't in any manner resemble the local neighbourhood alcoholic stereotype. He had an easy-rolling gait about him. When he came back, he had slid back into his chair and had sort of blended in with the dingy surroundings.

Shalini had to squint into the shadowy backdrop to make his features out. She knew there was so much more to Shinde and wondered if she'd ever be allowed to see what lay behind the veil.

Shinde lit a Gold Flake, took a large swig of his beer, and continued, "Yes, I did say that, but I need to jump back and forth in order to establish the timelines and for you to make sense of all of this. I do hope you aren't getting bored."

"Oh no, no, no. Confused, mystified, yes, but bored, most definitely not," said Shalini with a short laugh.

Shinde nodded with that very distracting smile, "Alright then. Drug dealers are the most vicious and paranoid animals on this earth, and Santosh Saukar was no different from the rest of his brethren. As I said earlier, he had no intention of ending up like his erstwhile boss, who now lay buried at the Grant Road Muslim cemetery. His bodyguards were carefully vetted, and Santosh was no slouch either when it came to drawing blood."

"Yes, you had mentioned that earlier. Not that it has ever stopped an assassin's bullet or knife, has it?" said Shalini wryly.

"That is true," said Shinde, "but it brought down the risks considerably. Wastra's hit squad ran a 24-hour surveillance operation on Santosh, and as I said, it was Amjad who spotted the weakness. Santosh, having never known family life while growing up, had corrected the tragedy by getting himself a fairly beautiful wife, who was a cousin of Madhya, the head of Paanch Pairi, and an inner circle warlord. She was an ex-dancer with whom he had two children: a son, aged eight, and a daughter, aged six. This did not mean that he did not stray, as those were the perks of his job, but he was a good provider and kept his wife and children in a luxurious, Worli sea-facing flat, far away from his area of operations. He was always surrounded by his bodyguards, except every other Saturday night. It was on those nights that, unbeknownst to anyone, including his closest bodyguards, he visited Pinky."

Shinde lit a Gold Flake, "Now you are going to ask, 'Who is Pinky?' and I will tell you. The dance bars, which were an integral part of Bombay's culture, had been shut for many years due to the whim of a minister who could not get one particular dancer he fancied to sleep with him. But before that, especially in the '90s, the dance bar, or '*chameli*' bar, was a part of the staple diet of Bombay's nightlife. The dancers of the hundreds of bars across the city came from as far away as Kashmir. Such was the lure of the dance bar lucre. They gyrated to all the Bollywood songs, past and present, but they were always fully clothed. They never stripped, and it's always been a bit of a mystery to me why grown men showered these dancers with money. They were not like the strippers in bars abroad. Here, the customers were lucky if they got a peek at some cleavage. The minister was a very sanctimonious, slimy man called Kulin Ashar. He had fallen head over heels for the dancer who worked in a bar in his constituency of Parel. But she wanted nothing to do with him, and no amount of gifts or threats could change her mind or feelings. Finally, the enraged minister declared all dance bars as immoral and bad for the youth and, through a state order, had them all shut down."

Shinde shook his head, took a big swig of his beer, and continued, "The immature actions of the minister put the dance bar owners out of business, and all employees in the trade found themselves suddenly unemployed. The backbone of the trade, the dancers, either went back to their hometowns or became a part of the prostitution rings that sprang up in the wake of the shuttered bars. These dance bars have reopened recently, by the way."

Shalini knew a little bit about the dance bar culture, having read about it in passing, but she wasn't very up to date about that particular fabric of Bombay's collage. It had never made any sense, and if what Shinde was saying was correct, then it had to do with the fragile Indian male ego. Shalini shook her head and shrugged.

Shinde cut into her thoughts, "It was inconceivable that fully-clothed women dancing on stage to Bollywood songs would excite the Indian male without taking off their clothes, but that's exactly what was happening in all the dance bars. The girls danced fully clothed, and the men swarmed the bars like bees to honey. You could buy exorbitantly priced garlands, which a bouncer would present to the dancer for whom it was brought, or you could just shower her with currency notes. This was the preferred means of entertainment for the jewellers, stock brokers, businessmen, and most importantly, the underworld dons and their minions. Most of the dancers had a lifespan of two or three years if they were lucky and if they survived. They were able to retire back to the distant home towns they had left behind, rich beyond their dreams."

* * *

Shinde poured himself a glass, and Shalini allowed him to fill hers. They both took a few sips, and Shinde continued, "Out of all these dancers, and there were hundreds of them, Pinky, by far, was the highest-paid dancer in all the '*chameli*' bars. She danced at Topaz, which was located on Grant Road. From the most famous of underworld dons to the richest of the Marwari jewellers, all of them flocked to see her dance, and they were not disappointed. Pinky was blessed by the Gods with a face that dreams were made of and a body to go with it. And she was rhythm itself. The lines of humanity extended for kilometres outside Topaz Bar around eleven every night, with panting males hoping to get a look at the most beautiful face in Bombay. It was rumoured that she made ten lakhs a night."

Shalini whistled softly, "Ten lakhs a night? That's a lot of money today, so imagine how much that was twenty years ago?"

Shinde nodded. "Oh, yes. She was very rich, and although she danced for everybody every night, her heart and body belonged to Santosh Saukar. She was tall, fair, beautiful and, most importantly, a man."

Shalini choked on her cigarette, and after she had finished coughing, she said, "I'm sorry. Did you say she was a man?"

"Well, technically, I guess the term would be transgender. She looked like a woman, but she had male genitalia."

"That's called making the best of a bad situation. So, all those poor saps throwing their money and cheering and screaming didn't know she was a he? That's poetic justice," Shalini laughed.

"When she was fully made up, she was more beautiful than any screen actress, and that's what people saw and paid for. It's all about optics, Ms Shalini."

"Oh, I absolutely agree," said Shalini, "To each his own. So, Santosh had a thing for the unusual. Good for him. Different strokes for different folks is what I say."

"Well, it's not for everyone, and not everyone would have understood. So, on the days Santosh went to visit Pinky, he only took his cousin Gautam along for protection. Gautam wasn't really his cousin because we both know Santosh's antecedents. Gautam had grown up with him in the orphanage and had followed him after his escape from that hell. To the world, he was Santosh's cousin and was the only person Santosh totally trusted, and that type of friendship comes only when you have seen death together. Now, Amjad also had a thing for the unusual and unknown to everyone, especially Santosh Saukar. He was also sleeping with Pinky. It was between the sheets that Pinky told him of Santosh Saukar's visits and his lack of security."

TWENTY

BADSHAH NO MORE

"You must understand that Pinky actually had genuine feelings for Santosh. He was her pusher and kept her high on company supply for free, but even without the drugs, Pinky genuinely loved Santosh, and he loved her back."

"So what was it with Amjad? With 'pretty boy,' it was just sex, was it?"

Shinde nodded, "Amjad was a dashing devil, and he had his own particular style that a certain type of woman went for. But Amjad was no different from Santosh. His good looks ran only skin deep. Under the bravura, when you cut below the epidermis, he was a cold, calculating killer. He had no feelings for any woman or man except for his pack. Pinky was blown away by Amjad's swashbuckling attitude and looked, and I guess a woman can love two men, but when she started divulging details about Santosh to Amjad, she had no idea that she had signed his death warrant."

"If this wasn't a thing between a drug dealer and a transvestite, I might actually be sad," said Shalini sarcastically.

"A tragic love story isn't always between two good and innocent heterosexuals, you know?"

Shalini reached for a Gold Flake to hide her impatience. She hadn't had time for love, and apart from the odd one-night stand, there was no permanence in her life. If you don't trust anyone, then you can never be betrayed.

Shinde continued, "They waited in the dark for Santosh to arrive. Pinky had let it slip that Santosh would be visiting her that night. The Mercedes Benz arrived at about 2 am, and Santosh got out and swiftly went up into the Bhayender Apartment, where Pinky lived. The Mercedes was parked facing the apartment complex, giving Gautam a clear view of the entrance. Prasanjit came in from behind, using the blind spot of the rear-view mirror to his advantage. He slipped into the backseat, slit Gautam's throat from behind in one short slicing motion, and held his head tight until his death throes subsided and the blood flow reduced to a trickle. They left him in the driver's seat and waited for Santosh to come. It was a couple of hours before Santosh Saukar returned to the car, well-satisfied, humming a tune under his breath. As he got into the backseat, he gave the order to drive. When Gautam did not respond, Santosh instinctively knew his old friend was dead and went for his gun. Then the door on the other side opened, and Arjun got in. Santosh was drawing his gun when he recognized the bar owner from Colaba. He froze for just a second, overwhelmed, confused, and shocked about the fact that his cousin was dead and that he had no idea what Arjun was doing there in his car. Then Arjun smiled a pleasant, friendly smile, and Santosh, in spite of all his years on the streets, fell for the easy smile and relaxed his grip on the gun. Arjun put two bullets in Santosh's stomach, and Santosh doubled up, unable to scream in spite of the agony.

"Santosh tried to speak, but nausea overcame him, and he vomited blood and mucus all over the expensive interiors of his Mercedes 500 SEL. Arjun leaned forward, dropped the gun into his lap, and with his right hand, yanked Santosh's head back by his hair. 'You should have left her alone,' he whispered quietly to Santosh. Again, there was confusion and fear, and he died with all these mixed emotions as Arjun slit his throat from ear to ear. Then they went up to Pinky's apartment."

"Why?" asked a shocked Shalini, "Why kill that poor dancer? I mean, she was innocent."

"No loose ends. Pinky might have remembered that she had spoken to Amjad, and someone might have made the connection. She was dead the moment she opened her mouth to 'pretty boy.' It was sad, but there were addicts dying every day in Bombay, and the fact that Pinky overdosed didn't surprise anyone. Her apartment was cleaned out by neighbours and some 'brothers' from Jaipur. She was forgotten in a month. There were always many hot acts to see, and the next Pinky was just around the corner."

Shalini found an unutterable sadness for the transvestite dancer and her unnecessary death, although it had happened years before. It must have shown in her face, and Shinde reached forward and touched her hand and said, "It was sad, but terrible things are done in times of war, and you have to keep a neutral outlook, Miss."

Shalini shook her head and said, "Is that what that was? War? I will be truthful, not neutral."

Shinde nodded, "It was the declaration of war, and you being truthful is more than anyone could ask for. Would you like me to refill your glass?" Shalini nodded back, grim-faced, as Shinde topped her off.

Shinde took a deep swig of his beer and lit up a Gold Flake, "The death of Santosh Saukar resonated all over the Bombay underworld and into the outer reaches of the state. Santosh Saukar was a dreaded warlord, and the promise of retribution had everyone running for cover. The commissioner of police issued a dusk-to-dawn curfew and IPC 144, prohibiting the gathering. More than five people in public went into effect. For all practical purposes, the city shut down after 9 pm."

Shinde took another swig of his beer and peered past Shalini at the entrance, taking in the influx of customers. At 10 pm, Sujatha Bar seemed to shimmer in an alcoholic haze and didn't seem so dingy anymore. A couple of well-dressed urban cowboys were grooving to some interesting music, in Shalini's opinion, which had suddenly come on. They were spurred on by their scantily clad girlfriends. This wasn't the bar that Shalini had entered in the morning. This was Bombay. Anything was possible, and any place could be a page 3 hangout.

Shinde continued, "The lieutenants of Santosh Saukar demanded a meeting with Wastra but got to meet Richard instead, which in itself was an honour. He wasn't just an insignificant Colaba gang lord anymore. Toting a gold Rolex, he was known as '*Badshah*' or King, and he received the Saukar faction in his Mohini Mansion flat and, after a couple of shots of whiskey all around, promised them revenge once the killers had been identified.

Mangesh, the second-in-command in the Saukar hierarchy, was vociferous in his demand for blood, but Richard wasn't taking orders from the likes of Mangesh, and he made that abundantly clear.

"There will be blood, but once we have figured out who killed Santosh and Gautam. Wastra will not authorize a hit squad until we know who we are going to hit."

"'Bhai, we have made you good money and have been excellent earners over the years. Now you have to fulfil your end of the deal."

Richard's face started to mottle with controlled fury, "You made your payments like everyone else. You weren't selling fucking vegetables in the market, you were peddling drugs, and when you deal in death, you better expect the reaper to come knocking on your door. Your boss was in Bhayender, which is out of our jurisdiction, without any backup, or informing anyone. That was careless of him, and he paid the price. But you better understand that he was my friend much before you even knew who he was. When I find out who did this, I won't need you, do you understand? I will kill the motherfuckers myself."

Mangesh knew when not to poke the bear. "I'm sorry, Bhai. I know you will do the right thing. We are ready and waiting for your orders," With a big salaam, Mangesh got up and left with his fighters.

Shinde lit a Gold Flake, "Richard was genuinely upset at Santosh Saukar's violent demise. They had come from the streets together. As one of the chosen few who knew the real identity of Wastra, Richard took the case to his leader and broached the topic of retribution."

"Whoever did this has to pay. They left him dead like a stray dog, miles from home. I still can't believe he's gone,' Richard was violently distraught, "Give me some soldiers from Antop Hill, and I'll take care of this personally."

"Wastra was cool in his reply, "Do we have any idea who killed him?"

"Not as of now. But somebody will talk. I've put the word out."

"Excellent. I will give you Antop Hill and Sundernagari fighters under Lhoncha once we know who the killers are. What was Santosh doing in Bhayender in the middle of the night? That's not under our control."

Richard replied in an embarrassed manner, "The rumour is that he was poking Pinky and had gone to see her."

Rasul guffawed, "*Arey*! Seriously, boss, that Pinky was making so much money. She had her own Lexus! But I had no idea that she was doing Saukar. Not bad for good old Santosh. Even though she was not a real woman, I have to admit that I wouldn't have minded some action with her. Really, boss, she could dance so well."

Wastra cut off Rasul before he could go any further and said, "Maybe this killing is a crime of passion. Bring Pinky to me; I want to question her myself."

"She was found dead in her flat," said Richard quietly, "The post-mortem results show her time of death around the same time as the shooting of Santosh."

"So now we have a connection. Could it be revenge? Was there another lover?" Rasul guffawed again, "That Hijra was getting laid way more than any of us!"

Richard ignored Rasul's inappropriate ribaldry and nodded in agreement, "Someone must have been upset with the romance and killed them both."

Amjad said, "I know who exactly. It has to be Nasirullah!"

"The drug lord of Matunga?"

Amjad nodded, "It's well known that he was in love with Pinky. She was his good luck charm. There is no way he would have tolerated Santosh Saukar boning his fortune cookie. You know how superstitious these drug dealers are."

Richard slapped his thigh and said, "That fucker is not under our umbrella and is tough as hell. Plus, he has well-trained fighters with him all the time. If we hit him, it's going to start a gang war, for sure."

Wastra squinted at the point behind Richard's back and said, "We have to hit him and hit him hard. But it cannot point to us. I'm giving the job to Ganguly."

Arun Ganguly, a gangster from Dagdi Chawl, had risen to prominence recently with his elimination of the dreaded Samar Khan of Dongri. He lived by his own rules but respected Strand and kept his activities concentrated north of the Worli border.

"He's independent, but he likes you, Richie, and wants an alliance with Strand. Let's outsource this to him. Ask him to make a temporary alliance with Mangesh and Saukar's guys. Give him all the necessary information, but do not get involved in the actual fighting. I know you want to avenge your friend's death, but I don't want any blowback to our operations.'

"And in this way, Richard unwittingly helped start the drug war that devastated the streets of Bombay in the the '90s like wildfire," Shinde reached for the Gold Flake.

TWENTY-ONE

JUDGE NOT, LEST YE BE JUDGED

Everyone knew of the riots of the 1990s. It had been a race war, Hindus against Muslims. Hindu fundamentalists had destroyed a mosque in the north of India because it was built on top of a temple, which had itself been destroyed by the Mughals during the regime change. There had been the traditional destruction of Muslim property, rape of their women, and murder of their menfolk and children. Up there in the north, it wasn't anything to write home about because Hindus and Muslims had been slaughtering each other since Gandhi had caved in and allowed the British to have one last hurrah before they were kicked out, dividing a five-thousand-year-old nation into two.

But in Bombay, everyone had been living in peace and harmony, or at least as much as the city allowed. Therefore, when Hindus started the slaughter of Muslim innocents and then the Muslims retaliated, it left the city in a numb state of shock from which it never really recovered. It was always believed that the riots in Bombay had been a direct fallout of the events up in the north of the country. Now Shinde was suggesting something else, that the catastrophic events in Bombay in the '90s had nothing to do with the occurrences in the north and were the result of something entirely different.

Shinde said as though he were reading her mind, "It's very easy to fan the flames of religious fervour to get people to do unthinkable things, but often the actual instigators have their own agenda. They use religion and the common man as their weapons to achieve it."

Shinde took a large swig of his beer and continued, "On the same day that Jamiroquai released their smash hit 'Virtual Insanity,' the combined forces of Arun Ganguly and the late Santosh Saukar, led by Mangesh, who had taken over as interim warlord, attacked Nasirullah in his Nagpada stronghold. The attack was carried out just at the break of dawn, taking advantage of the suspension of the night curfew. Nasirullah and his warriors were preparing for their morning prayers when the first rocket launchers breached the walls.

Caught completely by surprise, Nasirullah died in the initial attack, but his warriors were well-trained and regrouped quickly. Instead of putting up a standard defence, which would have allowed for an eventual invasion of their territory by the tactically superior force, they launched a counter-strike which caught Ganguly & Co. by surprise. They came over their walls, weapons blazing and took the fight to the attackers in five hundred metres of no man's land outside Nagpada, and in the fierce fighting that ensued, Mangesh took a bullet to the head and died with a surprised look on his face. Someone must have dialled 100 because all of a sudden, the police were there, and they joined in, killing gang members on both sides. They strategically retreated on a permanent basis after two chief inspectors and eight constables died in the return fire. With the boys in brown, they liked it best when it was a one-way street, and they were making the killing. After losing a few of their brothers-in-arms, they rapidly lost their appetite for battle. Still, the tragedy was that several innocent bystanders died in the indiscriminate gunfire. The streets were littered with the dead and the dying; the sharply rising temperature resulted in a palpable stench, as the bodies bloated and then started releasing gases into the Nagpada air."

"I had no idea you were musically inclined," said Shalini, completely off-topic lighting up a Gold Flake. She'd stopped drinking for a while now, unable to keep up with Shinde's unquenchable appetite Shinde was up to the challenge, for beer, but was able to match him in the cigarette department.

Shinde was up to the challenge, "Oh, but I am, Ms Shalini. Jamiroquai was a ground-breaking jazz-funk band with multiple platinum hits and mesmerized millions of fans worldwide. I am aware of Jamiroquai, but I'm amazed that you would know about them. They haven't had a hit in a while. Love their music, though."

Shinde smiled and said, "Judge not, lest ye be judged. Anyway, while everyone was still reeling in the aftermath of the Nasirullah assassination and ensuing carnage that followed, Bobby Mehta, a drug dealer from south Bombay with a penchant for underage girls, and his right-hand man,

Noel D'Souza, were shot dead at the Oberoi Towers in the early hours of a Sunday morning as they were leaving the night club of that hotel. Preliminary reports suggested that Arif Khan of Dongri was responsible, prompting a strike on Dongri by Bhai Thakur. He was Bobby's mentor and guide in all things that could be smoked, swallowed, or injected, and the strike left thirty dead.

"Suddenly, it seemed that the warring drug dealers had got polarised along religious lines, which was ridiculous because the white and brown deaths knew no god. But the attack and killing of Nasirullah had an unexpected fallout. Nagpada is Muslim-dominated, and hence the maximum number of casualties were Muslim. This attracted the attention of the famous Ibrahim Fawad, an Indian mafia don living in exile in Pakistan but with massive political and economic connections in India. He was related to Nasirullah by blood and used to run his drugs through him in Bombay and beyond."

"And beyond?"

"The Indian market was lucrative, but it was by no means the only end-user. The drugs came from Golden Triangle, which was controlled by the Chinese triads, and the Silver Crescent, which was controlled by the Afghans. The drugs came to India, and then they were carried on to the UAE, then found their way to Africa, and finally by land and sea to Europe."

"So India was the first port of call. But I'm amazed that you say that the UAE was the next. Isn't it really strict there?"

Shinde smiled indulgently, like a parent with a child, "Drugs and prostitution have been the backbone of the UAE economy since the 60's. I had seen Dubai when it had just one runway and cattle shed as an international terminal, and I have seen its development to what it is today. It is an economic miracle; only, people tend to forget how the miracle was wrought. It was on the backs of hookers, the blood of Indian, Pakistani, and Bangladeshi labourers, and drugs. Anyway, as usual, I digress.

"Ibrahim had been given safe haven in Pakistan, and he spoke to his masters in the ISI about what he perceived as atrocities being committed against Muslims. After a short in-house meeting, they gave him the go-ahead to send fighters to India, to bolster the ranks of the Muslim drug dealers. The average Pakistani from Karachi, for example, is not very war-like, but that doesn't hold for his relatives from the northwest provinces. These were more Afghan than Pakistani, spoke mainly Pashto, and lived and died by the sword and for their interpretation of their holy book. The ISI sent in these fighters, but they were all religious fundamentalists to the last man, and they came with their own agenda, which had the blessings of their masters. Setting up multiple command and control centres in Dongri, Agripada, and Nagpada with central command at Dombivili, they began to launch attacks against Hindu drug dealers in the beginning before branching out to target legitimate Hindu businesses.

They were well-armed and had the requisite military training, which the average soldier of the Hindu cartels did not have. It seemed that they would crush all their opposition, such was the ferocity of their attacks."

Shinde poured himself a glass of beer and proffered his glass to Shalini. She shook her head and said, "I'd like something more to eat, please."

"Of course. May I suggest something lighter? I highly recommend the *bhindi* and *aloo masala* with some *chapati.*"

"Thank you," said Shalini. Shinde signalled to the waiter, who leapt forward like a panther on a hare and placed the order.

* * *

Shinde continued, "The fundamentalists eventually came up against the wall that was Arun Ganguly, who rose to the challenge of the invaders and proved equal to the task. His fighters were loyal and well-trained. With his defence and effective counter-strikes, Bombay was soon locked in a not-so-covert street war. The night lit up with the noise of automatic gunfire, and dead bodies turned up in droves as the two sides battled for control of the streets. Wastra provided weapons and tactical advice but did not commit his troops to the battlefield. His plan of getting the drug dealers to eliminate each other was working to perfection, although the fact that non-criminal enterprises were also being targeted troubled him.

But no one in Wastra-controlled territory had been touched. The fundamentalists might have prevailed through sheer military expertise, which Ganguly's men didn't have enough of until they went and assassinated the owner of Regal Cinema Theatre, which fell under the protection of Wastra."

Shinde signalled to the hovering waiter who produced a pitcher of beer virtually out of thin air and said, "Even the best-laid plans—"

"—Of mice and men, they often go awry. Yes, I've read Robert Burns," said Shalini, completing the famous quote.

Shinde continued, "He was at the Everest Bar when Babu brought him the news that Jerry Sidhwa, the fat and affable owner of the iconic Regal Cinema, had been shot dead by unidentified gunmen. It happened while he was taking an evening stroll down Marine Drive. Further inquiries revealed that he had been the subject of several extortion attempts, to which he had not acquiesced. Inspector Beg provided some CCTV footage, which showed five burly, bearded men leaving his office, shooting the hapless watchman on their way out."

Shinde was sombre as he refilled his glass to the brim, "You are right, Miss. If Wastra hadn't killed Santosh Saukar, Ibrahim wouldn't have been able to establish a foothold in Bombay. He didn't care whether Muslims were being killed or not. He just wanted his business to be protected. The Pakistanis were another matter altogether; to them, an Indian Muslim was just another hated Indian. They sent their trained Jihadis to infiltrate the ranks of the Muslim underworld with the sole purpose of propagating terror."

Shinde took a deep swig of his beer, "Wastra was far too experienced a warhorse to dwell on the 'what might have been' situations. He made no excuses for what he had done, and he had no regrets. He understood clearly and unambiguously that he was now committed to battle. He summoned Richard, the inner circle warlords, Kalia Anton, and three top LTTE commanders to the war room, which was deep in the heart of the Sundernagari fisher village in Colaba, far away from prying eyes and loose tongues. Like the experienced war tactician that he was, he prepared battle plans and invited discussions on how to improve upon them. Twelve hours later, the final battle plans were transmitted to the field commanders through the inner circle warlords."

Shinde lit a Gold Flake, "War creates robots. Men in battle rarely question orders. Wastra had seen that in the Iran-Iraq conflict, where thousands of men rushed into certain death without any doubts."

"Or maybe they had doubts, but by that time, it was too late to act on them," said Shalini wryly.

"Duly noted. However, the point here is that no one among the street fighters questioned the dark-skinned fighters that suddenly bolstered their ranks. Over the years, they had become creatures of legend and appeared whenever the shit was about to hit the fan. What followed immediately after their arrival were some cataclysmic events, followed by relatively long periods of peace and harmony. Everyone knew that they fought for Wastra, so if they were here, then, most probably, Wastra was here as well. They kept to themselves, and it was obvious they didn't speak Hindi or Marathi. Command of the three platoons was given to Ghania, Ghungroo Salim, and Namdeo. But the dark-skinned fighters operated as an independent group within the platoon; this initially ruffled the feathers of the rank and file who were quite mystified that their field commanders did not take umbrage to this."

Shinde refilled his glass, and Shalini let him top hers off, "Then came the orders to attack the Muslim command and control centres. At 10 am, one sunny July morning in 1997, a three-pronged attack was launched on Dongri, Nagpada, and Agripada. The dark-skinned fighters led the attack, and that is when the Bombay street fighters saw real military ferocity up close, and it was eye-opening, to say the least.

"Using RPGs and mortars, the first wave broke down the defensive structures of the Muslim fighters. The second wave followed using Kalashnikovs and Uzis, decimating the initial resistance without the loss of a single man. Using knives similar to the green berets of the US Special Forces, their wet work was scary as they slashed and stabbed with blinding speed, twirling in and out of striking range and killing everyone that stood before them. The Muslim defenders melted like ice cream on a hot summer day before these fearsome warriors. You can understand that no one had any bruised egos after that," Shinde laughed, and Shalini joined in, both seeing the grim humour of the tale.

Shinde was on a roll as he took a swig of his beer and continued, "The fundamentalists were true to their creed and sacrificed the local soldiers in order to save their skins. Many of them had died, and the remaining retreated under cover of heavy gunfire. The chaos in Bombay was unimaginable… The streets reverberated with the sounds of gunfire, explosions, and screams of the dying. Wastra's fighters killed the Muslim fundamentalists and their associated drug dealers, while the fundamentalists, regardless of caste, colour, or creed, indiscriminately killed anyone that came in their range, trying to escape in the ensuing chaos and confusion. The police, true to their code of protect and serve, were completely absent. The news media, like hungry scavengers, circulated unsubstantiated and unvetted reports, given to them by the political servants of Ibrahim from within the state government, of escalating race riots in Bombay. Due to these reports, confusion and terror reign supreme. When they reached the slums of Behrampada in Bandra, which was Muslim-dominated, the fundamentalist fighters made a last stand. Using the fake news that Muslims were being killed by Hindus, the terrorists mobilized the uneducated Muslim masses in the slums into an angry mob that went on the rampage, torching Hindu shops and killing innocent men, women, and children.

PBP, a violent anti-Muslim party whose popularity was on a downward spiral, saw an immediate resurgence as thousands of sevaks, as they called themselves, descended upon Bombay from all parts of Maharashtra in response to a call to arms by their charismatic leader, Nagasaheb Bakre. In a matter of hours, they attacked Behrampada, slaughtering innocent men, women, and children. Interestingly, they never encountered any of the fundamentalists. The story goes that Ulhas Kakre, one of the Squad commanders, rushed into one of the lanes of Behrampada expecting easy pickings and ran into a regiment of fundamentalists. One RPG later, they scattered like dust in the wind." Shinde laughed loudly, and Shalini joined in. "So anyway, the sevaks avoided central Behrampada, where the fundamentalists were bunkered down and kept their heroics to the periphery."

Shalini took a deep swig of beer. She had heard of the atrocities committed on the Muslim population by the numerically superior Hindu forces. But how much of all this was true? If this story ever went to press, how many defamation suits were the paper looking at? She knew that Shantanu would weigh everything against readership and an increase in sales. Then she realised that she was here for something else. They had gone way off track. What was the connection between this story and the junkie on the railway tracks? Her questions must have shown on her face because Shinde raised his palm in a calming motion.

"I know you have so many questions, Ms Shalini, but you must listen to the whole story. It will all make sense very soon."

Shalini nodded, lighting a Gold Flake.

"Thank you. The riots spread to all parts of Bombay. Wastra had seen this type of mindless violence before and knew it was an infectious disease, and like the brilliant tactician he was, Wastra changed his battle plan. He pulled back all his forces and set up defence lines along south Bombay. From Worli and Walkeshwar down to RC Church, the combination of fisherfolk, street fighters, and LTTE commandos operated in tactical formation, their sole intention being the prevention of any violence from erupting. The word was sent to all political parties and religious communities that there would be no violence within the protectorate, against any caste or religion, on pain of death. The mystique of Wastra was enough of a deterrent, even with the political party leaders. If you check the records, Miss, you will find that South Bombay was relatively untouched by violence during the race riots of the '90s. But then again, not entirely untouched. And as usual, I must ask your indulgence if I don't seem to be making any sense."

TWENTY-TWO

INVISIBLE POWER

"Believe me, Shinde, all this will be checked and double-checked, but there's something that I have been meaning to ask you," said Shalini. The music was getting a little louder, though not entirely disharmonious to the ears. The main doors of the bar were closed and surprisingly soundproof, so the street was exposed to the noise only when the doors were opened. This required a certain amount of awareness, planning, and expense that were at odds with the dingy environmental settings of the bar. But the market had long since shut down for the night, and apart from the length of the chawl above the bar that stretched almost all the way down to the causeway, there were no residences. *Karate Vilas was probably getting a hefty cut for his patience,* thought Shalini with a small smile.

"Ms Shalini, I will answer all your questions to the best of my ability, but my memory is a little short, I must warn you. Probably caused by the alcohol."

If there is anything wrong with this guy's memory, then I'm a cane-whiskey-swilling Gujju, thought Shalini.

"I'm trying to build a profile on this Wastra. He was a real chameleon. That much is pretty clear, but you did say that he was a pilot, didn't you?" asked Shalini.

"Yes, he did his initial flight training in the US, then came back and joined Indian Airlines. Now it's merged with Air India. A disastrous decision pushed forward by an extremely corrupt aviation minister."

"I'm trying to wrap my head around the fact that he was able to juggle his day job with his extracurricular activities. In fact, it's amazing that he even wanted to have a day job. I mean, it's pretty much at odds with the rest of his career choices. If what you are saying is true, then it was a pretty nifty trick," said Shalini, as she lit a Gold Flake and checked her phone for messages.

Shinde took a swig of his beer, looked admiringly at the dusky, attractive reporter, and murmured, "How very intuitive of you, Miss. That was the beauty of it all. To perpetuate the legend, mystique, and unquestioned power of Wastra, it was of prime importance that there should be a clear distinction between Arjun and Wastra. Arjun became the pilot with a tendency to alcoholism, a volatile temperament, and quick fists. Wastra was the invisible unquestioned king of south Bombay's parallel universe. The pilot maintained his day job, and apart from a few colleagues who knew he owned a bar in Colaba, no one and absolutely no one had an inkling of his association with the legend. As far as the streets were concerned, he paid his dues to Wastra, like everyone else."

Shalini nodded as she took a sip of her beer, "I see what you mean about the tree and the forest. Hide in plain sight. No one will look for you there. They will be too busy looking in the shadows."

Shinde nodded admiringly, "Absolutely correct, Ms Shalini. However, his day job gave no joy whatsoever. Most of the pilots had procured their jobs through nepotism rather than merit and ability, and he found the quality and mettle of his colleagues to be rather mediocre, and it was this endless circle of mediocrity that did not sit well with the overlord of South Bombay who found his colleagues, with a few exceptions, mundane in the extreme. He found them to be a bunch of ass-kissing incompetents, but it was his official job on paper, and it provided him with the ideal cover."

Shalini laughed, her white teeth glistening in the dark. "I can, with absolute certainty, understand how mind-numbing he must have found his day job to be. He was the odd one out, the one who couldn't and didn't play by the accepted rules. Mediocrity has always been the nemesis of creativity. He couldn't have been very popular."

"Absolutely, Miss. But popularity is another fickle mistress, and he wasn't overly concerned about her. He knew himself well enough to know that he could win her back at any time of his choosing. The critical need was to create the persona of the arrogant, alcoholic party animal, and he did that to perfection. To his blinkered colleagues, he was an avoidable pilot that they could do without. He just came across as an unpalatable loudmouth, and he maintained and propagated that charade. He detested his colleagues, and to be fair, most of them detested him as well. There were a few incidents worth mentioning."

Shalini leaned forward interestedly, "Do tell."

Shinde lit a Gold Flake, took a large sip of his beer, and smiled at the expectant Shalini. Women would always be women, gossip above all else.

"For example, there was a Capt. Bamaji, who was in charge of administration, threatened Arjun with some disciplinary action, which may have, in all honesty, been warranted. The incident happened on a Friday afternoon. On Friday night, or more like early Saturday morning, Arjun sent Vasu and a contingent of fighters, all of them very drunk and extremely aggressive, to visit Bamaji at his residence in the Indian Airlines colony at Vile Parle. They dragged Bamaji from his fifth-floor flat and unceremoniously shoved him inside one of the ambassadors that they had come in. When he looked down, someone had placed a country pistol on his lap. Bamaji soiled himself and was then equally unceremoniously ejected from the car. No threats were made, and no names were ever mentioned, but Bamaji knew, and needless to say, felt no reason to pursue any disciplinary action against Arjun."

Shalini laughed loudly. It was an attractive sound, "Oh God! Bet he didn't see that coming."

Shinde joined in the laughter, "Then there's the story of Capt. Haveri, General Manager, also tried to have some disciplinary action taken against Arjun. Something to do with a female first officer that Haveri felt he had dibs on given his seniority in the airline."

"There we go," said Shalini. "The fragile Indian male ego."

Shinde took a large swig of his beer and continued, "Capt. Haveri wasn't necessarily of a bad sort. But after he found the female first officer constantly in the company of Arjun, he tried to have him suspended from flying duties on trumped-up charges of dereliction of duty.

To cut a long story short, on yet another Saturday night, more than thirty hardcore fighters stormed the plush Walkeshwar apartment complex where Capt. Haveri lived. Ten of the fighters held the building security guards, hostage while the rest went up to Capt. Haveri's luxury apartment. It was two in the morning when they rang his bell. When Capt. Haveri opened the door, the fighters dragged him out and pistol-whipped him and his son. There was blood everywhere, neighbours screaming, and father and son unconscious on the floor—it was absolute chaos. To make matters worse, the hit squad went down to the local police station and filed assault charges against Haveri and his son.

The sub-inspector on duty recognized the bar owner from Strand and had no hesitation in filing the complaint after a large envelope had exchanged hands. To add insult to injury, the cops brought the beaten and bleeding Capt. Haveri and his errant son Rishi went to the station for questioning. The news spread like wildfire through the airline, and attempts at intimidation against Arjun dropped drastically."

"I'm sure they did. This makes for some entertaining beer talk, but I feel that there is an underlying moral to these tales."

"And what is that, Miss?"

"Job satisfaction. If you don't choose a career that you want and are passionate about, you will never be happy in your job. Alternatively, if you do a job you love, you will never work another day in your life.

"That's the problem with India today. Most kids follow careers chosen by their parents and sometimes grandparents and end up with miserable lives. I suspect that Arjun was a victim of something like that. Bad career choice, coupled with unfortunate circumstances."

"Maybe he should have stayed a tennis player or musician. It's not only about money, you know? He could have maintained his cover doing something else."

"You could be right, but aviation played a significant role in his life, and without that, other events further south might have never occurred. But I'm getting ahead of myself again."

"There is another question," said Shalini. She was aware of the aviation angle in this story but could not find a connection. She was sure that Shinde would clear the fog away with a magical wave of his beer mug. A picture of Shinde in a wizard's outfit, waving his beer mug like a wand, came to mind, and she smiled.

"Go ahead, Miss."

"Wastra was a consummate professional, that much I have gathered. He was also not overly sentimental, and I'm sure he would not let emotions influence his decisions. Am I correct in my assumptions?"

Shinde nodded and said, "You couldn't be more accurate, Ms Shalini."

"There's no way he would have killed Santosh Saukar just because Lesley overdosed. The entire operation against Santosh Saukar has a personal feel about it, but Santosh wasn't directly to blame for her death, so why take him out in such a gruesome manner with no mercy?" Something flickered in Shinde's eyes, and Shalini took a deep breath, "Or was he?"

TWENTY-THREE

THE DOWNWARD SPIRAL

"You are very perceptive, Miss. And you are absolutely correct. There is a lot more to that story."

Shalini noticed that Shinde had actually not lit a cigarette or guzzled from his mug for a while. He had been rather intent on his narrative, and considering that there hadn't been a gap of more than five minutes in the last ten hours between his smoking or drinking, that in itself was something remarkable. Shalini wondered if he had finally hit his saturation point. Shinde reached for the Gold Flake packet, took one out, and lit up as if on cue. He topped off his glass and signalled to the indefatigable waiter.

"Lesley, if you remember me telling you, was an unusual beauty, and unlike most beautiful women, she was quite unaware of her effect on men."

"I think you might have mentioned that," Shalini was a trifle more caustic than she intended, and she immediately regretted her tone. But Shinde did not seem to notice.

"She was beautiful on the inside and the outside. She had a warm and friendly personality and was entire without guile. She caught the attention of Santosh Saukar, who saw her walking down Colaba causeway one morning with Greg."

"That was the boyfriend, if I remember correctly?"

Shinde nodded, "Now Saukar was quite a striking figure and was used to women giving him the once over. There was no shortage of women in Saukar's life, such were the perks of his trade, but we always desire what we cannot have."

Shalini said, "That is more of a male testosterone thing, in my opinion. Women, on the whole, are more easily appeased, I feel, when it comes to choosing a partner."

Shinde smiled, "I can neither confirm nor deny that. Saukar knew Greg in passing, and he had seen Lesley several times. But that morning was different. Maybe it was the way the sun set in those emerald eyes, or maybe the smile was more devastating than usual. At that moment, there was a wild fluctuation in Santosh Saukar's hormones, and he knew then and there that he must have her, Dev Anand, or any film producer be damned. He could not understand how an insipid-looking Greg had managed to win Lesley's heart when he was right there for the taking."

Shalini laughed, "Isn't that always the same with guys of all flavours? They can never understand a woman's heart. It's rarely about looks. She needs to feel a certain way deep inside her soul, and once she feels that with a particular man, nothing else matters. Of course, there is a high probability of a catastrophic mistake, but I like to believe what doesn't kill you only makes you stronger." They were both silent for a while, Shinde realising that Shalini was speaking from experience. He lit a Gold Flake and offered her one, and they smoked in companionable silence. Then Shinde continued.

"Santosh was used to getting what he wanted, and refusal wasn't an option in his world. But he was smart. He knew his chances of success with a direct approach were slim to none. He had to make her dependent on him, and he knew exactly how to go about it."

Shinde refreshed his glass, "First, he went after Greg. He found out that Greg went to the sailors club at Lion Gate for drinks and some gambling. He struck up a conversation with him there. He plied him with alcohol, and he soon became a close friend and confidante. This became a routine for them over the next couple of months. One hazy, vodka-fuelled night, he paid off his gambling debt to Greg's and further cemented the friendship. Then he introduced Greg to cocaine. Greg had his first mind-bending experience and was back the next night for more. Soon vodka took a backseat, and one hit wasn't enough. Greg wanted the drug-induced high to last forever and was ready to do anything to keep his mind in that altered sense of reality. That's when the white devil, very surreptitiously, took control, Greg slipped into addiction, and Santosh went from friend to ruthless pusher. He encouraged Greg to bring Lesley and Mario into the fold, which happened with relative ease. It is often the case when one person in a tightly-knit group gets hooked on drugs or anything for that matter. The rest of the group, or most of them, normally follow. With Lesley and

Mario, it was like giving candy to a baby. There was no resistance at all. And in that manner, Santosh Saukar was able to gain unfettered access to Lesley."

Shalini shuddered involuntarily and silently thanked her stars that all she was addicted to was her morning coffee. She was well aware of the devastating effect of addiction, having recently done a piece on drug addiction in the film industry. A famous star had been caught pimping his addict wife in order to finance their drug needs and had been the centre of a murder-suicide at a suburban five-star hotel.

Shinde continued, "Once she was addicted, Lesley was under Santosh's control. He began to use her as his own personal sex toy just by controlling the flow of his product into Lesley's nose and veins. There were no objections from Mario or Greg, or for that matter, Lesley.

They were too busy getting high on Santosh Saukar's supply. Greg was the first to overdose, somewhere near Kala Ghoda; he was found in a pool of his own excrement, drowned in his own vomit.

Lesley and Mario were too far gone, deep in the clutches of the white demon, to really care that Greg would not be coming home ever again, and in it lay the real tragedy; the destruction of true love by the insidious serpent of drug addiction. It wasn't long after that Santosh got tired of Lesley and her constant needs. As the drugs slowly erased her stunning looks, leaving her hollow-cheeked and dark-eyed, he lost interest and found that he didn't desire her anymore. One night, he smacked her around, broke her jaw, and threw her out into the streets and out of his life."

Shinde's face tightened as he lit a Gold Flake and continued, "The real downward spiral began after that. Unable to afford the expensive stuff, Lesley gravitated towards brown sugar, which was cheaper to procure. When the money ran out, she offered her body to the street pushers in exchange for a fix. It didn't take long for her to start offering her body to anyone in exchange for a few bucks. She just needed enough to get high. She became skeletal, with deep sunken eyes, and her teeth started to rot from lack of basic hygiene. It was the nuclear destruction of a beautiful rose."

"So that's what Rasul was talking about at the meeting of the warlords when he talked about Lesley's death and seeing her almost toothless sometime before she died, isn't it?" asked Shalini.

Shinde nodded, "It was a disaster of gigantic proportions in the heart and mind of Arjun. It had taken him a while to put the pieces together, but the entourage had been extremely thorough and had researched the events and timelines, through their various sources from the streets, before presenting the tragedy to their king. He blamed himself for the disaster, drank himself into oblivion, and when he surfaced a week later, he summoned his entourage to let them know of his decision to kill Santosh Saukar. As usual, he looked ten steps ahead of the game, like a chess grandmaster. He didn't just want Santosh Saukar to die. He wanted to kill all the dealers in Bombay or as many as he could. His plan was to kill Saukar and make it look like a gangland hit, which would hopefully spark a war between the drug lords of Bombay. It gave birth to another group called the 'white knights.' It was a plan that led him to isolate himself from the rest of his friends outside the gang world, creating the alcoholic persona of descending into madness; this would dog him forever, but he didn't care. He just dedicated himself to his ultimate goal of ridding Bombay of the scum of the earth."

"He had no idea that it would open the doors to the fundamentalists. Even the best-laid plans are slaves to the free radical, aren't they?" Shalini sighed and took a large sip of her beer.

***

Shinde ordered some more food. This time it was spicy chicken, served with *chapati* and *bhindi masala,* cooked the Malvani way. They both ate ravenously and silently while Shalini tried to get her mind in order, putting the pieces of this incredible story in sequence. She still wasn't getting the connection between the incident on the tracks and Shinde's story, but she felt they were getting to the end and the "sting in the tail" bit. They both lit up Gold Flakes, and Shalini waited for Shinde to resume his tale.

"Let's get back to what happened right after the Hindu-Muslim riots. There were a whole bunch of rumours about how it all came to an end, which normally follows in the aftermath of a disaster of that magnitude. Everyone wanted to take credit and gain mileage, either political or economic, as having been the one who stepped up to the crease. The most widely circulated story, and the one that I believe is true, is that in order to end further bloodshed on both sides, Wastra issued a challenge to the fundamentalist chief. The challenge was a fight to the death, with the guarantee that if the fundamentalist chief won, then he and his surviving soldiers would be allowed to walk free."

Shinde topped off his mug, took a large swig, and continued, "The terrorists were surrounded on all sides, and all avenues of escape were cut off. Behrampada was sealed off tighter than Fort Knox. The bulk of his troops, bolstered by the LTTE fighters, controlled all exits. The remaining fighters, under the command of Khalid Islam and Kalidas, blocked the entry of the police, the army, and interested political parties, like the PBP, into the conflict zone.

"Khalid, who would go on to become a prominent politicians, made the necessary phone calls to the people that were in charge, and subsequent instructions to the army garrison commanders at RC church and Bombay Police Headquarters were issued; they were ordered to stand down. The PBP, being the courageous organisation it was, backed off when it saw no help coming from the cops or the army. But Wastra knew the fundamentalist mind, knew they were ready to die, and would try to make sure that as many innocents as possible would join them in Paradise. However, he also was absolutely sure that they could not resist an offer to walk free. So, he made them an offer he knew they would find almost impossible to refuse. If the fundamentalist chief won, then he and his men, those who were remaining, would be guaranteed safe passage out of Bombay."

Shinde took a swig of his beer and lit a Gold Flake. Shalini felt her pulse race again.

"You mean a gladiatorial type of challenge? How could Wastra be so confident of victory?"

Shined smiled grimly. "Nothing is guaranteed in single combat. The briefest lapse in concentration, the slightest hesitation in striking, and a minuscule drop in confidence could be the difference between life and death, and Wastra was well aware of the pitfalls to victory. He knew that if he lost and the fundamentalists walked free, it wouldn't be very long, maybe a year or two, before they would be back, and that was something he was not prepared to allow. To this end, all inner circle warlords and the LTTE brigade commanders had been instructed to decimate every last one of the fundamentalists, regardless of the outcome of the fight."

"The fundamentalists must have known that there was a strong possibility of a double-cross?" questioned Shalini.

"I'm sure the thought must have crossed their minds, but their options were limited to non-existent. Either they died in the slums of Behrampada, which was a sure road to Paradise and the virgins who breathlessly anticipated their arrival, or they could take a chance on the possibility of a victory of their chief in single combat and delay the pleasures of Paradise for a little while longer."

Shalini lit up a Gold Flake, "I guess they decided to go with option two."

Shinde took a large swig of his beer, "Exactly that. Now, as I had mentioned earlier, the fundamentalists who had been recruited by the Pakistanis were Afghan and Pashtun fighters from the northwest provinces that bordered Afghanistan. They were uneducated and weren't the brightest stars in the galaxy, and; those are normally the ones you can mould into committing unthinkable atrocities. But what they lacked in intelligence, they more than made up for in brutality. Their leader, Ali Beg, was a towering brawny, red-bearded man, well above six-and-a-half feet, and it was amazing how someone who looked like him had gotten across the border undetected. He inspired respect and loyalty amongst his fighters and fear in his enemies. In their operational briefing, his handlers in Rawalpindi had told him to expect a cakewalk in Bombay, and his initial success had solidified his opinion of the basic lack of moral fibre of the ordinary Indian, with a massive magnifying glass on the keepers of law and order on the streets. He felt that they talked a good fight but were more adept at running rather than standing their ground. It was only after he had lost two-thirds of his men to those strange dark-skinned fighters backed by very obviously highly-trained street warriors did he realize that he was up against a very different organisational structure, one that he had not been briefed about."

Shalini lit a Gold Flake and took a sip of her beer. She knew there was a big hangover coming, but she still took a nice, healthy swig. *Live in the moment, Shalini,* she told herself.

Shinde matched her swig and continued, "So when the challenge was issued, Ali Beg was taken aback. When he was first selected as the head of the terrorist strike force inside India, he was overwhelmed by the honour and accepted the post without a second thought.

"He had not expected to return to his mountains and his wife and two sons; it was something his tribe had accepted, and in true Afghan style, no one had thought to ask his wife. The women were just sperm receptacles to facilitate the arrival of more sons for the Jihad. But as the sound of weapons fire drew closer and the inevitability of a sooner-than-expected meeting with the Almighty loomed in the near future, Ali Beg suddenly felt the need to feel the warmth of his wife again. She was the only kind face that seemed to come to his mind. He thought about his boys and realised that he had been away for so long that he could barely remember their faces. They were strangers to him, and he to them.

"Through all the blood and death, there was a sudden longing in his heart for home, and the challenge threw open an entirely new option, one that hadn't been there before. With regards to his operation in Indian territory, he realised, too late, that he was up against trained military personnel and not some dead-beat cops that he had been successfully dealing with until then. He could have even handled Ganguly, although it had not been easy-going with that vegetable vendor from Dagdi Chawl, but the sudden arrival of these dark-skinned, Kalashnikov-toting fighters had made the situation untenable. He could not understand where they had come from, but he realised he had made some error that had resulted in their activation, which had, in turn, resulted in catastrophic losses amongst his fighters. It had also escalated his street gang operation, where he was having considerable success, notwithstanding that upstart from Dagdi Chawl to an all-out ground war, in which he was on the brink of defeat. The challenge gave him renewed hope. He was an expert swordsman, and he had never lost in single combat. It was with this grim confidence that he accepted the challenge. He had no doubt that his men and he would walk. Once back in Pakistan, they could plan their next move. He needed to brief his superiors about this paramilitary force that seemed to think they owned Bombay. 'But then again,' Beg said to himself, 'if I can cut off the head of the snake, the body will just collapse.

These fucking Indians needed to see a real man at work.' With his morale boosted by these positive thoughts, he prepared himself for single combat."

Shinde lit two Gold Flakes and gave one to Shalini. They smoked in silence, taking in the music and the mixed aroma of booze, perfume, and chicken *masala*. It was actually quite heady, and Shalini felt the intoxication flow through her. It felt good, and strangely she didn't seem tired or sleepy. The story had got her by the nose, and she was hooked. Shinde continued, "They met in Brabourne Stadium. It had been the stage for many a cricket battle between Pakistan and India, and it seemed fitting that this war would also be settled on these hallowed grounds.

"Under the prearranged and agreed rules, each leader was allowed to bring three men, who would also do battle to the death. It would be four against four. Ali Beg arrived at the stadium a little after two in the afternoon. His chosen three had been with him since the days of their successful guerrilla war against the Russians. They were experts with swords, which was their weapon of choice, and were also skilled at unarmed combat, having been trained by the CIA, who had been their unofficial advisers during the Russian conflict. The stands thronged with armed fighters, and Ali Beg was shocked at the number of enemy soldiers in attendance. And these were the ones who were visible. He knew that hidden snipers had his men and him in their crosshairs. Pakistan needed to be apprised of this prevailing situation at the earliest and needed to avoid Bombay like the plague. A ripple went through the stands as Arjun presented himself on the battlefield.

"Everyone knew the bar owner, and the rumours that he was the chosen one of Wastra were obviously true."

"And Arjun came with his entourage, of course," said Shalini without any doubt in her mind.

"But of course. There had been heated exchanges at the war council as the inner circle of warlords vied with each other to be chosen. Rasul, Lhoncha, Vasu, Namdeo, and Ghania had been vociferous in their pleas, but Arjun told them that their duties lay with the rank and file, that they would need motivation if the fight did not go according to plan, and if he lost. 'There is no certain outcome in this fight,' he said. 'If I fall in battle, Richard will take over as leader of all operations. The LTTE commanders have been apprised of my decision.' There were some protests, but they lacked conviction. Not everyone had been happy with the decision of single combat, and Richard being chosen as successor didn't sit well with some inner circle warlords, but Wastra's decision, backed by the acceptance of the LTTE, derailed any potential opposition."

"Civil war following the death of a king isn't exactly unheard of in history. In fact, it's more of a standard operating procedure, isn't it?" asked Shalini.

Shinde took a large swig of his beer and nodded, "Arjun had stood up and looked around at his war council and had said, 'Don't worry guys, you'll be stuck with me for a while, so don't start planning any funeral arrangements just yet. Only the good die young.'

"Vasu had said, 'In that case, you will probably live forever,' and there here had been a round of grim laughter, which did little to elevate the sombre mood in the room. Everyone present knew of the danger that lay ahead for their leader."

Shinde lit a Gold Flake, "Arjun was in the centre, flanked by Prasanjit on his left and 'pretty boy' and Dharvesh on his right. They made an unusual-looking bunch.

Prasanjit had a katana in his right hand, while 'pretty boy' and Dharvesh, who was dressed in some sort of Buddhist monk type of outfit with flowing robes, seemed to be unarmed. Arjun had the strangest weapons the fundamentalists had ever seen. They were two identical long, ceremonial types of daggers, pointed only at the tips. The rest of the blade was round and smooth. These were known as "sai", but Beg and his men had never heard of them. Not that they cared a whole lot. You fought the enemy, not his arsenal, which was the one thing they knew how to do. All they saw were a bunch of medium-built guys of average height, with the exception of Prasanjit, who was closer to the six feet average of the Afghan fighters. All in all, they didn't look like much, especially the two jokers in the monks' robes. Ali Beg's spirits lifted as his group squared off with Arjun and his entourage.

"Beg looked down from his six feet five inches and spoke to Arjun, one leader recognising the other, 'You are the leader of this pack.' It was a statement, not a question. Arjun did not reply, and the daggers seemed to spin around his wrists like coiling serpents. Beg dragged his eyes away from their mesmeric dance with a little effort and unsheathed his sword that was strapped to his back. There was no need for any further conversation. As his men began to do the same, Arjun struck, and events seemed to unfold at the speed of thought as the entourage also struck at almost the same time.

"A gasp went through the stands as he covered the eight or so feet that separated the two groups with blinding speed, like a striking black mamba, thrusting off his right leg and dropping to his right knee, sliding while simultaneously bending backwards as Ali Beg swung his sword, catching only air, and the "sai" in Arjun's hand ripped open the stomach of the Afghan fighter. It was a mortal cut, but with the adrenaline and endorphins pumping through his system, Ali Beg was unaware of the severity of his wound as he roared like a mountain lion, pivoting to his left, trying to strike at the head of the Indian who had opened him up like a doctor. However, Arjun rolled to his right and was back on his feet, facing the Afghan chief. He did not hesitate as Ali Beg lifted his sword above his head, in the traditional Afghan fighting style of his forefathers, pivoted on his feet with the dexterity of a much lighter man, and swung his sword, slashing with ferocity, downwards from right to left, trying to cut the impudent Indian in half. Again, he struck the air, and another gasp rippled through the watching crowd of fighters. Arjun had flipped over the head of the huge Afghan like a gymnast. At his zenith, he must have been at least eight feet in the air. He landed behind Ali Beg, who was completely disoriented. Arjun spun around and went down on one knee, plunging both the sais into the broad back, under the ribs of the Afghani. He pushed further upwards, puncturing the lungs. Ali Beg felt a sharp, excruciating stab of pain and felt his immense strength drain out of him like water through a sieve. He roared again in agony, and gouts of black blood spurted out of his mouth as blood filled his punctured lung, and his intestines hung out of the clean-cut in his stomach. He went down on one knee, supporting himself with the sword of his ancestors that had been handed down for four generations. He saw something flying towards him through the corner of his left eye and felt something hit him hard on his shoulder…"

Shalini had drained her glass, and Shinde refilled both glasses, took a big swig, and continued, "Suleiman Yakoobi was a Bahraini who had left his life of luxury on his little island kingdom and had joined the Afghan resistance against the Russians. He had trained with Ali Beg and his fighters and had proved to be courageous under fire and loyal to a fault. He had critically appraised Prasanjit and had not been impressed. His choice of weapon was a curved scimitar that had been used by his Arabic ancestors all the way back to the crusades. He struck with above-average speed, but he met the cool crisp air of Brabourne stadium as Prasanjit pivoted out of the way, his speed matching that of his leader, taking the head of the Bahraini clean off his body with a short, powerful horizontal slash of his katana, as he came out of his turn. Suleiman Yakoobi had killed many Russians, brought down a helicopter gunship, and personally killed more than a hundred street fighters in Bombay. Ali Beg felt a momentary stab of grief as he recognised the object that hit him on his shoulder to be Suleiman Yakoobi's head, which was eclipsed by the blinding pain that seared his brain as his guts spilt onto the green AstroTurf of Barbourne stadium, and the great strength left his body.

"From the folds of their flowing robes, Dharvesh and Amjad let fly a stream of razor-sharp, star-shaped projectiles as they lunged towards their opponents. These were called shurikens, and they caught the two remaining lions of the northwest frontier provinces in their faces and chests. These were extremely painful and disorienting but not fatal. By the time they found their bearings, they were dead, powerful hands snapping their necks like matchsticks as the two members of the entourage crossed the divide like greased lightning and used their Krav Maga skills to full effect.

"Arjun stood before the kneeling Ali Beg, a king standing before a subject, and as Ali Beg looked into the cool brown eyes, he realized too late, like many before him, that he was not the hunter but the prey. Arjun brought both sais down into the skull of Ali Beg with such strength that the points of the daggers protruded through the beard."

Shalini found that she had been holding her breath unconsciously, and she exhaled slowly as Shinde paused to take a large swig of his beer.

"The soldiers of the inner circle warlords began the mop-up operations of the remaining fundamentalist fighters who had slipped away into the various streets and by-lanes, seeking shelter and refuge from collaborators and sympathizers. It took a couple of months or so and a few more lives, but in the end, the operation was complete."

Shinde lit a Gold Flake and continued, "And that is how the violence in Bombay came to an end. At least that's the way I'm almost sure it happened."

Shalini poured herself a well-deserved glass of beer, "But that's not the end of the story, is it? Obviously, there has to be more. Otherwise, we wouldn't be here, drinking all this beer and putting all this undue strain on our lungs, would we?"

Shinde said, "We are not at the end, but we will be there very soon."

"There's something else that struck me," said Shalini. "Manzar was kept out of the battle at Brabourne. Why?"

Shinde smiled as he blew a smoke ring, "Why, indeed?"

TWENTY-FOUR
PARANOID WRECK

It was one in the morning when Shalini checked her cheap but flashy Casio wrist watch. Shinde had gone to the men's room, and she took the opportunity to step outside and get a few breaths of fresh air. They had been at it for more than twelve hours, but she didn't feel tired or sleepy. It was a bit like the times at the Madh Island raves, except she wasn't high on any chemical substances this time. The high was the story, and she was the willing addict.

The market was shuttered for the night, with tarpaulins wrapped over the numerous hand carts that dotted the centre of the narrow street leading to the Colaba Causeway. The lights were still on in nearly all flats of the high-rises to the right, and there was a fair amount of traffic on the Causeway. Bombay was a city that slept late, if at all. Ganpat, the laconic manager, came and stood next to her, smoking. She turned to look at him, thinking that he might be amenable to a chat, but he just signalled for her to get back into the bar. Shinde had returned. Shalini shrugged and stepped back into the dark interior and the shaded lights, leaving a puff of smoke in her wake. Shinde was talking on the phone as she approached the table. He hung up and refreshed her glass before she sat down.

"Do you know how the British rewarded Churchill after he led them to victory in the Second World War?"

Shalini nodded, "Yes, they voted him out of power. I've always felt that was very classless, giving the old man the boot after he guided them to victory."

"Victorious kings have always been the targets of coups and assassinations that have followed in the wake of their campaigns. They feel omnipotent, and then they let their guard down, which is when they are most vulnerable. The face of the betrayer is never immediately apparent; more often than not, it's always the ones who have ready access and are close to the throne."

Shalini thought about that for a moment. There was a lot of truth to that going as far back as the post-Trojan War, where all the returning Greek kings had been murdered when they returned back to their kingdoms after razing Troy to the ground. The murderers had been their wives and the lovers whom they had taken to their beds during the ten long years that their husbands had been away, trying to get Helen back. Ulysses was the only king to escape assassination because he decided to go looking for the Golden fleece instead of returning home to Greece. Shinde lit a Gold Flake and continued, "Arjun was a keen student of history and knew about the inevitability of betrayal. He knew there would be a coup or an assassination attempt, but it wasn't because of the lessons of the past."

Shalini sipped on her beer and lit a Gold Flake, "Something else must have happened to trigger his suspicions. You can't be in such a position of power without becoming a paranoid wreck," she said.

Shinde nodded, "During the riots, Wastra had explicitly decreed that there would be no violence against Muslim families by Hindu-dominated mobs, and vice versa. He knew about the fake news being circulated by the media and was aware that these unsubstantiated news clips that were playing on all the television channels would do more harm to the civilian population than any fundamentalist action ever could. But his edicts were followed up with a few exceptions, which were within acceptable margins. It was towards the end, following the slaying of Ali Beg, during the mop-up operations, that the PBP surprisingly developed independent thought and did not heed this command."

"How long did these mop-up operations last?"

"The surviving fundamentalists had melted away into the various neighbourhoods like Dongri, Agripada, and Nagpada, and it took a while, a couple of months, to flush them all out. The entourage and the inner circle warlords found out their locations through the vast network of informers that they had on the ground, but, in spite of that, it was hard work and took some time to eliminate the last of the terrorists. People who helped them either out of fear or due to some misguided sense of loyalty were also put to the sword. During this time, innocent Muslim families in South Bombay started getting targeted by PBP. It began to accuse all Muslim families of sheltering the fundamentalist survivors. First, they resorted to destroying their property before getting bolder. There were beatings and rapes, and then the lynch mobs went into play. This led to the resurgence of fear and dread amongst the Muslims; they began to band together, forming resistance groups, and for a while, it looked like the entire furnace would be set alight again."

Shinde paused as he emptied his glass and signalled for yet another pitcher. "Arjun met with the elders and representatives of the various Muslim and Hindu communities as the emissary of the great Wastra. He was able to, after huge efforts, allay all fears. A lot of things were done to help the Muslim minority with the help of moderate Hindus, like changing all the Muslim names on boards of the buildings that showed the names of the flat owners to Hindu ones. Rampaging Hindu factions looking for Muslim residents were confounded in their efforts, and a lot of Muslim lives were saved. LTTE fighters were allocated protection duty at buildings and localities that had Muslim dwellers whose lives were at risk. A few gunfights later, the brave *sevaks* lost the desire to salvage the Squad pride, and gradually the attacks petered out completely, but a lot of lives had been lost unnecessarily to mob violence."

Shinde lit a Gold Flake, took a large swig of his beer, and waited while Shalini poured some black *dal masala* onto her plate. She broke off a piece of *chapati,* dipped it in the spicy gravy, and shovelled the mixture into her mouth. Shalini had discovered that the drinking and smoking were stimulating her appetite, and also knew she'd be on the treadmill for a month after this, and sighed inwardly.

Shinde continued, "At a meeting of the inner circle warlords, there was no information put forward regarding the sudden growth of the PBP backbone. Rasul shook his head in confusion. 'They seem to have grown a new set of balls. I had a conversation with Rajesh Shendge, the *shaka pramukh* in Worli, and he was saying that the order to attack all Muslim households had come from the big man himself. Now you know that these guys are useless, boss, but I could swear they were looking for a fight with us."

"Wastra looked around at his war council. They had been with him since the beginning. They were his trusted and closest confidantes. They had willingly put themselves in harm's way for him, and he for them, yet he found himself facing the most unpleasant of facts a leader can ever face."

"Somebody within his organisation was colluding with the Squad," said Shalini, filling in the blanks.

Shinde nodded grimly, "The fact that they had attacked with such impunity, deep within Wastra-controlled territory, raised another unpleasant fact."

Yet again, Shalini filled in the blanks, "It had to have had the blessings of one or more of the inner circle warlords. Oh wow! This has disaster written all over it."

Shinde continued, "Now Arjun knew it could not be any of the fisherfolk. He had been one of them almost since birth, and no one, especially some politically blighted party workers, could ever change a mindset deeply ensconced in a thousand years of loyalty to the tribe. But the collusion meant something much more disastrous."

Shalini nodded, looking into the beer mug, and, almost as if speaking to herself, said very softly, "It meant that the identity of Wastra was no longer controlled information."

TWENTY-FIVE

SILENT TOAST

Shalini took another break to visit Karate Vilas' dwellings. As she left, she saw Shinde talking on the phone again.

That was the second time, she thought and wondered whom he might be talking to at this advanced hour. God knew that apart from Shantanu, she couldn't call anyone else who wouldn't be pissed at this time.

Okay, maybe there were a couple of guys, but she wasn't a booty-call type of girl; if you rang a guy at twelve in the night, you knew he would be expecting only one thing, and it had nothing to do with deep, meaningful conversation.

Karate Vilas was watching TV when she knocked on the door and stepped in. He quickly got up with a welcoming smile and gestured in the direction of the washroom. The two bedrooms on the right were dark, and she guessed the family was asleep. They must have come in while she was with Shinde. She wondered what his connection to Shinde was.

Karate Vilas didn't seem to be a person who enjoyed the occasional vodka shot, he was obviously a family man, so she couldn't understand their relationship, but it had to be deep if she was being allowed to use the facilities whenever she felt like.

Shinde was still on the phone, talking in a slightly agitated manner, when she got back. Karate Vilas was a true gentleman and had escorted her down the unlit stairs but didn't enter the bar.

He hung up the call and started talking, picking up where Shalini had left off.

"You are right, Miss. The big worry was whether Wastra's identity had been compromised and, if so, how many undesirables now shared the closely guarded secret. That could explain a lot, but it didn't explain why they hadn't come after him directly. After all, if he was dead, then so was the organisation."

"Maybe they lacked the moral fibre to pull off a coup d'état. After all, they must have known they couldn't take on Wastra and the entourage. Not to forget the LTTE fighters who were blindly loyal to him. Everyone had seen what happened to good old Ali Beg and his band of merry men. I don't think anyone would want to bell the cat after a display like that. What do you think?" asked Shalini.

Shinde laughed and continued, "It most probably was something like that. If there were colluders amongst the inner circle warlords, which seemed almost impossible, they knew that any attempt on their leader's life, if unsuccessful, would result in the perpetrators joining Ali Beg and so many who had gone before him in the afterlife. But Wastra was no fool, and in his opinion, if it looked like a duck and sounded like a duck, then it was time to get the good old shotgun out and go duck hunting."

Shinde took a deep breath, lit up a Gold Flake, and continued, "After the killing of Ali Beg, it became a custom for Kalia Anton to drop in at Strand on Friday evenings. He would go to Ghungroo Salim's ground-floor apartment in Ghoo Gully, the entrance to which was a hole in the wall in Kamala Mansion between two Malbari shops. He would then send word to Arjun, who would drop by. Anton brought news of the war in Lanka and of the great man. Arjun brought the alcohol.

There were always at least four or five LTTE fighters along with Anton, some new to Bombay and some who had been in the fundamentalist war and knew about or had witnessed the killing of Ali beg and his men at Brabourne Stadium. Arjun was escorted to Salim's place by at least two of the entourage, who would then merge into the canvas of passers-by on the streets, keeping a lookout for any possible threat to their leader. It was foolproof and an impregnable procedure, which was not known to anyone outside the entourage, and it worked like a charm."

Shalini tried to make a joke, "A gathering of the good old boys? I can understand the camaraderie that must have existed. Nothing like a bit of blood-letting to get a bunch of guys to bond over a few drinks, huh?"

Shinde continued without smiling, the humour totally escaping him, "Normally, the drinking would continue late into the night. It was at one of these meetings that Arjun made a very radical proposal that would be received with much interest by Vellupillai Prabhakaran. But I will digress since that would be a story for another day. One Friday evening, Arjun was invited to a party outside Colaba. After the fundamentalist war, he had stopped socializing outside Colaba, and his visits to other bars had come to a grinding halt. The work of consolidation was exacting; unknown to most, he was also conducting a mole hunt, trying to sniff out the Squad collaborator in his army. But he had been unable to come up with any leads and had started to think, with no amount of relief, that maybe he was wrong and that he was seeing ghosts where there were none.

The invitation was from Amarnath, an old friend from the time he frequented Hyderabad estate on Napean sea road, and because he felt a trip 'far from the madding crowd' would help with the spring cleaning of his head, he left the gathering at Ghungroo Salim's place early. While leaving, he asked for a thousand pardons, which was granted with some ribald comments about how he'd have to make good by providing some action for everyone at the 'Blue Nile Club' in Fourth Pasta Lane. He came back in the early hours of Saturday morning, quite honked and happy; he went straight to bed, had ten hours of untroubled sleep after a long time, and received the news late in the afternoon."

"What news?" asked Shalini.

"About ten minutes after Arjun had left, Anton had come out of Ghungroo's place to buy some cigarettes. In the time he took to cross the road, a hit squad lobbed two grenades inside Ghungroo Salim's place. The twin blasts levelled Ghungroo Salim's apartment and the adjoining flat, killing everyone in a ten-metre radius. The hit squad then stormed the apartment and gave it a once over with their automatic weapons, just to make sure. It was a bloodbath, and no one inside survived the carnage. Anton, having the proverbial luck of the devil, took advantage of the stampeding crowd and made his escape, but Ghungroo Salim and LTTE fighters were killed."

Shinde topped off his mug, and Shalini lit a Gold Flake. Both were silent for a bit, Shinde taking a deep swig, allowing Shalini to digest the information.

Shinde continued, "This was not a seek-and-apprehend mission. They were not there to take prisoners. The hit squad made sure that no one was left alive. Then they just melted away, allowing the local cops to take over. It was as if they had never been there.

One of the dead was Sada Pawle, a dreaded shooter of Arun Ganguly and a good friend of Arjun. He was one of the few, though not in the inner circle, who knew the real identity of Wastra. The police, true to their scavenger blood, extorted a lot of money from his wife, saying that Sada was still alive and would be returned once his wife paid up. Once they had extorted all they could, they dropped off his lifeless, broken body in front of his house."

Shalini grimaced with disgust. She was well aware of Bombay's pride and joy. There were many Billimorias around. The questions welled up inside of her like a torrential flood after a heavy monsoon downpour.

"Who could do something like this? These guys, the hit squad, were ghosts, not unlike the LTTE fighters of Wastra. The Squad could never have organised this themselves. They didn't have access to these types of men, and certainly, no one in their ranks had the type of training these killers had. This type of training is only available to private security and military soldiers. Was it a government-sanctioned hit? It would have taken so much planning and so much bureaucratic compliance. Of course! I get it now!" exclaimed Shalini, the lights in her head suddenly switching on.

Shinde said, "It was not that Wastra underestimated any threat, however insignificant. It was not in his nature. He had thought that the prevailing turf war between Arun Ganguly and the Squad forces that followed the fundamentalist war would be enough of a distraction for the cartoonist while he searched for the mole in his organisation. What Ganguly lacked in numbers, he more than made up for in ferocity. His fighters had fought alongside the LTTE soldiers and Dagdi Chawl, and Arun Ganguly's headquarters had been turned into a training ground, not unlike the Antop Hill training grounds. They were more than a match for the *sevaks,* who suffered several successive demoralising defeats."

"But Wastra underestimated the PBP leader, didn't he? I know stories of the grand old man. He wasn't a natural fighter and surrounded himself with sycophants, which is never a good mantra. But he was a survivor, and in spite of several setbacks over the years, some being really demoralising ones, he still had the capability and charisma to attract men to his fold, and he wasn't someone who could just be counted out."

"You are right, Ms Shalini. Wastra underestimated Bakre and his resolve. You can't teach an old dog new tricks, but you better be careful of the tricks he already knows. At a secret meeting with the Chief Minister in his residence in Malabar Hill,

Nagasaheb Bhai came up with a plan to kill all birds with one stone. The Chief Minister had initially been rather unexcited, to put it mildly, to meet the Squad chief. He didn't share the extreme views of the Nagasaheb Bakre, but after his aide-de-camp had recommended highly that he take the meeting, curiosity more than anything else had motivated him to extend an invitation to the Squad supremo."

Shinde paused to empty his glass and refill it before continuing, "He had expected to hear usual rhetoric about Maharashtra for Maharashtrians, but when Bakre dropped the bombshell, it had taken several minutes and a couple of shots of Glenfiddich to stabilise him. It seemed absolutely unbelievable, totally preposterous that a small-time bar owner was actually Wastra. Could it be that for so many years, the one true God of South Bombay was an alcoholic pilot-cum-bar owner? The feedback had been that he was on a downhill spiral, unable to get his addictions under control, and had not been considered a threat at all.

"But the facts presented were indisputable, given the credentials of the source. It had all been an elaborate cover, a master plan that had taken him off the radar; it left Arjun to rule with unbridled power while everyone looked for the invisible King everywhere except in his direction. It was an absolute genius, and when Nagasaheb made his proposal, the Chief Minister grudgingly accepted his proposal. It seemed that he was surrounded by men of superior intellect to him by several degrees. But the Chief Minister was no fool when it came to money, and he saw the financial rewards he could reap with the demise of Wastra and the death of the urban legend. South Bombay would be his for the taking, keeping the PBP as a junior partner."

Shinde topped up his mug again. Unbelievably, he seemed to be picking up the pace of his drinking again, "And so, the plan was put into motion. The Chief Minister approved the use of Special Forces, validating their use for action against terrorist forces operating in the urban jungle that was Bombay. Then they waited for the right time to strike. They kept the circle tight, and operational information was restricted to only a few key officials. They needed to eliminate as many high-value targets as possible in one go, but their main target was Wastra. Initially, the plan was to hit the Everest Bar and take the collateral damage on the chin. Anything could be explained away if they could eliminate the pilot. However, they backtracked once they were made aware of the extent of the security placed in the bar. They knew they would get only one chance, and failure meant that they would be looking over their shoulders for the rest of their lives. Then their source inside the Wastra umbrella told them of the new Friday evening get-togethers at Ghungroo Salim's place.

The best of the best undercover agents were tasked with preparing a detailed report of the Friday night soirée.

One Friday evening, they received news of a God-given opportunity; the news was that the security was lax, as none of the entourage had been spotted. It meant that their target was relatively unprotected. Yet, they hesitated because the God who protected Wastra seemed stronger. But the Squad chief was confident of success and pushed the operation forward, forcing the green light. Tactically, it was absolutely marvellous.

There was no warning to anyone around of the imminent attack. Right up to the end, Ghungroo and the LTTE did not suspect anything. They died with whiskey glasses in their hands, which in itself is not a bad way to go," Shinde laughed mirthlessly.

"There were no survivors. In the aftermath of the attack, although several bodies could not be identified due to the extreme nature of the destruction, there was no doubt that the bar owner had been killed in the attack. The fact that they got Ghungroo and what seemed to be a group of heavily armed men was an added bonus, but the prize was the head of Arjun—metaphorically speaking, of course, because they couldn't identify several bodies."

Shalini exhaled silently through pursed lips, overcome with the twist in the story, and Shinde lit a Gold Flake, "After the reports of the death of Arjun were made public, it became obvious that there was more than just a close relationship between Wastra and the bar owner. For Arun Ganguly, who had risen to the challenge of the Squad menace after the defeat of the Muslim fundamentalists, it was a disaster. His men were well-trained, and although they were numerically inferior, Wastra had made sure that they had a continuous supply of weapons and ammunition.

But the death of Arjun resulted in a vacuum that was followed by an immediate severance of his military aid, and the sevak troops pushed Ganguly back until he was locked in from all sides in his bastion Dagdi Chawl. He bitterly agreed to a truce, although it was more of a conditional surrender, and the PBP took over ninety per cent of his operations, both legal and illegal. He went back to his roots, selling vegetables and running the market in Dagdi Chawl, which was where he had first started. This was the only latitude granted. It was either that or the promise that he would end up like his good friend, Sada Pawle. The LTTE just melted away like the ghosts they were, receiving orders from their supremo to evacuate Bombay. Suddenly, it seemed like they had never been there. The Antop Hill training grounds could never be found. They were so well hidden, and so few people knew about them that after a while, people started doubting they ever existed. They faded away into folklore."

Shalini lit a Gold Flake and felt like her heart was breaking. The road had been long and winding, and she had been a more than willing traveller. The twists and turns had left her dizzy and breathless, but all that was overwhelmed by the sense of loss she felt with the fall of a king.

Shinde took a large swig of his beer, "The fisherfolk retreated back into their territories where they were untouchable. Ghaniya and Namdeo took over leadership of the fisherfolk after Lhoncha abdicated his post, sick in his heart over the loss of his king. He retired to Elephanta Caves, and not much was ever heard of about the ferocious giant again. The entourage disappeared as if they had never been there. There were wild rumours about how they were in hiding, waiting for the right time to strike, and all the various guilty parties thought it best to stay cloistered in their homes, surrounded by bodyguards. But after a few months, this threat turned out to be unfounded, as there were no reported sightings of any of them.

"Then, the negotiations began in earnest as to how Bombay would be divided. Everyone wanted a piece of the pie, and while the northern territories were profitable, the tastiest portion of this pie had the south written all over it. The PBP and the Chief Minister's party locked horns, as was to be expected, with neither side ready to concede any ground. Eventually, it seemed that the Chief Minister was ready to give in to several demands by the Squad, and there were mini-celebrations in various Squad strongholds. But in their eagerness to celebrate their victory, Nagasaheb Bakre, the Chief Minister, and all their lackeys made one fatal mistake."

Shinde said, "There is a saying: *don't count your enemy dead until his body is cold in your morgue and you've put your fingers in his wounds.*"

Shalini said, "There is another saying: *assumption is the mother of all fuck-ups,* excuse my french."

They raised their glasses, making a silent toast.

TWENTY-SIX

UNFATHOMABLE BETRAYER

Shinde signalled for another pitcher, which arrived with the usually remarkable alacrity. He poured the unresisting Shalini a glass and topped off his own. He lit two cigarettes and handed one to her.

The twists and turns in the story had been, to say the very least, a very fast-paced ride, which had been chased with copious amounts of beer and a very forgettable amount of cigarettes.

Shalini waited eagerly for the icing on the cake, the sting that was in the tail that would bring this saga to an end.

Shinde took a sip and started talking, "Kasargod Nivas was the residence of the PBP chief. A palatial estate in the eastern corner of Santa Cruz, the huge bungalow was surrounded by high walls and rolling greens of carefully tended grass and palm trees. The main entrance was a huge steel double gate adorned with paintings of the Hindu God of destruction, who also happened to be the symbol of the PBP power.

During the fundamentalist war and the following clash with Arun Ganguly, the gates had always been shut, with heavy security on all the walls, guard towers erected with deep penetrating searchlights, and entry restricted only to known persons. But following the massacre at Ghungroo's, the surrender of Ganguly and his forces, plus the restriction of the warlord to vegetable markets of Dagdi Chawl, the gates were now open. The security was down to two jeeps at the entrance, with a single-armed driver in each of the jeeps. The guard towers were empty, and the lights no longer automatically came on at sunset. The command-and-control centre at the rear of the bungalow was now manned by a single *sevak* in a six-hour rotation cycle. There was still a contingent of *sevaks* within the walls, but their military firepower was housed in the command-and-control centre, and only the senior-most *sevaks* carried pistols on their persons.

This was more for show than anything else because it had been more than six months since Colaba had gone quiet, and the PBP now ruled the streets, the Chief Minister has given in to several of their key demands. After all, no one had any doubts as to who had been the architect of the downfall and destruction of the great Wastra. The Chief Minister was a pragmatic man and had listened to his counsellors. As long as they got their share of the profits, the advice was to let the PBP have control of the streets. The last thing anyone wanted was another armed conflict, and everyone knew that no one would benefit from a protracted war that would surely follow if the PBP strongman was denied his place under the sun."

Shalini took a sip of her beer. This was not what she had expected. "Are you saying that all of Wastra's men, the fisherfolk, and his inner circle warlords all just succumbed to the new power without even a semblance of resistance? Didn't anyone know that he had survived and was very much alive? And what about Wastra himself? Why didn't he strike back immediately? After all, he had prepared for this eventuality, hadn't he?"

Shinde smiled and raised his hands, palms facing Shalini, "We are nearing the end of this tale, Ms Shalini. A little more patience will go a long way."

Shalini said, "That's fine. We've been here for a long time, and I understand how you work your magic. I'll have a Gold Flake and some beer with my patience, please."

Shinde smiled again as he lit a Gold Flake for her and replenished her glass before continuing, "It was a very pleasant Friday evening in Mumbai. The sun had disappeared into the Arabian Sea and washed Bombay with a deep orange glow and the promise of a clear starlit night. A cool sea breeze blew inland, and the news on the radio was that a blockbuster movie starring Shahrukh Khan was about to be released.

"The critics were gushing with praise at the acting, the songs, and the new actress who was starring opposite the icon of Bollywood. Vishranth Tambe was manning the command centre inside the Squad bastion when one of the TV screens that monitored the western wall flickered and went dead. He tapped at the screen and bent down to check the connection. It seemed alright, and he straightened up, wondering whether he should call it into the guards at the entrance when the screen flickered back on again."

Shalini felt her pulse pleasantly quicken again, and she poured herself another generous glass of beer and fired up a Gold Flake.

Shinde continued with a small smile, "There was a knock on the door of the command centre, and when Vishranth checked the closed circuit monitor, he saw it was Shantabai, one of the household maids, with a tray. "Ah, finally! Some *chai* and *vada pav*," Vishranth was starving, and he opened the door with a smile. Maybe he could entice the maid for a quickie. He had heard she was game if she liked the guy, and Vishranth fancied his chances. His smile was wiped out like one of those small islands in the Indian Ocean after the tsunami.

"Instead of Shantabai, Kalia Anton stepped in, followed by about ten dark-skinned fighters. Vishranth knew about the dark-skinned fighters, and he knew what was going to follow and his last thought, before Anton put a bullet between his eyes with his silenced Glock, was that the chief was so fucked."

Shalini lit another Gold Flake, her hands shaking ever so slightly, and Shinde took a big swig of his beer.

"At the time as Vishranth took his last breath, a taxi pulled up at the entrance of Kasargod Nivas. Shivraj Patil, sitting in the jeep to the right of the taxi, motioned the driver to get out. The door opened, and both he and Suresh Natekar relaxed when they saw the handsome young man accompanied by a rather attractive young lady in tight blue jeans and a green t-shirt that accentuated her breasts, get out and approach him. It was well-known that the old man's appetites eclipsed both his sons and that both youngsters approaching him would have their hands full tonight.

The lascivious grin died on Shivraj's face as he saw what was in the girl's hand. He tried to shout a warning to his partner, but there were a couple of spitting sounds; Shivraj took a bullet in his left eye, and his partner in the other jeep took the other one straight between the eyes. Namdeo pulled the dead sevak out of the driver's seat, got in without a backwards glance as the body hit the cement, and flicked the headlights of the jeep on and off while the rest of the passengers in the cab got out and formed a defensive perimeter at the metal gates.

In the far distance, in response to the prearranged signal, the lights on several vehicles came on, and the train of lights moved forward, accelerating towards Kasargod Nivas.

Nagasaheb Bakre was sitting in the huge conference room, presiding over a meeting of the victorious dons. To his right sat the Deputy Chief Minister of Maharashtra. He was a short, fat pig of a man with a thin moustache and stained teeth; he was called A.G. Sharma. For some strange reason, as is the case with several Indian males, he felt he was rather attractive because he was extremely fair of skin and had the misconception that this would cause his ugliness to get bypassed. The PBP chief was not impressed by this fat, ugly man and knew him to be a coward who had stayed in the background during the wars. He was the typical politician whom he despised, but politics and wars make strange bedfellows, and he was forced to accept this poor excuse of a human being at the table. He also knew he could never have accomplished his victory without the Special Forces, and this meant he was beholden to the Chief Minister, who would try to call the shots through his mouthpiece.

Nagasaheb had marched with the great Mahatma and was cut from a different cloth to the present-day mobsters who occupied Mantralaya. In another time and place, most of the gathering would not have found a seat at this conference, but this was the reality of the time, and the PBP chief had no choice but to roll with the punches.

Shinde refilled his glass and continued, "So you see, Ms Shalini, the PBP chief, was in a contemplative mood when the doors of the conference room opened. He turned irritably to see who had had the gall to interrupt the proceedings and was understandably confused and shocked to see Kalia Anton stride in, flanked by Kalashnikov-toting, dark-skinned fighters. He clearly recalled the police report that had stated that all occupants of Ghungroo Salim's house had been eliminated.

"There was a sharp staccato as some members of the Surve gang who tried to go for their weapons died in a swift hail of gunfire. But the rest of the members at the table sat frozen, careful to make no move that might have been construed as hostile. And then Arjun walked in, flanked by a giant, took the Glock offered to him by Anton, and Nagasaheb Bakre knew the police reports had been grossly overexaggerated because the one known as Wastra was very much alive and once again, against all odds, held all the cards."

Shalini's face was flushed with excitement, but she held her tongue and did not disturb Shinde, who lit a Gold Flake and offered Shalini one, which she accepted without any fuss. Shinde continued, "Arjun ignored everybody at the table. He was searching for someone and found him sitting at the far end of the conference table. Their eyes met, and Vasu felt a violent spasm rock his entire body. The shock of seeing Arjun alive was more than his system could handle. He had been absolutely sure that Arjun was dead. He had multiple confirmations, from eyewitnesses to the massacre to actual interviews with the police in charge of the post operations and even reported from the streets and the inner circle warlords. He had been so sure that he had mobilised support and opened a confrontation with Richard for control of Strand. He had been given tacit police and Squad support and had been able to topple Richard from power, sending him into exile in the suburbs of Malad. He had even comforted Arjun's grief-stricken parents. A second spasm shook his body as he realized everyone in Strand Company knew of his betrayal.

"He realised how far out of the loop he had been kept. He had been locked out, which meant that he had been under suspicion all the time. His heart spasmed again, and he felt a sharp pain shooting down his left side. He was Brutus in this play, with the only difference being that Caesar was still alive. There would be no need for a Mark Antony."

As she drank her beer, Shalini wondered about this alcoholic, sitting in this dingy bar, and wondered how come he was so well-read. Shinde continued, "Vasu's elder brother Prabha sat next to him. He had been instrumental in turning Vasu's heart into the black lump of envy it had become. He had never been allowed into Wastra's inner circle and had developed close ties with several Squad stalwarts instead. He had had his suspicions about the identity of Wastra, but Vasu had never broken the faith. It was only after Arjun made

Richard the next in line to the throne of Strand in case Arjun fell in battle against Ali Beg did the insidious coils of hatred encircle themselves around his heart, and after a night of heroin and Stolichnaya vodka, he had broken the sacred covenant and confirmed his brother's suspicions. All that was needed was the charisma of the Squad supremo and his fox-like cunning, and the plan fell into place."

Shalini took a large sip of her beer and lit a Gold Flake, and said, "Even the best-laid plans."

Shinde nodded, "The chance factor that favours champions.

Prabha had hated Arjun since he was a child. From his smug parents, the fucking upper crusty school he went to, to his stupid fucking tennis rackets, he had hated everything Arjun stood for. The money and privileges that he and his family had been denied. Then this soft boy had pulled off the hit on the Shettys. He hadn't even known about it until Vasu and Arjun had become partners in the Everest Bar. He had tried to turn Vasu against Arjun several times over the years but had been unsuccessful. It was only later, when he found out the identity of the king of south Bombay, did he understand why. But by then, Vasu had been wooed over to the dark side and had brought down an empire and a king. His hatred got the better of him, "You betrayed all of us by protecting those fucking Muslim families. You gave Strand to Richard when it should have been Vasu who sat on that throne. You didn't give a shit about your closest friend," Arjun didn't even bother to look at him. He kept his eyes fixed on Vasu and emptied the Glock into Prabha.

The bullets stitched a pattern, and Prabha danced like a puppet before collapsing, broken and bullet-ridden, on the floor.

Arjun looked at Vasu. He remembered Ramona and Harinder Bagai and Cuffe Parade. He remembered happier days, his first chai with Vasu, Deep Purple playing in the background, and then his first Old Monk and coke. The Kahlua party in his car when they celebrated Nerissa's twenty-first birthday. He saw him coming out of the mist one December morning after his abandonment and the beating of his parents, his long black hair making him look like a rock star, taking the pain in his heart away and giving him the courage to go to war. So many memories!

"The betrayal was unfathomable, but it had happened. In spite of his vast experiences in different theatres of war and always expecting betrayal from the most unexpected of sources, Vasu's act of treason had hurt him more than it enraged him, and it had cut him deep in his heart. It had taken more than a month after the massacre at Ghungroo's for the truth to emerge. Only Ghania, Namdeo, and Lhoncha were parties to the subterfuge. Arjun knew that once the truth of Wastra had been leaked, the kingdom would collapse. It was only a question of time. He arranged for a smooth transition of power in critical areas, with the exception of Strand to his three trusted captains. Lhoncha abdicating the Sundernagari leadership had been a veil to cover his true intentions. With Lhoncha out of the way, Arjun had been sure the traitor would reveal himself. He had received new orders in the wake of the massacre at Ghungroo's, but he needed to unearth the traitor first before leaving Bombay. Still, the identity of the traitor remained unclear, but Prabha's sudden rise to prominence pointed the finger of suspicion in an unbelievable direction. It was only after the entourage disappeared and Vasu approached Namdeo and asked him for his help in toppling Richard did the real picture begin to emerge. After that, Richard was given orders to surrender Strand to Vasu so that the other rats would come out of the sewers. The kingdom was lost, and now the only thing that could be done was to rid the earth of the vermin. Anyway, there was another war that was beckoning. Then it was all a question of waiting until they were gathered together under one roof, and that had taken longer than expected. Nagasaheb and the Chief Minister hadn't reached their positions by overplaying their hands. Arjun and the entourage took up accommodations, melted into the urban jungle that was the old city of Hyderabad, and waited for Namdeo and Ghaniya to let them know when the time was right. The rest," Shinde shrugged, "followed a natural course that led to Arjun standing in the conference room of Kasargod Nivas. The truth is often stranger than fiction," Shinde finished off his beer.

Shinde refilled his glass, and Shalini demurred. He lit a Gold Flake and continued, "Unlike his dead brother, Vasu had calibre. The reasons for his betrayal were not important any longer, and he would not justify it to his erstwhile king, and he would not beg for his life. He knew it was forfeit, and he pushed back his chair and stood up. The silence in the room was deafening. No one at the conference table dared to move as their lives hung on a knife's edge. Vasu came around the table, ignoring the cocked weapons trained on him. Arjun signalled to Anton that everyone else was to stay in the conference room and turned and walked out, followed by Vasu."

Shalini took a deep breath, topped off her glass, and took a swig that matched Shinde's, "This is terrible," she exclaimed, "I mean, there can be only one end. I don't think anyone in that line of work believed in the 'forgiveness is divine' bit, do you?"

Shinde nodded in agreement, "Vasu had been with Arjun long enough and had dealt with potential traitors himself to know that there was no coming back from this. Arjun lit two cigarettes and offered one to Vasu. They stood in the courtyard, which was a beautiful garden with a tulsi plant right at the centre.

They smoked for a bit in silence, taking in the ambience, and Arjun said, "I wouldn't be here if it weren't for you, bro. You've been my rock. I didn't give you Strand because I didn't need to. You ruled it all with me. I thought you knew that. Everything I had belonged to us. It was you and me against the world. If I had fallen in battle against Ali Beg, you would have inherited my mantle. Not just Strand, everything. Wastra would have lived on through you. Maybe it's my fault that I did not make that clear, but I swear I thought you knew."

Vasu didn't reply. There was nothing that he could say that would wash his sin. The enormity of his betrayal was more pronounced because he had been caught. Absolution of guilt is always easy if you're never suspected of the sin in the first place, but here he had been caught with his pants down. He didn't feel guilty about the betrayal because that was the game. He had known that when the poison of envy had infected him. But getting caught was unforgivable, and he knew he would grievously pay for his sin. Vasu wondered for how long Arjun had known. And he understood that all the inner circle warlords, from Rasul to Lhoncha, all of them had known, and he felt overwhelming admiration for Wastra.

Now there was a king, he thought. When would another come to take his place? And then he felt a deep desolation as he realised there was no going back from this one. Like many before him who had gone to the happy hunting grounds in a state of disbelief, he realized too late that he had underestimated his boss. He wondered if he would be given the chance of falling on his own sword, and if so, would he have the guts to see it through?

"And then," said Shinde as he lit a Gold Flake, "Vasu's body came to his rescue. His body spasmed a third time as a blood vessel burst in his head, and he was hit with an aneurysm. The sudden, cataclysmic turn of events had put a devastating bill on his body, one that it could not pay. He collapsed, and Wastra dropped his gun and caught his falling comrade before his head hit the ground. A sharp call and several fighters came out of the conference room, while Anton, adhering to the strict military protocols, kept a contingent with him, controlling the conference room."

Shinde lit a Gold Flake and continued, Shalini seemed lost for words, "They took Vasu to Nanavati Hospital, where surgeons were ordered to work their magic. But it was all in vain. Vasu was paralysed on his left side. There was no need to execute him because life had taken care of that by turning him into a vegetable. He was retired to a small flat in Navi Bombay, and his body was found a few months later near the water decanter in his kitchen. The coroner placed the time of death at around four in the morning. The assumption was he had got up to drink some water and didn't make it. Arjun wasn't there at the cremation."

Shalini was silent as Shinde continued, "Wastra returned to the conference room.

"He spoke to the PBP chief, "You cost me a lot over the last few months, old man. A lot of good men have died because of you. I am not one to wait on the banks of the river, waiting for the body of my enemy to pass me by. I'm sending you down the river where you can ask forgiveness for your sins."

The Old Lion had had many close encounters with death over the years, but the fates had always smiled on him. At times he had been forewarned, but a couple of times, it had been sheer dumb luck. He cursed that very same luck that he had listened to Billimoria when he was told that that the body of Arjun had been identified, and then, in a flash, realised it had not been Billimoria but Inspector Beg who had been in charge of the entire post-investigation following the massacre at Ghungroo Salim's. He looked around and saw the Inspector standing in the far corner, weapon holstered, and realised that maybe he should have conducted his own damn mole hunt. He had envisioned a peaceful death, surrounded by his loved ones. He felt a deep sense of regret as the one known as Wastra put a bullet between his eyes, sending him to the great beyond, the smell of urine filling the room as Ashok Sharma, the Deputy Chief Minister of Maharashtra, wet himself, thinking that he was next."

Shinde stubbed out his cigarette, "And then Wastra turned to the surviving son and nephew of the PBP chief and made his proposal."

TWENTY-SEVEN

THE END OR THE BEGINNING

As Shinde started to pour himself another enormous serving of beer, preparing to continue, both his and Shalini's phones started ringing almost simultaneously. Shalini answered her phone first. It was Shantanu, and he was shouting on the phone, almost hysterically.

"Where the hell are you? Are you still with that fucking drunk? Have you any idea what has happened?"

Shalini glanced at Shinde, who had answered his phone and was listening very attentively to someone on the other end. Shalini had a feeling both calls were connected.

"Yes, I am. And no, I haven't," she said as calmly as she could.

"Fuck," yelled Shantanu, "Talk about Nero playing the fucking fiddle."

"What are you talking about, Chief?" asked Shalini as goosebumps began to run unabashedly up and down her shapely arms.

"Try to listen carefully. While you were in this bar getting sloshed, the devil and his minions descended upon George's Hospital."

Shalini had a sinking feeling in the pit of her stomach, not unlike the one you have as you go down the steep slopes of a roller coaster.

"What happened?" she barely managed to croak.

"Around midnight or so, three doctors came to check on the junkie. They had been sent by the Dean and had all the necessary paperwork. The only thing is that they weren't really doctors."

Shantanu took a deep and audible breath, "They killed everyone. Every cop who was assigned to the junkie is dead. Billimoria got special treatment. They hacked off his head, placed it on the junkie's bed, and then positioned the bed in such a way that it was the first thing everyone saw when they entered the room."

Shalini thought about the Parsi brute who had sent so many innocent people to their deaths, and all she could think was "just desserts." And then Shantanu answered her next question before she even asked it, his words stumbling over each other, "The junkie has disappeared. This was a damn rescue mission. There are dead bodies everywhere. And one of the orderlies has also disappeared. They are searching for his body."

Shalini instinctively knew who it was and knew that Moti Singh was long gone and wouldn't be heard from again. The hit squad hadn't got access to Babu's room just by sheer luck. She bit back a smile as she thought about the plump, smart Nepali. Boy, had she underestimated his loyalties!

Then she saw that Shinde had put away his phone and was looking past her and felt the bar go very silent. She felt the hair on the back of her neck rise, and she turned to see what was going on in Sujatha Bar at this ungodly hour.

He was older, and he still looked very fit. She knew she was looking at Wastra, and her breath caught in the back of her throat. There were many men around him, flanking him, a protective shield. She recognised 'pretty boy', Dharvesh, and Prasanjit from the photo and knew she was at the end of her journey. No loose ends, and she was the very definition of one. That damn photo! She didn't recognise the other men but assumed many of them were the famous inner circle warlords. She looked for signs of dark-skinned, Kalashnikov- toting men that she had heard so much about in the last twelve hours. If Wastra was here, then it stood to reason, so were they.

He smiled, answering her unspoken questions, and she was immediately smitten. There was something so pleasant about his smile that it was impossible to believe that she was in the presence of a legend, that standing before her was the bogeyman she had been listening about over the last twelve or so hours. He seemed furthest from a paranoid psychopath as anyone could ever be. He just seemed such a nice guy.

Maybe a little too old to take home to meet mom and dad, but then again, not entirely out of the realm of impossibility.

"Miss Shalini, I have heard a lot about you this evening, and it's all been good. You will get to meet Anton and the boys very soon. I know they are looking forward to meeting you. They are just making sure the perimeters are sewn up tightly. We wouldn't want our trusted law and order enforcers to crash this party, would we?" The voice was deep and measured, and her heart skipped a beat. It was as if he had read her mind.

He gestured to a lean, tough-looking gentleman with grey sideburns and aquiline features to his right, "May I introduce Najeeb?"

Shalini nodded and said, "Also known as Miya. The lion of Dhanraj Mahal! You were at the shoot-out at Gateway, cutting off any escape for the Shettys to the north."

Najeeb and Wastra looked at each other and grinned broadly. Wastra said, "You are right, Ms Shalini. This is indeed the lion of Dhanraj Mahal. He has been living a quiet life in Hyderabad and has come out of retirement just for me. You cannot choose your family, but you definitely have a choice when it comes to your friends."

So that's where Wastra and the entourage had lived for the six months following the massacre at Ghungroo Salim's, thought Shalini.

And then, a figure stepped through the door of Sujatha Bar, blocking out all the light from the street outside. Shalini saw Lhoncha, felt an electric shock go down her spine, and thought the same thing many people before her had thought when confronted with the vision: *My God! There really is a giant in the Strand Army.*

She turned to Wastra to ask him the most important question of all and realised that she was mistaken. A million questions were storming her overwhelmed brain. She saw that Shinde had got up and was standing almost to attention as he shook hands with Wastra, and they exchanged a few words she couldn't quite catch. They smiled, and for some reason she could not immediately fathom, she realised that she had been accepted into an inner circle that she was absolutely, one hundred per cent sure she wanted to be a part of. She had been so sure her journey was at an end that her last known location would have been Sujatha Bar and had wondered how Shantanu would explain her disappearance to her family. Then the man known as Wastra turned to Shalini, and as she got up and took the hand offered to her, she realised she had been so mistaken. Her journey was just beginning.

GLOSSARY

- **Adda:** A social gathering or hangout spot, often used to describe a group of friends chatting and spending time together.
- **Asli maal:** Slang term for high-quality drugs or narcotics. It is also used as a term for sex workers.
- **Banyan:** A type of loose-fitting shirt commonly worn in South Asia.
- **Beedi:** A type of thin cigarette made from tobacco wrapped in a leaf.
- **Chai:** A popular Indian beverage made from brewed tea leaves, milk, and spices.
- **Charas:** A type of hash made from the cannabis resin.
- **Chhakka:** Slang term for a transgender person.
- **Chooth:** Slang term used for someone.

GLOSSARY

- **Chotey:** Slang term for someone small.
- **Chutiya:** A derogatory term used to insult someone as foolish or stupid.
- **Daaru:** Slang term for alcohol, usually referring to hard liquor.
- **Dukkar taxi:** A rickshaw or auto-rickshaw, a common form of public transportation in India.
- **Ganja:** Slang term for marijuana.
- **Gardulla:** A slang term for someone who is considered to be a tough or strong person.
- **Hafta:** Slang term for a weekly bribe or payment made to a corrupt official or organisation.
- **Hawala:** A type of informal money transfer system used in South Asia and the Middle East.
- **Hawaldars:** A rank in the Indian police force equivalent to a sergeant.
- **Jhingha masala:** A type of spicy shrimp dish commonly eaten in India.
- **Kaamwali:** A domestic worker, such as a maid or housekeeper.
- **Kattas:** Slang term for a gun or revolvers.
- **Lathi:** A type of long wooden stick used as a weapon or tool in India.
- **Lungi:** A type of traditional garment worn by men in South Asia, similar to a sarong.

- **Maal:** Slang term for drugs or narcotics. It is also used as a derogatory term for sex-workers.
- **Maska:** A term used to describe a type of butter used in Indian cuisine.
- **Mawashi-geri:** A type of martial arts kick used in karate.
- **Naan:** A type of flatbread commonly eaten in India and other parts of South Asia.
- **Namaste:** A respectful greeting or farewell commonly used in Indian culture.
- **Pathaka:** Slang term used to call someone as hot as a firecracker.
- **Pavs:** A type of soft bread roll commonly eaten in India.
- **Pawli:** Slang term for a police station.
- **Raes:** Slang term for someone who is rich or wealthy.
- **Sadela:** A slang term for something which is filthy.
- **Sevak:** A term used to describe a member of the Indian armed forces.
- **Shaka Pramukh:** A term used to describe the leader of a local branch of a political party in India.
- **Surmai:** A type of fish commonly eaten in India.
- **Tikka:** A type of marinated and grilled meat dish commonly eaten in India.
- **Tres Dramatique:** A French term meaning very dramatic.
- **Ustara:** A term used for a razor that street barbers use to shave.

ACKNOWLEDGEMENTS

My profound thanks to Kevin Missal who took a chance on a first-time author.

To Abhijeet Kataria who has proven to be a true friend.

My gratitude to Navya Singh, Deepika Sarkar, Vini Bhati and the team at Hubhawks who worked tirelessly and with such great enthusiasm to make *Wastra* into the book that it is.

AUTHOR BIO

Rohan Kailasam was born in Chennai and grew up in Mumbai. After finishing college and finding his MBA course uninspiring, he went to Texas. He became a commercial pilot before returning to India and joining Air India, initially based out of Mumbai. He has since worked for several foreign airlines.

An avid fitness enthusiast, he plays tennis and holds a black belt in Ishin-Ryu karate. He is currently a student of Brazilian Jiu-Jitsu. His other passion, apart from writing, is music; he plays the piano and is the front man for the Chennai rock band, Helmsdeep.

Wastra, his first book, is a crime thriller set in Mumbai and written entirely at 40,000 feet on long-haul flights from South East Asia into Europe and North America.